A NEW SHIRT

A NEW SHIRT

Desmond Hogan

faber and faber

LONDON · BOSTON

First published in Great Britain in 1986 by
Hamish Hamilton Limited, London
First published in this paperback edition in 1987 by
Faber and Faber Limited
3 Queen Square London WC1N 3AU

Printed in Great Britain by
Richard Clay Ltd, Bungay, Suffolk
All rights reserved

© Desmond Hogan 1986

British Library Cataloguing in Publication Data

Hogan, Desmond
A new shirt.
I. Title
823′.914[F]   PR6058.0346

ISBN 0-571-14911-1

For Caroline Tonson Rye

Nessan, the holy deacon, loves
Angelic pure devotion;
Never came outside his teeth
What was untrue and guileful.

Martyrology of Donegal

Dublin, 1984

I had a dream last night in which the old man whom Nessan was acquainted with in Chicago after Armistice day was transported from his exile in that, the early part of the century, the first parcel of his years in exile, and placed here, in O'Connell Street, in this city, at evening in summer – it is summer now – among the young people in their ties of aquamarine and vermilion, with their black, shining shoes topped by white socks, their hair – that of the young girls – creamed into gold fusses, their hands holding one another's, and left to wander – he who wrote of swans in a poem to console himself – past the newly cleaned pillars of the G.P.O. – Georgian pillars are about all that's clean in this city – among the young people with skin blanched the white of swans and eyes vacant from rippling drugs. They in turn are transported back to his time, to the parties, the colonnades, the Greek goddesses in the gardens among the bamboo. My own garden, overlooking the Irish Sea, has thrown around tiger lilies now. This bungalow where I live, the last remnant of my mother's and my father's combined wealth, enjoyed by an aged, well-nigh celibate man, who parades his genitals among those of

1

other men on the slab which constitutes the men's bathing place on the Vico Road. Naked old men saunter among the nudes ready for autopsy. Occasionally a young man starts out of the white sheets of my bed in the morning. I have attracted him with liquor, with Swiss chocolates, with perhaps the relics of my youthful handsomeness. And, in the hot summer, youth and nakedness incline me to think of Nessan and another world – of the matchstick skyscrapers signalling towards the blue-balloon sky, of the girls I nonchalantly took home with me in the labyrinths between those skyscrapers after the second war, of the songs and the tunes which linked those skyscrapers after the war, the meandering tunes or the delicate smoky croonings of Art Tatum, of Billie Holiday, of Hot Lips Page. I berthed in New York on a Sunday at the end of August 1948 to a tune by Colman Hawkins. I had come to try to outline the wraith of Nessan. I alighted in a panama hat and a white suit, certain of my future quarry. I had come from a world over which war had cascaded. But I'd been safe, or semi-safe, in the emporium-like cafés of Lisbon, spies, in white suits and in neatly creased hats, grovelling before their cups of coffee and the white, smoothly shining bowls of sugar. Newspapers and letters had trickled through my hands. I was the only child of a Spanish aristocrat and an Irish industrialist. My mother could not match the one-eyed Ana de Mendoza but she squinted with her right eye and made it seem an area of darkness. My father once erected a lavatory bowl full of flowers on a dinner table prepared for the Protestant bishop of Dublin in our home in a valley in Wicklow. The bishop, in his magisterial robes, had disdained to look. We moved to Ireland, permanently, before the Spanish Civil War, but I could recall the fires of Andalusian summers – we'd just spent summers in Spain – the reds of manifold flowers and the sprites of Sevillana dancers' dresses. After I'd completed a B.A. degree at University College, Dublin, the second war lured me in the direction of Spain, searching for the magenta colours of my childhood, but I got only as far as Lisbon and dallied there, eddying about one or two cafés, for two years. I had heard of Nessan at university but instead of writing a thesis on him, because I was rich, I decided in Lisbon – it was the war and its encirclement of my figure in a white suit which made me think in turn of Nessan, his possessed, onion blue and red skin, the guilty smallpox marks of childhood over his white suit in his last

2

years, and of the little fluttering of his poems I'd read at university – to attempt a book on him, and so, a few years after the close of the war, much wine consumed in the meantime, many lavatory floors splattered, I set sail. Dublin was a diamond I was leaving behind. Fascists had oozed out their songs over pianos in this diamond during the war, soft, milky songs, songs sung by women about Hitler's Adam's apple. I knew I'd never return to the same city. My parents were sliding down the marble stairway to bankruptcy. I took my share of my inheritance, Spanish and Irish and, dark eyebrows combating with Connemara coast blue eyes, confronting the Atlantic, abandoned Cobh, a church on an island which had seen many people of this nation take leave of history in search of food, clothes, shelter and their posterity.

Prologue

Bonnie Muir had started dying on the 6 of August 1945. She was being assisted in protracting her act of dying by sisters in white attire who cared for the gentile poor – of any Christian persuasion – in a home in Brooklyn near the sanatorium where, in the early 1920s, Nessan had befriended a young, flaming black-haired, tubercular case, who, in his white silk shirt, lacerating his chest with sweat, wrote poems in which he predicted the near-end of the world at the end of the century, an end narrowly avoided by some optimistic cosmic smile. In my first few weeks in New York I took early strolls from my hotel room to witness the morning sun become a spot of amber in front of the rooms Nessan had occupied on East 13th Street for many years of the twenties. The orange walls were being licked by a sun which already tasted of autumn. I would carry a cane on these mornings, sit in an appropriate café and have bagels. Bonnie Muir had welcomed me as though I was a stranger she'd been expecting for a long time and who had taken form out of hallucinations she'd been having ever since the cloud had reared over Hiroshima and made her think of a great wave she and Nessan had encountered once in California and to which he'd said – she'd been carrying a delicate, tall, mauve umbrella – that deluges can be bested by hempsoles – he'd been wearing white Hollywood hempsoles, white shirt, white, neatly pressed trousers – and umbrellas.

7

One

There'd been a harp hanging from an elm tree in the garden which, when the wind blew, seemed to sing of its own accord songs about the abandoned palace courts of Ireland. Nessan, a child, would listen into these tidings. His face worried and his quiff newly spruced by his mother. The house was on a hill, near Mr. Muir's candy factory. In one of the valleys boys wrestled on certain festival days and, in the verdure, boys in white surveyed the baseball balls. To these gatherings came automobiles, men in duster goggles, women, as erect as trees, emerging from the automobiles, hats on their heads like mauve Himalayan mountains, so sheathed were the hats in chiffon that it seemed the mountains were garbed in cloud. One broad shouldered young man Nessan would fixate on as a child. This young man wore a cream, mustard coloured at the edges, baseball jersey instead of a white one, though his trousers underneath looked white as he raised a javelin. Nessan's blue eyes would follow the upward progress of the javelin. The young man was blond. Nessan mentally called him brother. There were no other children in Nessan's family. He was a lone child, and would desultorily return to his parents' picnic cloth. Nessan's parents had met over a picnic cloth in these low hills. Nessan's mother had journeyed from her city to sing songs at a picnic organized by a young ladies' charity organization. The funds from this charity were directed at black girls in the cities. Bonnie had come reluctantly that day. These hills, this area of houses on hills and small lakes where contentedly quacking ducks could be divined was beyond the realms which attracted her – even for charitable purposes. She had a reverberating, regal voice which she dipped her head in a lowly way to use. She hoped an impresario would discover her. In white with flourishing black dots she dipped her head in her usual lowly fashion to sing that day, leaning forward on the ground. Bethuel Muir heard her. He was amazed that he, a Bohemian Jew, who pretended to be a Scottish Methodist could fall in love.

He drew the ladies back to his home late in the afternoon and on the veranda they cooed about the view, heights being rare in the Mid-West. His cigar ash seemed to have stubbed into the edges of his hair. What a comely middle-aged man. Still something of an austere and manly early twenties about him, more than just a hint, a prominence of youth about him as if youth was rising like the sun in him. Bonnie at first refused the candies. She turned her liquid, jade-black hair from him. Her mouth was put on that day like a pagan red rose. She'd treated them at the end of her singing to 'The Last Rose of Summer'. Her favourite. But the rose in her mind was always white.

At the picnic he'd approached her, introduced himself, bowing his head. She'd sorted him out with a glance. He was an oaf. Bonnie's spiral of ambitions ascended to Broadway. She intended to act, sing. Only men of the theatre and men of the arts interested her. But he followed her even to her city and in the elm-lined avenue, on a day her mother threatened suicide for the umpteenth time, Bonnie O'Dowd accepted the discreet proposal of Bethuel Muir.

Bonnie's widowed mother, whose tiny receptacle of a waist was usually swathed by white blouses, had suffered all her life, had been commanded by depression. Herself appointed a beauty in her youth, she had been less than true to her ambitions to marry into the dizzying Olympian echelons of society, but her husband, Páid, had accumulated more than modest wealth from his timber business. There was in her brain a shard of Irish history, a shard of Ireland merely maybe, something that caused her to tear at all who surrounded her and to pluck out her own emotions as if her heart was just made of tissue paper. She was an elegant beauty pursued by the small city, dilettanteish artists – those whose legs stuck out as if they were on ephemeral stilts – and a melancholic. She always had the story of her family, the Finuacanes, near at hand. As close as the trespass of her lace handkerchief on her dark skirt as she was seated in the broad drawing-room looking out on the peaceable elms.

Whatever else they had in the sense of their family aesthetic, the Finuacanes had a sense of some former treasure being in their family possession, of glamour, of aristocracy having instantly been radiated by the family name once. To understand their concept of themselves one would have to understand something of the trek of the Irish nation west in the 1650s – or the trek west of the gentry of that nation. For the Finuacanes were convinced that they'd had a holding on the east coast of Ireland and had had to vacate it on Cromwell's orders. They'd ended up in County Leitrim and, if you were to believe Bonnie's mother, Jesuits spent most of the eighteenth century going up and down chimneys and crawling into priest holes – the largest one behind a painting of the Valley of Glendalough in the east of Ireland which was vintage 1575 – in a big house in that county where they'd renewed their aristocratic status. But the Penal Laws and an eventual row with a British colonel – a redcoat who confiscated Catholic mares and beat them to death when he was drunk, or caused them brain damage, from his enthronement on their backs, with a Chesire-made cane – eliminated their good fortune and brought financial ruin on a house at the bottom of a mountain, a house which had risen from bog and was almost as black as bog. And the Finuacanes left, for America of course, bearing the painting of Glendalough across the Alleghenys in a covered wagon. The painting had saved those Finuacanes' lives for it was given to an Indian chief in exchange for their lives. The Valley of Glendalough faded into the foothills of the Alleghenys and the Finuacanes went on to find themselves in a settlement among Quakers and Lutherans. Stones in the ground marked the graves of Quakers smitten by New World germs. A city grew up here and the Finuacanes were one of the first families of it, starting a leather and meat factory and producing women like Bonnie's mother, indefatigably slim at the waist. Bonnie's mother made the mistake of marrying an Irishman, a poor one, but one who quickly improved his status, not only through his marriage connections but also through the trees in a patch by the lake – he'd started a timber business, and pines seemed to shoot up as quickly as they fell – he'd brought the certainty of miracles from the holy wells of County Limerick. Bonnie's father died when she was five. She had two elder sisters and a younger brother. Her mother did not mention her father. She looked onto a street and spat curses at horses drawing carriages of people with English names.

Páid O'Dowd had looked back on his people in County Limerick on an autumn day in 1847, when the hilltop on which they stood, looked gold but the only harvest was in the incarcerated fields of English landlords. A huddle of people stood on a hilltop, shawls dripping from the women. They would die that winter unless he could collect money quickly for them. Limerick was alive with the movement of corpses and the trundling of them in barrows, bodies piled on bodies. But the worst stories came from afar where women were said to have eaten their new-born young – a woman in Skibbereen ascribed with the act of eating new-born twins – and in Galway where five adjoining villages were wiped out and the survivors hanged on ash trees for having made away with turnips and mangels from a landlord's grove. Páid was leaving behind home and country. He was leaving behind heritage and lovers. He was leaving behind stones and crosses, holy wells and mass rocks. He was leaving behind the future harvests and the prayers of Father O'Shea over a possible wedding. He was breaking himself from his mother and father, sisters and brothers. He would walk to Cobh with his pittance. From there take a ship to the New World. The ships leaving Ireland were already burdened with the dying, and the dead were said to snap from them like fleas.

On his journey by foot and in a milkman's cart to Cobh he was numb to the sights that surrounded him, to the dying, the dead, or simply those crying, rat and greenslime skinned, and bonily reaching out. Shawls that fell off women's backs were themselves mouldering corpses. He was numb to these things because inside him always and inside his posterity would be the moment when he exiled himself from the last hillside of his townland and from his parents and from his sisters and brothers and from the little crop of land that should have been his and should have yielded sustenance to his wife and children and replenished the heavy malleable breasts of his wife, white as the milk left out for the galleon-full of cottage kittens.

'Off to Cobh,' the milkman had said to him, 'But sure you'd be better off flying to Mars.' The milkman gave him a carrot, a spindly carrot. The carrot had a long octogenarian's nose. 'This will keep you going until you reach Amerikay.'

When Nessan was very small, in the city, Grandma O'Dowd would load him with stories about the funeral of the Liberator Daniel O'Connell, how his body was brought back to Dublin from Genoa where he died on his way to see the Pope, how the ship bearing the body paraded in spring rain before the city of Dublin, the Archbishop on it and bishops from Tasmania and America, the body in a shrine of Genoa velvet of rich crimson and the coffin draped in turn in black cashmere. Sometimes rain fell on the ship, sometimes in her stories it sailed through a blue, balloon-light day. But always, always there were crowds waiting for it, including her father, especially crowds on Richmond Hill. These vast, black crowds converged to see the body being delivered to a mausoleum in Deans Grange Cemetery, the widow descending with the coffin, men with tall black hats standing at the side of the mausoleum, the masters of ceremony. The St. Vincent de Paul Society representatives were allowed to follow the widow and leave a token of O'Connell's good deeds to the poor in the mausoleum. Charcoal fires burned Ireland's grief late into the night and the crowds were treated to soup of split peas and spices in the Protestant-run soup kitchens of Dublin. Grandma's husband returned to Limerick with a gold tassel from a banner and a lily crushed under black heels, bare feet and hooves. O'Connell's pudgy face, his heavy locks and the aristocratic upward tilt of his face became synonymous with a clean, sunny, tree-lined street in the Mid-West, visible through lace or on particularly fine afternoons through open bottom-halves of windows.

*

15

Nessan was seven when his mother brought him West. They shared a bed in the train and they shared beds in San Francisco and Seattle. San Francisco still had ruins that smoked with rain as if still fulminating from the earthquake. Nessan's mother sometimes tucked rosemary into her bosom before she slept with him at nights, hugging his body to the scents in gigantic, marine-light beds. In Yosemite she confronted him with a bunch of wild orange, he in white short trousers, white dickie bow, a mountain rising behind him topped by a clown's white peaked hat.

San Francisco would be a toy he'd take into memory, the pink and lemon colours, the nursery blues. But competing with the colours was the fungus of earthquake ruins, some still spiralling, untended, in poor areas. They were isolated from their fellows which were long destroyed and they were said to constitute no public danger, either waiting to be repaired or, failing that, knocked down, but they crept into Nessan's imagination. 'For here we have no lasting city.' The areas around these ruins were slushy.

Three naval ships came into port when Nessan stayed in San Francisco and in the street Nessan saw a lost Geisha girl, umbrella over her head. His grandmother had told him the story of Puccini's *Madame Butterfly* which a friend of hers had seen in Paris the year of the earthquake. Nessan followed the Geisha girl before his mother caught up with him and the hilly streets devoured the girl. His grandmother often sung an aria which she pretended was from *Madame Butterfly*. She always brightened with talk of theatrical tragedy. A child, Nessan had seen Madame Butterfly die on his grandmother's clean blond floorboards, Madame Butterfly's black hair torn from its braids and slashed on the ground, her hands punctuating the boards with the movement of dying as drops of blood spilled in egg-cup full dashes. If Madame Butterfly visited San Francisco so did Lieutenant Pinkerton. He was the young naval man in a white jacket in a restaurant. The orchestra played 'My Old Kentucky Home'. Coloured lights on the esplanade outside seemed to travel into the black water. Lieutenant Pinkerton sat upright. Nessan undressed him and found he had a chest which was not tanned but the pale colour of fawn sausages. Lieutenant Pinkerton faced them. The woman he was faintly conversing

16

with was turned from them, but she was in white with a pink bow in the shape of a turkey at the bottom of her back. San Francisco, Lieutenant Pinkerton's slurring voice, the fungus of orphaned ruins would crowd into Nessan's mind and become the perennial, glad and sometimes pathetic city by the ocean.

Lisbon, during the war, had the face of many other cities; exiles or passers-through read their cities into its buildings by the sea and flashed glances across imaginary bridges on the Tagus as if the bridges connected Lisbon with their own countries or cities. Lavender shirts blossomed here and a variety of colours prospered that anywhere else would have seemed obscene at that time. White hats were knocked down over the lines on spies' faces. Big noses were everywhere, noses that curved downwards after a certain point, suggesting wealth, aristocracy, health, or Jewishness. Mount Ararat I christened one swarthy and darkfaced young man's nose under the young man's white hat. The oleanders led me and him to the river one day. He was Romanian. Jewish. Wealthy. I told him about Dublin, and I saw Killiney Bay on a fine May day from the house on the hill in which an uncle of mine lived – an uncle who had renegued on a partnership in my father's paper-mill business in order to devote himself to writing a massive novel in which all the characters were bees – a summer-house in the garden, on a slope, in which I had addressed an imaginary companion called Manuel when I was a child, at the end of summer on our return from Spain, the grass on the slope untidy and having a kindred smell with the harvest, the light in the summer-house blanched from the one window. Wartime graffiti in lavatories in Lisbon revived the fantasies and the desires of that single light.

Nessan sat in awe of downhanging, male, American genitalia in the changing-rooms after baseball games on Sunday afternoons. His father would take him to the changing-rooms which were in a circular building white as vanilla ice-cream. Unknown to his father, Nessan worshipped male genitalia every Sunday. He'd seen his father naked many times. He knew his father made abundant demands on his mother. He'd once seen him making love, standing, to his mother. He should have been at a picnic that day with the school, but Miss Dinani, herself a tall, poised butterfly in white, had recently called him 'a drowned

17

grasshopper' and, at the last moment, he'd changed his mind about going, returning with a bag of chocolate covered chestnuts. The fruit of his father's candy factory. Through a half-open door he spied his parents. He sped off, devouring the candies in the shrubs, his white, heavenly blue rimmed, sleeveless jersey quickly smeared by runny chocolate.

On the way back from the West his mother befriended a young actor who'd been playing in San Francisco. His name was Buddy. Nessan's mother's face lit up when she spoke to him and she constantly slapped his shoulder, crying out 'Buddy' as she did so, as if his name invited this conduct. She interrogated him about the theatrical scene in New York and she told him his name should have been Pedro or Antonio as he looked southern – he had black hair slicked in a bold quiff on his forehead. His mouth too was small and bold. 'He's a friend,' she informed Nessan when she was drunk. When he got off at a nameless Wyoming station for some unknown reason – to visit a shady relative maybe, to seek out an old tutor who was in clerical cloth, Nessan's mother ventured – she kept complaining about the discomfort of her corsets and pulled them upward from behind as if she was a chicken who could scratch its bottom.

There was always a stomach-aching, an inner-pinching feeling of loss when casually encountered strangers, swiftly assimilated into her most out-going emotions, went. After Buddy left she allowed a train-hand to stick his penis, huge at the base, into her in a toilet on the train. Nebraska's wild cherries went by alongside the railway tracks outside. They were almost home. I heard Bonnie's confessions years later. That had been the first time there'd been sex with someone else in her marriage, which was strenuous with sex.

When he got home Nessan felt like a cherry tree from which all the blossoms had just left in a single shaking. Virtually every last one. In a grey suit, trousers to his kneecaps, he presented his daddy with his gift, a Bible from Bohemia, in a Slav language, in which one of the colour-bursting illustrations was of Abraham about to sacrifice a quiescent Isaac, Isaac's frail legs bound under his toga and the boy, his hands behind his back, looking up towards God, apparently oblivious of the meal for God he was about to make.

★

All his life there would be that feeling of loss in Nessan, of abandonment when casually won acquaintances went, the sailors on Hobonken Waterfront, the paper-vending boy with skin white and solvent as a gull in the air of Atlantic City.

I too understood loss. I had been brought up in deranged wilfulness by my parents. My mother was of a Spanish family who, if you were to believe them, claimed princesses and princes before Christ. More likely they were Moorish upstarts. Gold was thrown on the Moorish-type house we stayed in when I was a child. The kind of gold it was reminded me of my mother in an Irish spring and convinced me she was a Moor. She'd been studying in Dublin when the 1916 rebellion erupted, bangs from boats on the Liffey; studying at University College, Dublin, the Catholic university, and, for refuge, this Spanish girl in a black coat and hat, slipped into my father's arms. Way back, his family had been Catholic but they changed during the Penal Laws to hold onto their property because at that time the first relative to become Protestant could claim all the family property. So they all became Protestants. The paper-mill, which had long been in the family hands, was supposed to have been supplied – apart from wood from our seven woods in Wicklow and wood from Sweden and Finland – by disused family silks to make paper. To marry my mother my father became Catholic. I was raised Catholic. Catholicism was screamed at me by my mother and chucklingly pulled from me by my father. My mother had wanted a Velazquez princess, so when I was a child she dressed me in trousers that looked like a hooped dress. My hair was first gold, wavy gold, beaten into serene subjection by my mother's brush. The house in Andalusia that we went to – at first for six months of the year, around the summer months, then for shorter periods, June, July, August – had been a resting house for my mother's old and disabled relatives. To-ing and fro-ing made it seem to me that everything in life was double: I was Irish, Spanish, Catholic with a heritage of Protestantism. My mother's people had been from Castile and to a mansion on a hill there we were carried in a pony-drawn trap a few times, breaking our dormant stay in the south, the pony with its head down like a diffident Spanish lady in black. There were wobbly bowls of golden sky between hills as we sauntered there. I was the Irish boy miracle. My hair

19

was dark now and I had a dark-looking Moorish face. Going to Spain involved abducting me from school. That did not matter. My father was too well-known to accost. So my schooling wavered. We saw Spain for the last time in 1934. I was twelve then. Then it was Dublin, a Catholic school there, buses home in the afternoons to Wicklow when there were school holidays. Priests, mangy looking priests in black soutanes suspiciously eyed the ermine of boys' penises curling upon themselves in showers. If they rose, those penises, they were mentally beaten down. My father gave me the Cambridge jacket of a friend of his for Christmas one year. I'd turned seventeen that December. I was nearly grown and I wanted to return to Spain but Franco was there so I went instead to University College. 'Please get me out of here,' I often told myself. Priests sneaked along corridors. The same black soutanes. The same stooping backs. When it was over I began travelling and my travelling with a break of three years saw me ending up eventually in a cold hospice ward in Brooklyn.

Gulls came to the window when I first spoke to Bonnie. I was doing a book, I told her, on Nessan. My father was rich and my mother was rich and they were my patrons. It was strange how once I'd finished at college my parents indulged me; I'd done the requisite suffering and now I could be a kite, a brightly coloured kite, to fly into the sky. But the war had been on. The war had reinforced my image of Nessan's face. We shared the same blue eyes. That was all we had in common. Because Nessan was fair and I was dark, though once having been fair and my darkness having a knowledge of that fairness.

Nessan's fairness came from his father, of course, a confusing fairness because his father's people had been Jewish. Though an ancestor of Nessan's, walking away from a hill in Limerick, had been fair too. The people of Nessan's father had all gathered together at some point in the late eighteenth century in Prague and fled from that city. A child in that group had been required to attempt to write out the Talmud over and over again because always he faltered in writing it. Spinning, many coloured toys he took with him. The Jews had to leave Prague. This group went to Edinburgh. The child had been told over and over again how the Jewish people had wandered since the

Romans demolished the temple. But a part of that temple remained in their hearts despite the obliteration and the butchery that went with it, and they caressed and stroked this remaining part of the temple in them each night. The Jews gathered their belongings, left, and this group, with all the sacred trappings of Judaism, became Methodists in Edinburgh. Eventually. And a section of this group set sail. For America. Bethuel Muir was of the first generation born in America. The only surviving child of a profusion of offspring. Home had been set up in the Mid-West near a white chapel. The candy factory was one of the evangelical, sudden hallucinations of the 1870s. When Nessan was born it was painted white like the chapel.

The brand of religion practised in that chapel was spurious; Sunday school, when Nessan was growing up, was taught by an Italian Catholic who imparted the tenets of Protestantism. Sometimes he and his mother took carriage rides to a French Catholic church ten miles away. There an Irish priest turned up for a while, his cheeks like broken red Christmas crackers. 'Ah sure, I'm Father O'Hennessy,' he kept reiterating, 'Ah sure, I'm, Father O'Hennessy.' He might have been saying 'Ah well, I'm, a toad.' He looked a bit like one in brown. Nessan was brought up a Protestant then but with advances on Catholicism – his mother brought him to mass as if to the grand opera, always crowning her head in meringue whispers and alleys of veil and a white hat – and with a many patterned background of Central European Judaism. 'The trees of the Lord are full of sap; the cedars of Lebanon which he hath planted.' There were cottonwoods between two hills, smoky and golden in spring, smoky and golden and copper in autumn, which spoke of no religion but offered ever-yielding paths for those confused about the multiplicity of their backgrounds, and shelter for little boys fleeing the rancour caused by the clash of their parents' different backgrounds – fathers' leaden declamations, mothers' billowy and shrieking condemnations – the little boys' white sleeveless jerseys, white shirts, white trousers quickly issued with dirt by the trees as if with passports to carry goats' legs further into realms where there was no jurisdiction except that of high flying cisterns of light and of gaggles of leaves, craning in conversation with one another or in rapport with little boys.

*

21

Nessan's mother made a big show of going to confession when Nessan was about nine. She dressed all over in black, a runaway from a Verdi opera. Her costume and her appearance were in fact a requiem. The only adornment of colour was the nectarine, almost puppet-like blotches on her cheeks. Her skin was smattered with powder. Cartoon big eyes leapt out of this powder or eddied before doing so. Mrs. Muir was going to kneel before a French priest. There was a young, sweet smelling French priest attached to the church then and it was him she acquired. After twelve years Bonnie Muir had confessed her sins and was discharged into the spring air, western breezes blowing over the cornfields and over the meadows penetrated by edges of yellow.

Confession was short-lived though; soon Bonnie was screaming at her husband again and, in an inadvertent secret, had a farm-hand make love to her. After he made love to her he pointed in the direction of Nebraska and said that he came from out there. The occasional bison would be poking towards the honey coloured grass at this time of year.

In the summer squatters gathered around the railway tracks. They drank whiskey from jamjars and sometimes their conversations sounded like moaning. Purple lilac encroached on the railway tracks in early summer and, later on in the summer, golden rod roamed the horizon. Nessan heard one man's song. 'I'm from New York. Going West. My ma was a whore, my wife is a whore, my daughter is a whore and my son is at sea. I'm going where there's gold. A few coins of gold for the trouble of a man's life.' Smoke enveloped a cannery and it swung around squatters' backs, their mouldy, vermin-ridden, gangrenous coats. These coats were bedding at night and emblems of status in the world during the day – the status of squatters in a summer which was just about to meander on its course.

It was a railroad squatter who first took Nessan's penis in his hand. He examined its mouth though didn't do anything with it and commented. 'You have a neat little thing. It will voyage far.' Nessan's penis lay desultorily still that day. Both Nessan and the squatter looked at the penis as though it was an object, a world it and its surrounding area – separate from them.

*

One squatter was Dante. He was young. He was from Illinois. The rainbow, perched over dark, wet, wooden farmhouses and contagions of white, newly washed, bustling geese in farm fields, had been the cause of his uprooting. He'd abandoned the farm-holding of his family and left, to posture under rainbows. The rainbow was the only guarantee of surety. But the further West you went rainbows dissolved into blank blue skies. He should be thinking of heading north-east again but now the tug of his journey held him. He was travelling, like Christian, to a holy city; or a holy certainty. 'The pimply arses of San Francisco's whores', one toothless, ash-faced, fathomless cheeked old man was distantly heard to mutter. Weeds were cherished in wine bottles by a squatter with an eye for the decorative, purple ones. With the upward slide of summer old squatters doffed their maggoty coats and some their shirts and you saw ladders of hair going down narrow chests. Dante headed West on August 15, feast of the Assumption of the Virgin according to Nessan's mother, a strange day for a young man from a family of of singing and dancing Protestants to go, someone who knew the sacred steps of an evangelical spring-celebrating dance.

Nessan's mother, in white, looked West herself. 'That's where I must go again in spring. To see the sandpipers in Monterey.' She sang that winter in a Christmas show and, as a Catholic church had opened near them, she practised her faith regularly now, taking the equanimous Nessan with her.

Bonnie Muir looked up at me. Her eyes were snails in mustard lassitudes of lines. It was one of the first times in hours she looked up at me. She begged something of me without saying anything. 'You're a bright boy, aren't you? What do you make of this, our city?'

Charlotte was from Maryland. I'd met her at a restaurant on East 5th Street. I took her home, down East 13th Street where Nessan had lived. The haloed space of red brick around Nessan's rooms was not even punctured now. It was dark and grey. Charlotte could not believe I was Irish. She herself was a vapour of blue taffeta. Her scented and powdered hand reached from the blue taffeta into my hand – pointed decorously, an

23

eel's head. Laughter gurgled from her. Twin spirals of alternative shades of laughter. Her accent was vaguely southern but restrained by Vassar inflections. In bed she told me she had no doubt I was Irish. I had not made love to a girl for a long time. What was the destructiveness of Ireland towards sexuality even if you were very upper class Irish? My sense of my own genitalia was torn long ago. By what? I made love to Charlotte many times, and when she was not there, there were other girls, balloons of girls, brightly coloured balloons, though mainly angelic blue, floating and hesitating – dropping suddenly and stopping as if to eye me – around the white walls of my life. Lizzie told me I was a prince of Aragon. My black hair grappled with my forehead and I sat, legs apart, in a black suit, way back from her as she raised her left leg at an angle from her pale slip on the bed, the leg terminating in bunched down toes, the raised leg meant to reaffirm her point.

I sailed around New York, my genital area blown apart by lightness. Parachutes dropped through this lightness. But in my customary café over its bagels I was making love again in Lisbon to a Romanian Jew who had the spacious buttocks of an Irish bullock and whose body was generally grosser and darker than mine. I was the boy in the summer-house again wanting to be dominated by someone older and gentle, more masculine and the epitome of the male capacity for masculine friendship, wanting to be sealed between this boy's loins. But the only place I was sealed was in a first holy communion photograph in which my shoulders were fraught and my stance was debilitated. I was in a white shirt, long pale trousers and I carried the status of my parents' union, I was a one man state, an ikon, an autistic child, never meant to be reached or to reach out, a kind of rare ceramic bowl on a mahogany cabinet in Wicklow, an inveterate but untouchable symbol of a delicate but disdainful marriage, a point of mediation between two parties and at the same time a point from which to withdraw back into the autonomy of self and nation.

So I could tell Bonnie Nuir that I loved this, her city. Its luminous blue pointing wafers of skyscrapers were a mirage of escape for me. Its maze of passages between skyscrapers were alleyways from multi-form old selves for me. The shadows of

24

Auschwitz and Bergen-Belsen survivors on street crossings were inflections of a new movement in me. The hesitancy in an old Polish woman's face before she crossed a street was a reminder, a reminder that touched an annihilated cityscape of grief in me, but the morning's newly grinning blond and russet bagels were a resurrection of laughter and comic quips and zany and agitated comedy routines. But the waiters' white jackets and the upheld trays of bagels and the pavement tables could not quite make me forget that it was on my parents' fortune I was living and that the new happiness of Europe was a mortgage from other countries. But I still sat there, grinning, my shoulders in a black jacket slightly crouched and a vestige of butter on my napkin.

Nessan dressed in pristine white to bring Angeline Goldfarb to a school dance. It was to be held in a little hall among the baseball changing-rooms which were in the circular building. Angeline dressed like a Confederate belle in a blown-out blue dress. It was the last year of the war and the boys of the orchestra, themselves in white, surveyed the prospective dancers before starting up the music. Esther Killianball excelled at the cake walk, naughtily fluffing up the snow of her undergarments, her pale stockinged legs sliding into violet pink shoes and her eyes tossed back, as though she was holding marbles in them. Juvenile mandolines became giddy with music. Angeline's blue dress was difficult in a foxtrot but it was the waltz at the end she'd saved up for. Her dress spread into Nessan's groin. In the orchestra, a chopped-hay headed boy with hare front teeth and a face that dropped into his teeth, salivated over his banjo. A whole row of orchestra boys salivated towards the end of the waltz. Blue decoration fell from the ceiling and clad Esther Killianball's right breast like a fox fur. She was glad of its caress and stopped to savour the sensuality. A waltz rolled in from the Carpathian mountains as Nessan took Angeline into a changing-room. She wanted some 'preevacy'. 'I hear you write poetry,' said she. 'I do.' She surveyed his groin. 'I like your trousers.' His legs looked military in the tapering neatness of the trousers. Her voluminous and quivering lips invited a kiss. Her dark ringlets under a strawberry banner of a ribbon threatened to shoot from her head. No kiss forthcoming, Angeline declared that she was cold. Nessan dropped his eyes to the cream circles at the tops of her breasts. In the dark and the cold Nessan saw the phantoms of naked men. 'I've got to go,' he said. He turned abruptly, making off, sleeping that night with a childhood teddybear, sucking his thumb beside the teddybear's head.

That was Christmas 1917. Nessan had turned fifteen that December. The war ended the following November. In the meantime Nessan applied himself more to poetry and got his first response, a letter from a renowned literary hostess in Chicago.

Nessan had found poetry in a field of cropped corn on the slant of a hill. It had been a book of seventeenth-century English verse. He'd been three. Faithfully he'd toddled in to his mother with it. A white shirt with fussy pale blue embroidery on the breasts covered his body. She accepted it. Light slinked on the shining tan of what his mother called his 'perfectly curving' legs under the shirt and his curls spurted out like those of the ghost of a seventeenth-century angel.

At eleven he was a sturdy poet, strangely strong limbed and upright at that age. He'd stand on the corn-coloured slants of low hills in autumn, savouring some latest piece of inspiration with his nostrils. When he'd be standing on the slant of hill near his home his mother would sometimes come rushing out in a slattern fashion, white skirts rolled up, one over the other, wrenched from some household task, flour and baking powder dispensing themselves in particles from her hands, a sudden knowledge in her, a sudden intuition of Nessan's fresh burst of inspiration. She knew of his talent, of his obeisance to poetry and was determined to see this talent run its course.

'Poetry comes in tunnels through the blood,' she said. If so the aggregate of elements which made up poetry in Nessan's blood came from such diverse sources that it would cause a whirlwind in the mind to contemplate, the big wheel at a fun-fair, going around and around, a swirl, paths of colour. These colours found their way into Nessan's blood and rested there, though

26

only at odd moments, in odd photographs, would he rest with them.

*

It was a factory worker more than anyone who defined the particular width of the course Nessan's talent would run. A youth nibbling straw at lunchtime outside the factory. Violets poking their faces at him. Blue. Nessan came upon him, sat beside him. The youth gave him a riddle. 'On my hand is a sore. It is both cured and always there.' Nessan gaped at it all right, fiery, blue and red. It was an explosion yet a disappearance. The colours faded into a respite of ordinary skin, very pale at this juncture. 'It is the colour of my soul,' the young man said. Nessan had taken the hand and looked at the colours more closely. He wrote a poem about this sight and his father found this poem and trembled. It was the first he knew of his son's poetry. In a chocolate suit, he stumbled out the words, 'A son of mine. Poetry. Poetry is for cat-faced ladies.' What would echo from these words would be 'of mine'. Bethuel Muir had strongly invested in Nessan.

Undaunted Nessan went on writing and on his fifteenth birthday, 1 December 1917, found that, to his mind, he was a poet.

She wrote to say that she thought the poems he'd sent her – in a long brown envelope, poems on airy paper which made no resistance when you bent the envelope so light were they – had already the manifestations of a very pure talent, of an ethereal, somewhat contorted but very sturdy view of the world. She would welcome more poems and hoped their correspondence be kept up. Nessan, back slightly bent in a sleeveless white jersey, trembled with the letter in his hand. The bones of his face were like her description of the poems, ethereal, somewhat contorted, but giving the overall impression of sturdiness in their anxious state.

The correspondence was kept up and resulted in an invitation to Nessan to participate in one of her soirées at Easter 1919, staying with her in order to do so. The rambling back gardens of her house were struck by apple blossom, punctuated by dignified arbutus blossom, whisked by mignonette gusts. She sat in this garden, on his arrival, on a stone bench, herself a

27

mausoleum of purple, purple tulle over a purple hat, falling over her face and a purple dress on her. A hand reached from her frog figure when Nessan was escorted to her by a black maid who took no chances with him and remained beside him for his initial conversation with the hostess. The maid was in black and white, with a bustle in her black dress. Nessan had taken a direct train to Chicago, his luggage in a small schoolboy-type case. He was packed into a neat dark jacket. His thorax was a vessel in that jacket and his fingers had a frailty on the case. He was nervous. His fingers showed it. He stayed beside the train window. The window showed pictures of a spring countryside, horses in the clay fields. Now, after arriving, he was shown to his room. His hand had trembled in hers and he examined it in his room. It had swum into another person's hand. For the soirée people sat among floral wreathed wooden trellises which broke up the room unevenly. Women's heads surfaced above white fox and men stirred cocktails with wafer-like spoons. On the white, laid tables were bowls bearing orchids. Nessan understood that these bowls were to be drunk from and that these orchids were aphrodisiacs, but, as it turned out, no aphrodisiac was needed for those standing, mainly men, streaming out their poetry. Nessan, youth from the cornfields, took the place of honour, his hair yellow ochre and brown, a neat wedge of thick hair over his forehead and the sides of his head closely cropped, a tomato coloured tie on his white shirt and his legs poised apart in impeccably pressed white trousers. The paper fluttered in his hand, there were chasms in his voice, but in his delivery there was ultimately no doubt. The heads festooning the hall like decorations alerted. Women's heads particularly stirrred over their white fox. The hostess's large purple hat had been exchanged for a tiny pink one which fitted on her black hair like a shell and it too made a movement as if to say that people should immediately desist from forcing their attention on her. A weighty hush was quickly despatched from one member of the audience to another, the flat, sonorous inflections lapping over the bowls bearing orchids, particularly reaching the ears of Mr. Barrett, the Irish Poet, whose bald pate was surrounded by a creamy tuft and whose delicate earlobes seemed to disappear into the blanched and tender landscape of his neck.

The leaves on the wallpaper had climbed, pale green, rhythmically spurting pink rose-buds. The baby had slept in this room in the early years of the 1890s. Ladies, their brows worried about revolution, their eyes bowed to the ground, tripped by on the broad grey pavement in the quiet, vestigial Georgian street outside, hands often consumed by white muffs. Mr. Barrett, in his late thirties then, had snapped up a young wife in the late 1880s and brought her from the country with its swans and its battering of legends to this house. He was already famous for his poems and his songs and into this house trailed the Olympians of Dublin, some looking somewhat doubtful about their Olympian status, or their inspiration, or else rebuffed by the shade of wallpaper which met them. A young wife after years of celibacy: a child. What more could a man ask for? His hair had mostly fallen prematurely and the rest of it had slid into grey, with edges of white, but still there was a compensating pillar of happiness always in front of him. Of a simple country background himself, he had prospered. He had entered into and been accepted by the highest echelons of society. Yet he never lost his Midlands' accent. Derravaragh. That was the lake near his home where the Children of Lir had rested as swans for three hundred years in their trek through the British Isles. A boy baby's pink fully exposed genitalia. Why had they reminded him of pink waterlily centres on Lough Derravaragh? Both had a vulnerability. Life in and around Lough Derravaragh, among the reeds, was both precious and vulnerable. Mr. Barrett had grown up among manifest vulnerability. Swans' eggs among the reeds had taken his mind to the adventures of the Children of Lir, a collection of tawdry looking eggs. But eggs could be destroyed by other boys and lives prevented from being lived. The romances of swans' lives, whether they were the Children of Lir or not, could be aborted. The basis of Mr. Barrett's work had sprung from the swans and the drovers and the alcoholics and market people of his home; through the scenes went a shiver of a tricolour, a faint pattering of military feet. Ireland was rising again, that old woman, rumbling in her resurrection, a drunk who'd been asleep all night. Mr. Barrett's work caught the tingle of innocence that remained in these times and showed a face despite what might have been behind that face. He ensnared a mood. Optimism, but perhaps a sudden devilishly smirking mask behind that optimism. His boy was Daragh – oak. He'd been born in December in 1890.

The angels of Irish myths which had brought Mr. Barrett much money had watched over the little boy, mercantile angels. Mr. Barrett's young wife often checked the flock of angels to see that they were doing their duty. Once or twice she faltered in doing this. She felt that they might not be altogether reliable. Their unreliability proved itself. When the little boy was three he died mysteriously in his bed, having swallowed his own vomit, having got sick when both Mr. and Mrs. Barrett had run out for a few minutes to breathe the air by the canal – they'd been in all night reading by the fire. Daragh. The dead boy's hair had been the colour of oak on the pillow. Lacquered oak. The little boy's soul had gone to join the spirits of the Children of Lir and the host of other doomed innocents from Irish legend, and for Mr. and Mrs. Barrett there was no option but to go somewhere where legends, if not left behind, could be assimilated into life without their flourishing and their active reality. Ellis Island received them, a country mesmerically drew nearer. Mr. Barrett had brought a package of streets from Dublin, a memory of a city where people wandered through fogs thrown up by the 1890s, looking for inspiration or human contact or assuagement. He and Mrs. Barrett would never return. From their arrival, they would live in America renewing their empathy with Ireland through myths and poetry and dispensing smiles from that country, pale generous smiles, at parties. They were destined always to represent the country which had killed their child. Mrs. Barrett's dress grew shorter when she was playing this role. You could see her legs now. She held her hands nervously. Her shoes were scarlet at banquets in New York but her dresses were mustard coloured and her smile, like her accent, that of a lost Irish country girl.

The fact that they became friends seemed inevitable afterwards; the boy had just shaken off the nervousness of reading, the tremor in his voice and in his limbs, when she approached him. Mr. Barrett's pale face was the galaxy of Irish literature. There was a smile there. But in her face there was warmth, there was abundance; her hair that was black still and parted evenly in the centre was scintillating in stripes as if from warmth for him.

She carried herself to him with dignity; she held herself erect. Her hand reached for his and as it touched him he felt drawn into her current. The fast flow of her emotions and her loss. 'There's Irish in you somewhere,' she said. But they did not spend the night speaking of Ireland. Instead they spoke of his home and the grandeur of that part of the Mid-West. Ireland, he realized afterwards, was left for dessert.

His father more than his mother recognized the change in him. Part of him had been abducted. His father, stood, looked towards him, preened himself for argument, but there was silence. In the night his father dreamt of Prague and Jews leaving it with their sacred books, the colours in their illustrations a covert extravagance.

'And Nessan. Where did you get your shirt?' Way past Easter now, his shirt had an Easter whiteness. Nessan was back in Chicago, virtually a runaway. His mother had packed his schoolboy-type suitcase though, party to the gesture of runaway. It was June and magnolia was ferociously in blossom in the hostess's garden. 'South,' she'd told him from her stone bench, 'You'll need the south someday.' He exchanged words with Mrs. Barrett now. They were seated on a veranda overlooking the garden and among an audience of pots of petunias they faced one another. 'I feel so drawn back to Ireland sometimes,' she said, 'But I know I'll never go back.' He'd asked her specifically about Ireland. She and her husband housed Ireland in the United States. 'And you,' she asked, 'Will you go there?' 'I will,' he replied definitely.

On a pillow, he was rubbing against her starched cheek. The pillow was in his room in the hostess's house. Sometimes Mrs. Barrett's face, though she was glowing with a smile, was shockingly pale. There were rifts between mountain ranges in her cheeks. 'Nessan,' she said his name as with the familiarity of one's own child's name. His head corroding the pillow on early summer nights, the windows open, she kindled in his mind for him.

At that point his mother grew jealous. She recognized the presence of another woman in Nessan's life. But she was deferential even in her jealousy. She knew that Nessan was sailing along the path of poetry and that was the most important

31

thing. But in the summer she dipped her head melancholically towards a picnic basket as she strode with it through the fields. She looked tall and splendid that summer, a new tree, much, much younger than before; it was as if competition had braced her and that the fact, the intrigue of Nessan's other life had imbued her with a new life which rose from within her like the ignition and dazzle of sparks from larva. 'Nessan.' She called to his parallel life sometimes. But he did not hear her.

She didn't follow him though. She didn't try to follow him. It was too early yet. Instead, that summer, she went to stay for a long stretch of weeks with her mother in the city. Mrs. O'Dowd was talking back to her Gaelic past through the window. Bonnie had decided to brave her many depressions. She could cope with them now. Mrs. O'Dowd rumbled something about the War of Independence being fought in Ireland. 'May God bless . . .' She called the rebels 'the good lads'. She looked away from Bonnie towards the War of Independence in Ireland. The pageant unfolded on the summer street. Mrs. O'Dowd shot a woman of English family name in her buggy – with her eyes. Cars rushed up and down, guns spitting from their windows. The streets became a ribbon of roads in mountainous country in Ireland. 'May God bless.' Beside her mother, Bonnie embroidered an apron with Saint Patrick expelling the snakes from Ireland. Bonnie's red and blue fingers suddenly poked themselves into my hand, they were blotched like sausages. 'Mateo.' There was a shock in hearing my name. It was as if I had not heard it for years and that here, now, in New York, it was renewed, a wraith of a Statue of Liberty governing all the notes I was making. Bonnie Muir had jumped from the summer of 1919 into the near-carcass of an old, slattern, almost tinker, grey-haired woman.

She wondered visibly why she was telling me all this and then she relaxed at the sight of me and continued; where was her imagination? At a white apron embroidered in scarlet in 1919. Yes, she'd been right to trust me. There was a familiarity, an ease there which she had to question every now and then, had to rail against. She'd said my name in a kind of panic, as if I wasn't the person she'd come to accept me as. Then she was back, in the city streets again, summer 1919, as I watched her eyes, hypnotised by their rolling journey from side to side.

It was like an affair. Her head came close to him, those bony cheeks with the wide creases. Nessan was truant that summer from the candy factory with its mortar of saccharine smell in the air, from the railroad squatters, from the purple willow herb which shuffled along by the railroad. Candy winds blew from his father's factory but they were dispelled by the smell of Mrs. Barrett's gleaming red lipstick. Daddy watched a son go mad. He wanted to drag him back and not just leave him but get him metaphysically involved in the mechanics of the candy factory before it was too late. But Nessan was having alternative candies – more than anything he devoured lemon sorbet, shot through by strawberry chips, under the gaze of Mrs. Barrett.

Nessan's prolonged absence created the first noticeable division in his parents' marriage. Mr. Muir at home, Mrs. Muir residing with her mother. There was a vacuum of silence between them. Late afternoon sun fell in the front room of Mrs. O'Dowd's house. Bonnie reclined there, silently, in white.

Nessan sat talking to Mrs. Barrett, on the veranda, at evening. The summer evening was a southern Mississippi-type red sun. The sun's radiance was packed into itself. It sat in the sky. There was a noiselessness in the air as if a fear the sun would wake.
    'But you write poetry too.'
    'No, no I don't,' she said.
    'But you do,'
    'I write reminiscences.'
    'Of Ireland?'
    'Yes. And I scribble my own versions of folktales.'
    Nessan asked, 'What do you miss most?'
    'Water.'
    Nessan smiled. A long smile slanted across his face. His teeth were very white. And she touched his smallpox scars on his left cheek as though they'd bite.

Nessan slept with her in his mind. His sleep took him very deeply into his own being and into the being of others. It was as if he was falling down into an interminable well. The sun-weary, dust-laden purple lilac by the railroad, the squatter's broken cups of red Californian wine, the harp hanging from the

33

garden elm all merged into an image of her, Mrs. Barrett, on Grafton Street in central Dublin. She was a little ruffled by the crowd, though she fought her way through it, holding up her dress a little with her fingers, her pale face looking straight ahead. There was a fear in her eyes. The crowd, the street, the moment disclosed some premonition to her. Nessan in the United States took up this woman at the tail-end of the outcome of that premonition. They laughed over a white laid table on the veranda, a table which seemed especially laid for them, but always there was the sense of what she'd been through, of the gap in him, of the ocean of knowledge which separated her from the young, slightly flinching woman on Grafton Street in Dublin, Ireland.

All tides bring you back to the same moment. Nessan was the success of a literary scene in Chicago. Hats flew off and were tossed in the air for his youth. There were detractors. But he insinuated himself into many people's hearts with his good clothes and his good looks. But there were losses that summer too: a loss between his parents, a loss, for all the ribaldry, in him.

In a poet's bedroom, a paunchy, fungus faced New York poet, Nessan having gone there, in lieu of a black maid, to deliver pineapple vinaigrette on a white plate, Nessan was seduced. He wasn't unwilling to be seduced. In fact he was waiting for any experience which might help him towards the early corrosive maturity he thought appropriate for a young poet. The New York poet pulled down his trousers and his underpants from behind. 'What sleek buttocks you have,' the older man complimented him, 'Lamb-like white.' His large cold hand flat on Nessan's naval, inside his shirt, with the other hand he caressed Nessan's buttocks. Nessan tightened them, arching that part of his body until he was in the same position as a Cupid about to fly from a wedding cake. Matters proceeded when the older man calmly strode to the door, turned the key, returned to Nessan who was still a static Cupid or a ballet dancer transfixed in motion, not knowing what to do next. The man munched his pineapple in front of Nessan and then, with the oil on his fingers, touched Nessan's penis while his own penis tried to get inside Nessan's backside. It was very big. In minutes Nessan's penis was in the man's mouth. 'I love your hairs,' the man said. 'Red. Chestnut. I would not have guessed at them. Come deep.' He did come, and later he took the man's penis and played with it. He held it like a toy. A disconnected thing. For some years Nessan would go through life collecting penises as if they were disconnected things. When the penis had collapsed in size the only legacy of the encounter was an image of his mother scrubbing his backside as he stood in the tub when he was a child and of her suddenly paying stringent attention to his buttocks, telling him he had those of a frightened billygoat. Apart from the physical legacy that was. Nessan washed semen and vinaigrette from his groin and thought of Quaker graves, endless patterns of slabs of stone in a dizzyingly expansive meadow near his home, especially at evening, when light struck the stones and illuminated them as if illuminating the untarnished and brave souls of pioneers to this place.

Mr. Barrett's elfin, delicate smile, that baldness poised among white surrounding hair and white skin, loomed behind Nessan's exchanges with Mrs. Barrett. There was nearly always a gurgle of laughter in his eyes, some mischievous tale ascending from his throat. In fact he kept people up late into the night with his tales. There were red roses on the wallpaper in the room in which he kept people up and he launched into a fresh story on the final cadence of another. Moonlight on stone fields in Ireland, Invincibles, White Boys – secret societies rummaging and darting about with their business among the stones, fairies hopping off stones in moonlit fields like grasshoppers off sun broiled daylight stone, Spanish wine caskets among rocks on beaches in the West of Ireland; these were the stuff of his tales. Banshees, revolutionaries with midget caps dragging carts of arms, the ropes over their shoulders, the hanging of corrosively handsome young men. On such a simple diet millionairesses in crimson, hooded capes stayed up through the night, seated, listening to him. Mr. Barrett's brogue had a velvet assurance, a tickle of mockery, a self-mockery, mockery at an audience who were so taken in by his stories. When not entertaining others he seemed to be giving advice to young poets. Nessan came up the aisle towards him for advice and ended by going away with the altar gifts – the fruit, the flowers.

*

They made a trip in unison to a lake beach one morning, Mr. Barrett, Mrs. Barrett, Nessan. The sky seemed more a canopy raised from the perimeter of the lake so luminous was it. Every figure, mules by the lake, striped changing tents, had a theatricality, an emphasis; within this theatricality a Punch and Judy show proceeded, Judy was bludgeoned on the head by a catatonic Mid-Western drawling Punch. Nessan strode between Mr. and Mrs. Barrett, but a little ahead of them, their mutual child. He was hungry for the water. He splashed and raged in it. The strawberry coloured bathing costume was tender to his skin. His face from water, hands gripping a wave, back bent, looked to Mrs. Barrett. She stood on the shore, a woman abandoned by a sailor. Afterwards, towards late afternoon, Nessan, in a brown suit with an ice-cream, was more tanned than ever, his gold hair licking his forehead and his head looking arrogantly – like that of a precious English public schoolboy – to the condensation of sunset on the water. 'Now you have water,' he told Mrs. Barrett. But she said, 'Not the ever-present water of Ireland.'

Nessan changed in a lemon and lime striped tent. Alone, naked, alone with his body, the white patch glaring agonizingly, he masturbated. Semen fell on a rose nucleus of sunburn above his knee. Some day someone commensurate with his idea of love would do this to him.

Brown bog water of Ireland, soft, luke-warm water, water which rippled with dapples of buttercups in its brown and with little threads of slimy contorted green when you stroked it, was the water she pined for. Water which had surrounded her body first time he saw her naked. They'd been walking, she and the older poet, when he suggested she go for a swim. He just stood there, fully clothed. She entered the water for him. He made love to her there, under a white hawthorn tree in blossom. He found her virginity among her thick and formidable-looking shield of pubic hair. 'A dark girl,' he called her. He often asked her to undress in the fields of Westmeath and she walked naked beside him, holding his hand, among the manifold heads of buttercups. There was enough space in Westmeath not to be seen. Anyway she was a model, his model for poetry and it did not matter to her if Westmeath labourers saw her bum as she

36

walked with a lavender parasol above her, her arm in his, her feet picking their way alongside his clerically black suit from George's Street in Dublin.

The morning they'd gone to the lake beach Nessan had been slouched on the sand when a man in a bathing costume with a heavy black moustache and an uncertain crust of black hair, thick at the base, balding on top, approached him. The man stood over Nessan and asked him if he'd like to hire a mule. Nessan said no. The man did not go away at the refusal of his offer but stood there, threateningly. Then he turned to Mrs. Barrett and Mr. Barrett and asked them if they wanted to hire a mule. They said no. 'That son of yours, he'll turn out no good,' he mumbled and turned, going on his course.

Fat women in striped bathing costumes, women with balloon bellies and balloon bottoms, had gently tossed balloons in the air in little groups on the beach. Mr. Barrett had awkwardly emerged from a changing tent in a bathing costume. His skin had been pale and his legs, especially at the knees, looked undernourished and deprived of a lifetime of sun. Mrs. Barrett had taken to the lake, entering it, like its owner. A camera had pronounced a shot of the trio and a literary photograph had been ordained for the albums, three people in bathing suits on the blanch of a lake beach; Nessan's cheeks seemed to have collected ruddiness in them like those of a healthy, innocuous farm boy and his eyes had been lit up like lanterns. He'd been straddled on the beach between Mr. and Mrs. Barrett.

Going home – there was always going home to be done after these triumphs – the sinking in, the paling of the blood. Nessan was aware of the tribulation in his blood vessels on trains taking him home. He stayed beside train windows, baggage often beside him, as if he was about to make a getaway at a village station along the way. Essentially he'd been the rich boy having a number of holidays that summer and towards the end of summer his father put his foot down. The old man confronted the young man, both in cocoa coloured suits. 'You were not brought into this world and brought up to be an idler. You'll have to set your mind to something. If not to the factory to a position. This man's' – he was talking about himself – 'dollars

37

are no longer going to be fed to you. You're going to have to pirouette, if you want to do that, to your own earnings. And this poetry. And those poets, pederasts, I know.' It was strange his father should have mentioned that word so early in Nessan's career. Nessan's mother shrieked a little speech on his behalf but her heart wasn't in it – her son had drifted from her and she wanted him back or wanted him punished. Poetry was meant to consolidate their relationship not to damage it. And she could not help noticing his carnal eye as he looked from the hill on which their house was to a procession of hogs in a field below.

But there was one more trip to Chicago. Nessan managed to extract the money from his grandmother in the city who was dawdling by the front window at an uncertain point of Irish history – there were Elizabethan English soldiers in it, there were profuse forests clothing Ireland, forests later felled by English malice, there were unkempt wolves, but there were also debonair young men running frantically about on the business of revolution, wearing cravats – she handed it to him in a flash, seeming to take it from inside her skirt. She had in fact had it in the hand furthest from him and blocked out by her dark skirt. Nessan took the money, uncertain as to how he should react, wavered giddily in his stance for a moment or two, then made off as if he'd just performed a smash and grab raid, muttering thanks to the old lady as he headed out the door, facing away from her. Her eyes twinkled sagely towards him, then, mentally, she resumed counting the corpses at some English massacre of Irish people, looking out the window, the figure of Nessan flitting by in a charcoal suit, in later summer sunlight, interrupting some companionable and unbelligerent shire horses at the Battle of the Boyne.

What brought him back to Chicago with a measure of desperation? It was she. Mrs. Barrett. They were leaving Chicago, the Barretts. Nessan had to see them, had to be with them. He had to fulfil some inkling, some troubled, cloudy notion. They were waiting. She was waiting in a garden of dahlias. Clothes dripped from her. She was melancholic. She talked about her baby. She moaned about her baby. She turned away during her first encounter with Nessan, her back going into a purple, inky blast of sunset. There were funereal tidings from the flowers. 'I wanted so much to go back,' she told him later,' when I first came here. So much to go back and find the little grave of my child in the Dublin mountains. I imagined it, each spring, flowers about it, and a limestone school nearby. Daffodils. The first vain, shaking daffodils. It was as if by going back I'd find in the spring wind why. But America took me over. And my husband's fame. But always in me, or at least deepest at night, there's a loss, a cry, a wailing, an impotence. Some room was destroyed in my house and all the grand rooms, the wallpapered rooms of America can't make up for that. I fled my own guilt and took up in a waltz with your country.'

'But it's not my country. Ireland is my country.'

'No, no, my lad,' she faced him pointedly, 'you're American. It's written all over you. American.'

The wind in the night, the stillness, the hush before the wailing, the tumultous shrieking of the banshee. Stone walls in Galway, low hills, the sudden tremor of a banshee in the air. They tell you these things aren't true, logic itself tries to dispel them but there's something stranger than logic and America's electric vacuum cleaners. There is something taller and more spindly than skyscrapers. The remembrances of youth and of nation. The terror on a young, black-haired girl's forehead. Sweat came to Mrs. Barrett's forehead, one, two, three jewels of sweat, an anointment. It was towards five in the morning, the wave towards the latter part of the night and she was full of regrets, of disappointments, of her own rocky inner abrasions.

That a boy should have healed her. How strange that was. Life was tugging at her hand again like a child and inviting her forward. She stared at a big bath for five minutes before removing her clothes and entering the vessel. She knew she had to leave here soon. There were labyrinths being made into her emotions; narrow roads gesticulated through bogland under pencilled grey skies in Ireland. She held her pale palms out in the bath and examined them. The lines in them were scarred with pink. There'd been ravages inflicted on her on life's course but here for a moment, in a house in Chicago, there was merriment before winter, multitudinous and noisy drinks before Waterloo.

★

For Nessan it was giving himself to a river, the parties made a current through the nights, scraping out bits of the bank. You just went along with it. Your body was taken along with it. His glass was continually replete. Eventually at night, his body shook with the impact of drink, it shook around the spine. But he continued drinking and his body, at that place, seemed to revolve. He was entering into a routine, there was a tunnel and at the end of the tunnel there was more drink. For Nessan, Mrs. Barrett was an object in the crowd now, a pink rose on the right side of her velvet grey coat which hung from her, her face directed towards him under her wide grey hat and her eyes clearly sending out signals to him occasionally. Her pink rose floated in the debris of the party. The mind was a holocaust. There was burning in it and it left craters like catacombs in ancient Rome. Nessan's thoughts still lived in these catacombs and disturbed him. Then there was his body. As he became more drunk his genital area became more flagrantly alive. His penis sometimes almost visibly poked out. Nessan was up for grabs by a few middle-aged men. They were men who paused around the edges of parties. Nessan gave his bum to plump, puffy-faced and puffy-eyed middle-aged men in their rooms. And as he did so he thought of his father and willed vengeance on him – for what? The sexual rapaciousness he'd shown to Nessan's mother, the humiliating subjection he'd forced her into, those positions – Nessan imagined them though he had never seen them – particularly his father riding his mother from behind as though she was a female Alsatian and his mother's thread-like fingers grabbing a piece of brocade on a cushion, the pale thread-like fingers clenching that brocade tighter as his father became more heated and more Alsatian-like in love-making, a streak of gleaming green phlegm slanted over his upperlips. On one occasion after having been made love to Nessan threw boots from him. He should have taken them off earlier. Now, the boots near the door, he nursed his pale feet with their florets of pale, curling toes. A puffy-eyed man – the balls of his eyes like two mice – slinked out of the room, Nessan's room, those eyes still on Nessan as he backed towards the doorknob, turning it.

The remorse which set in, shocking in a way, his own cargo of humiliation, his seared rectum were all swiftly oblivionized by

40

another rush of drink. Nessan had only to hold his hand out at parties for a half dozen men to take it. 'Your shirt, it's getting grimy,' someone said of his shirt cuff one night. Later that night under a marble staircase Nessan showed his famous marble white buttocks in an act of daring to an older man. The older man caressed them and said they should be positioned on the end of the bannisters. It was very late. Nessan heard footsteps and pulled up his trousers in the alcove. Mrs. Barrett passed through the stretch of hallway outside. She did not see them. The footsteps ascended the stairs and the man requested Nessan to pull down his trousers again. But Nessan did not. He retired to bed and detected a wailing in the autumn breeze.

The emotion was becoming clearer to her, this winnowing of breeze in her. She was in love with the intractably blond part of the hair that should have been her son's, or a possible image of her son's, but was Nessan's, impeccably waved, the focal youth of this autumn in this house. She and her husband had in part created the stage for Nessan and now that it was there they were somewhat removed. When Nessan was going about his business, she had time to think about her early life, about the girl with the black hair in a heavy bun at the back, and parted on top so evenly that it had scintillating shapes like swallow adornments in it, from near Mullingar, who'd encountered the poet on one of his return visits to his flat native soil, how they'd nearly bumped straight into one another beside a lake, the young female literary devotee making forcefully for the famous poet before he faded from her reach and the famous poet making ruefully for the scent of a fresh young woman before she vanished into thin air. The girl from the country who invested the town literary society with her enthusiasm was taken up by the poet, her grey dress seeming to blow further out for him, so far that she seemed to levitate from the meadow flowers, as he tugged himself along beside her, her purple parasol reaching into the Westmeath spick and span sky, her other hand going occasionally to her troubled voluminous dress. Their friendship changed its tone when their hands reached for one another's over the dome of her dress, which was quite an athletic achievement considering its offputting width. Eyes narrowly gawked. The event was noted behind a thousand hidden black shawls. But the only people who saw them first make love were the scarecrows, some with black shawls over them. Magic, a kind of innerly summoned magic, kept the eyes away when she gave her thick and flourishing virginity to him under a white hawthorn tree, arching that part of her body to meet what emerged of him from his clerically black suit. Low, stone-walled hills in Galway welcomed them, hills rolling and dancing and sometimes getting drunk. They excavated Irish legend, she secretarially taking notes for him. But in Galway, between two hills, she understood a profound chasm in her. She had moved away from her kin. She had soiled herself in their knowledgeable eyes. In the townland she was from and in Mullingar she was a cross between an illuminated Jezebel, a particularly spectacular piece of fireworks which had leapt from a staid and prayerful young woman, and a girl made commercially good. On her marriage in Our Lady of May-white in Dublin, a bouquet of small, unopened pink roses trembling in her hands, there were those in and around Mullingar who whispered that God would avenge this audaciously carnal relationship demonstrated to the world. Ladies of note moved up and down the street and milled into their house. One woman came with a hat like a basket of roses on her head, pink chiffon wrapped around the roses. Gloves were swiftly removed for fear any conversation would be missed. Their house was noted for 'conversation'. Revolution and war were at hand and with war and revolution came a glass of wine and the perusal of new and shining books of poetry. Mrs. Barrett always looked at other people's books of poetry. She was a midwife for poetry. But she knew she had her own literary world inside. A child came. A child briefly came into the world. The child was the child of literary men like old billygoats who lived in cottages veering towards the heights of the Dublin mountains and of mad young playwrights who ran into the Barretts' house early mornings searching for pages they'd left behind the night before. Daragh was cradled in a word and he left a legacy of a word. Oak. Their years of exile they would have to be oak to survive and like oak after rain soft and almost pliant to touch. Letters still came from Ireland condemning her. In America Mrs. Barrett discovered her own genius and penned volumes of Irish folktales. Demure in grey, outlandish in emerald with vermilion linings, royal in black, she stood and received the accolades placed on her and her husband's shoulders and heard speeches of commendation meted upon them. But still in her, biting her with sharp teeth, lashing at her, was the knowledge that they would never love her where she came from, that they felt God had been wise in punishing her, that the image of her would always be the same in their minds, that no amount of awards or commendations would alter that, that they had elected to see her as a drooping, debilitated and grey-faced old lady whose life had been parched once by a ghost, that no amount of loving or creative travail could lead her true image back to them, that of a woman who could still have a place in her emotions for a sensual boy.

Nessan came to her one night, when she was in the bath. He knocked on her door and understood she said to enter. The door of her bathroom was open. He sat on the side of the bath in his charcoal suit. She had on her head a ridiculous white rubber bonnet, banded by elastic and frilled at the bottom. Her right breast investigated the water. He pressed her hand in his. 'Nessan, pet,' she said. She still had a smear of red lipstick on her lips and a whiff of daylight's perfume emanated from her. He left then, saying sorry or something under his breath, sorry for entering, sorry for –; he clanked along the corridor, putting his body to bed after this wild escapade with his mind still leaden with drink.

Vicarious love lasts only a night or two; a few nights later Nessan got very drunk. In the middle of the large banqueting room he declaimed some of his recent poetry to a plump man with oily skin like a seal's. Mrs. Barrett was standing at the side of the room alongside her husband. Both of them had their vision steered on Nessan. Mrs. Barrett was in that strange grey coat which hung on her like a drooping flag on a flagpost. People milled around the hall, less than before, mainly very erect men, often in pairs, like sentries. In a sudden upward dramatic rush of his arm in declaiming his poetry Nessan fell on the floor. The oily skinned man laughed. Mrs. Barrett abandoned anchorage and drifted towards him. A slender arm reached to him. He rose with seeming ease. Less drunk, not wishing to leave Mrs. Barrett out in the cold, Nessan began declaiming poetry at her too. She turned to the man and, in a very polite, articulate voice began to speak to him about poetry. It was the first time she had ignored Nessan. Very peeved,

Nessan began shouting about the abundance of his recent poetry on fresh white sheets of paper, raising his arm in the air to demonstrate that abundance. In doing so he hit Mrs. Barrett on the chin. She walked away. Two shadows merged into one another, Mr. and Mrs. Barrett left the room together. The erect men still circulated, even fewer than before. Outside on the veranda red carnations shivered in paroxysms in vases before an autumn breeze sent by a thundery sky. Nessan was still shouting about the retinue of his poetry which had emerged from that autumn when he excreted in his trousers. Part of the excrement was left on the shining floor, most of it in his white underpants which were halfway down. Rain poured on the garden outside, flecks spattering the shivering carnations on the veranda. Even the oily skinned man didn't want Nessan then.

Although he would have many humiliations in his life this would be the worst. People turned their eyes from him in the morning. He heard a whisper that the Barretts had gone but he could never be sure. Shunned, he crept out with his baggage having cascaded backwards from being a young already admired poet to being baby.

The rain in the air that night would creep into his bones and augur an early death or an inherited memory of Irish famine bones. Going home on the train he remembered sailing up the Mississippi once with his father when he was a child, and how the dreadful autumn rain had spoilt the holiday and how they'd both stood in shelter on deck, staring with fixation at the autumn rain which was insinuating itself into their bones and cloaking them in the premonition of a winter which, with summer prematurely tossed out, would offer no respite and weigh on them with the weight of death. The little boy had shivered, in this, one of his first inklings of death. Nessan gripped the rail beside the window and thought of the winters long ago, which followed premonitions in the autumn rain, when the dead seemed to stalk the hills, stopping and starting, wraiths eddying to and fro until they made an unstinting onwards course over trees and bushes fixated in the grip of the long and unbudging winter.

The huge purple clouds of autumn banked up over the flatness and the low hills of Nessan's home. Nessan wandered to a point beside the house said to be the oldest in the neighbourhood. A cottage really. White painted timber with whiskers of dead and cobweb-like flowers around it. Bruised, he was back in the terrain of his fathers, a minion of the mountain ranges of cloud above. He drew comfort from this soil. In fact comfort and solidity seemed to flow from the earth and embrace him. It was a warm evening so he just wore a white shirt. He stood very still and it was as if a procession of old men rose from the soil like smoke from a cavalier cigarette and embraced him. He was being fondled by his ancestry. Dusk plunged into darkness and he groped his way home, leaving the deserted house and entering upon his mother's pale dishes with emerald patterns standing on the dresser.

Nessan stayed a year working for his father as a clerk in the factory. Often newly acquired black glasses dug into his nose. A position was found for him in New York as an assistant in a solicitor's office and in September 1920 he travelled there, inhabiting rooms on East 13th Street donated by a New York landlady relative. Sunlight hit the auburn façade outside the window. It reminded him of the sunlight which bore in on him in his father's office, when, black glasses on, sunlight catching sawdust on the floor, he penned poems instead of office details, poems about young male workers with hair the colour of sunlight on sawdust and Norwegian blond floorboards.

In the room to which he'd moved his possessions in the first few weeks, he was able to contemplate the manner of his going. His grandmother had pressed a profusion of dollar bills into his hand in her front room as though they were rubbish she was trying to dispense with. Her hands seemed like elongated scrolls. She held them out flat when he'd taken the money in a gesture of beseeching for him. His father stood stoically as he was leaving. He hardly said goodbye to Nessan. He was military in his composure but Nessan noticed something unusual, a red handkerchief in his breast pocket, a splash, as though for symbol or carnival. His mother came with him in the buggy to the station. She wept a lot and loudly before he left. She said he must stay pure and 'handsome'. She looked very handsome that day, Nessan noticed, tall, graven-faced, erect, the skin of her face eventually a dusky parchment. A few calm tears on it. The breeze blew a tear away. There were dahlias growing on the platform and begonias sat in a vessel hanging from above. 'My, my,' his mother kept saying, amazed at the bigness of the event of Nessan's going. A woman wrapped in a black shawl stood on the platform. Black tassels on the shawl. A Slav. She pulled the shawl to her but she was calm before whatever history those railroad lines conjured. She was meditative even, totally still. The stillness was repeated in an Indian man in a flashingly embroidered waistcoat. His history was nearer at hand. Beyond the railroad station was a conquered land. Women, they too in black, but younger women, held baskets of red berries, ferrying them from one station to another. They were not communicative with one another and stared ahead. Truculence came when Nessan's mother cried again, saying. 'Nessan, I hope you have not deceived me about anything.' What did she mean? Nessan was bland faced. 'That your heart will still be here.' Nessan looked at her. His face was pale and there was a sunrise of questioning freckles in this pallor. During this facial hesitancy the train came. Mrs. Muir embraced her son. She virtually walloped him with her kiss. Nessan parted in a pendant screen of blond late afternoon sunshine in which the odd, blind, groping spot was left.

In the weeks after his departure, Mrs. Muir wandered the low hills, distraught, demented, frozen hearted and jubilant in turns. Jubilant for the movement in his life, painful for her, for the triumph of his move. She willed his life to poetry now and contrived to direct him that way. His first poems were published in New York. They came in a magazine with a sheer white cover. Mrs. Muir eagerly searched the pages for them. They were in tiny, frail print, print so frail it seemed scared to meet the pages. Mrs. Muir celebrated with the geese at the back.

New York was more than just a current which subsumed Nessan in the early 1920s; it was a spot in the general current. You knew you were part of the current and yet you knew you had an identifiable location in it. Nessan's head bobbed up and down in the crowd, the young man confidant that he could be picked out in his lumber jacket with its mauve, blue and brown colours. And yet sometimes he was content to dive into the anonymity of the less ostentatious heights of the crowd. Lemon shades threw a midsummer illumination over Fifth Avenue sometimes at night and into this Nessan loved to wander; its borders were a passport to possible romance. Or at least to edification of self and of every passerby. Even the horses looked alluring. But a sailor suit was finest in broad daylight. Nessan purchased a flock of chalk ducks for his friendly sailor lover at a streetside Jewish market, lemon beaks on them and tails that peaked rudely into the air. He handled the fine part of one of their tails and pointed the duck at the sailor. Later in his room, as late afternoon winter gloom consumed them, there'd be love. Nessan wandered into the nights, looking for the love and the companionship a Mid-West childhood barred him from. But it usually led to cleaning a penis over an East 13th Street lavatory bowl which had a mahogany coloured seat.

Bonnie Muir, on her deathbed, tipped me off about places to go and, in late October, around Hallowe'en, I wandered through backstreets off the main avenues, mainly to the east of the convergence of Fifth Avenue and Washington Square, and found myself savouring morsels from Singapore or the Lebanon. Gastronomy was not the reason for sending me to these parts. Nessan's life lived in slanted shadows across these façades, moulds of even shadow on them thrown by the opposite block of houses on a narrow street. Alley-cats arched their backs in repulsion to innovation in music and young men still arched their backsides as they sidled along or acrobatically stalked from shadow to shadow. Bonnie sent me into the bowels of New York for Nessan's life. But it merely awakened a whole other life in me. I'd gone to find Nessan and I ended up by reinventing my own life. Hallowe'en found me on top of a skyscraper, listening to piano keys jabbed by black fingers and sitting opposite Mathilda from the north eastern outreaches of Upper New York state, her gold hair in Limerick sausage ringlets at the back and those ringlets checked by a carmine ribbon and her pale, slightly anaemic face, eagerly craning forward. 'Gee, I never knew Irish people spoke like you.' Planes dipped outside as though coming to hear the piano music or investigating the skyscrapers. Planes rocked like cradles over New York. They suggested the motion of the entire city, a

47

rocking, lulling, soporific motion. It put trouble to sleep and exacted only the iridiscent from the spectacle of one's experience. New York that night was a craning of skyscrapers into the sky, their necks speckled by luminous windows and the luminous windows creating an overall aureole which received the sky and the visiting lights of aeroplanes. Mathilda undid a bar of chocolate and ate into it. I watched the chocolate smear her white and delicate chin. Eager not to miss any of it she created a trail of dots from the already runny chocolate onto her chin. Finished, she sat back and wiped the chocolate with a napkin. One dot had reached her left breast. That reminded her. 'We'll be off,' she said. I paid the waiter and half-way home I got scared I was escorting a piece of confectionary.

Nessan's mother paid her first visit to Nessan in New York, the spring of 1923. He had not been home since he'd left. She'd got a bit haggard looking and a bit older looking. Life with Bethuel Muir was not going well. Nessan still had the rooms, paying rent to a female relative he never saw. For a few days she was like a stranger and behaved as a recently bereaved stranger. Nessan could not really believe it. Her hair had turned grey and was caught in a loose bun behind, at the bottom of an abundant fall of hair, and she stooped a little. At first these changes seemed integrated in his general expectation of her and it took a few days for him to unravel his memory of her from what she was now. But the grey hair did not overwhelmingly age her. It merely produced a different person. After a few nights and a few days —days of large spoonfuls of couscous or yellow rice in Village cafés or cafés near the Village – old customs were revived. Mrs. Muir left her room, entering the adjoining room in which Nessan slept, in a dressing-gown speckled with a thousand tiny pink roses and slept with him, in his double bed, as she did when he was a child, the hulk of her troubled body leaning towards him and her arms about his unresisting neck.

Two

Varela was from a Southern American country. He was Nessan's first real love. He moved in with him to those little rooms. He was a rich man's son. A few years younger than Nessan, he gave up wealthy surroundings to live with him. While Nessan worked in his office Varela tended plants on the roof. There was an estate of which he was due part waiting for him in a north eastern country of South America. The prospect lazed. In New York he wore dungarees and smiled a lot in his plump, puckish face which was surrounded by playful and irregularly protruding tufts of onyx black hair. He did his plant tending in these dungarees. Varela was of a country where lascivious, often mountainside estates swept to the ocean; his own father's estate was low-lying, next to the ocean, cotton and cocoa growing there, bananas, sugar-cane but room also for steeds on which his brothers and he had ridden. Distant mountains tossed to the ocean. The capital city was in the right hand mountains. Tufts of cotton clouds got entangled with the nonchalant mountains. In a cove a swimming pool had been constructed and Varela's mother – herself educated in Europe – brought pans of fried vegetables to the boys whose long legs

51

writhed in the water there. Behind the mountains were copper and iron ore mines; the wealth of the country was addressed to the ocean-side; where there weren't cotton or cocoa or coffee plantations there were impeccably gardened estates adjoining the ocean, rows of sealed off camellia bushes and men on horses playing polo. The Spaniards had come here once, dropped anchor, collected bananas and papayas from the mountain-side forests and returned then to the ships. Varela, growing up, had often half expected Spanish galleons on the ocean. But there was only the whip of the tennis racket on the tennis ball to break the silence in him, boys in white shorts with legs the amber of dollops of fried banana shuffling on the tennis court. So he thought to go to sea some time himself. In the city, in a café on a rolling street, you got ice-cream you were told was made in New Orleans. But after these excursions it was back home, to a swimming pool that looked like a Roman bath. The changing-room alongside it too looked like something from ancient Rome, a temple, white. In this temple boys changed raiments. They fidgeted with garments. With this fidgeting, when you were with a fat country cousin from the copper mining area of the mountain forests, other things happened too. These events were paused over, giving them time to register, to be philosophized over, or for the wonder to be drawn out. Two years Varela spent at a clerical school in the mountains, in a bit of land dipping in the middle like a hammock. Priests armed with huge sticks patrolled his fantasies. The priests had the faces of the monkeys of the kings of Spain and were hunched at the shoulders. Or rather the faces of the after-death monkeys of the kings of Spain and were gnome-like at the shoulders. Lemon broom shot out over priests' heads, they did not notice it. It was a signal to leave. Varela joined the navy and sailed for two years. His father had an apartment now in New York for business purposes and, off a ship on one occasion, he ensconced himself there, smoking marijuana in a shirt a sailor with one eye and a studied gold earring in his left ear, from Persia, had given him – a pirate handkerchief over his dark face with its pouting mouth and its eye that watched for the first event of the near-lavender shirt on Varela. So much for the sun flashing, benevolently signalling waves of home, the flashing steeds. Here in a fulsome shirt you sat and smoked. On red satin draped couches. The red that crowded into the couches anticipated Nessan and his set. They were the red of brothels or of licentious South American women's drawing-rooms. Nessan rescued him from the couches and brought him into the streets. They met in a café on the Hobonken Waterfront – Nessan's stalking ground – they smoked cigarettes, they bantered with Mrs. Clancy, they heard a Cork sailor dribble and spit 'Mary from the Banks of the Lee'. Nessan hunched in a black donkey jacket. Varela moved in with him, giving up the red satin couches and listless modern painting decorated apartment. Home was always a legend, Varela's home, the flashing, distant tides, the cocoa plantations, the Roman bath-type swimming pool, sequestered, white – the bottom of a boy to be seen in the changing-room, a rouge towel going to his face and giving it quarter. It was left a legend; daily routine was got on with. Nessan lived in domestic happiness. He eyed Varela as he might a young wife. But Varela was anything but feminine and the nature of their relationship often seemed not homosexual. More a platonic comradeship. That was an observation of people who could not guess what they got up to at times. Varela's torso when he was half naked was a collage Nessan had built up from his life, the statue-like billows of the muscles of his arms, the rush of dark hair towards the amber conflagration over his chest, the out-lying regions of red, disparate sun spots. Varela stood in casual trousers and sometimes folded his arms as if expecting to be admired, fluidly pushing out his chest, grinning. Some of the plants from the roof wandered into the apartment, cacti and crocuses. Literary society from parties spilled over into the apartment, ladies coming to have a look at a sculpted head Nessan claimed he'd found among empty pea cans on West Street, by the waterfront. The head, needless to say, was that of a young man, who looked by the expression on his face as if he'd just been shot in the stomach. Beth Hibbing said she'd seen a young man like that at a literary party at which a coal fire had ignited the house. It must have been his head. 'He was very *bonhomie*,' she said philosophically. The rush of party people stayed on one side of the room they'd entered. There was a strange, quixotic, non-literary smell here. Nessan burrowed himself into his black jacket after one of these intrusions and went walking by himself. It was as if he suspected these people of some ill-intent. In his years in New York – it was now 1924 – Nessan had become part of a literary set that seemed to move in unison from one party to another, a kind of mobile suffusion of people, glasses, and erect conversations. Some of the women virtually foxtrotted in literary conversation. Mystic ideas visited this group, sexual rancours flew through it, odysseys were made by individual members to the ends of the earth – one man came back from inside Mexico after having realized he'd forgotten his Arkansas, young manhood wellingtons. In fact he'd just come back for the drink and was soon seen guzzling beer, in his black and yellow ochre check lumbering shirt, at literary gatherings, the only difference being that he now wore his wellingtons everywhere. Nessan's poems had been published in a promiscuous cross-section of magazines but their airing centred on the organ of this literary set – a magazine an old man twitched his beard into in editing it. The selection of material caused visible flutters of jealousy and more than once a fist fight at parties. In fact fists were very prominent among the men at these parties. They seemed nearly always clenched and were almost all muscular, not effete. It was a time for the muscular, tufted chest man among literary people. Against that was set the tenderness of Nessan's voice in poetry, though his voice in speaking was often wheedling, occasionally high-pitched, and very often aggressive. Hunched shouldered, big eyed, he hauled Varela around at parties, often in circles. It was at a party one night, sitting on the ground, glaring, Varela speaking, standing, to a lady from Louisiana, that Nessan was struck by the idea of his longest poem. Feet on the ground, a maze of feet in front of him, he had a vision in that density of a cluster of young civil war soldiers in nursery blue facing one another on a verdant battlefield, in desultory conversation before or after battle or maybe just filling in time before the real factions, to which they did not belong, arrived, when they would somehow disappear. 'Real Factions'. That would be the title of Nessan's poem. And that's how he saw himself. As belonging to no real faction, a kind of intermediate, who would forever somehow obliterate himself when the dinosaur forces arrived. The magenta taffeta dress of the lady from Louisiana flickered in Nessan's eye below her knee. Her shrieking syllables rebounded in the room and her cream and delicate Adam's apple pulsated.

Varela and Nessan got a train to a place in New England where a playwright had a house on a peninsula. They were both cloaked by jackets. They presented themselves as though they were autumn apples, the innocuous products of autumn, and set about taking a holiday, walking, observing fowl, pegging stones at reeds in lakes. A truck passed up a dirt road near the house at the same time each morning, heading north. A woman in angelic white came to the house and she kept veering towards Varela as if she was going to have an accident with him. Nessan realized that he was not entirely a source of physical attraction for people any longer, that there were flaws, that the smallpox marks of childhood had made deeper indentations on the left side of his face, that his face was worried looking and his yellow hair shot up like a proclamation, more than anything that his blue eyes seemed often to roll in madness. But his body still shot up like a tree trunk from his middle and it seemed to concentrate with a sturdiness at his hips.

It was at a New Year's party, which Nessan had foolishly deigned to give in his apartment, that he first realized that there was a concerted plot surrounding Varela. Varela had become singled out as an object of attraction by the literary set, as a focus of sensuality; he was elevated to a position of prowess by them, as someone to approach and touch, if you could, and have some sensual transaction with and, if not, a smile. In short he'd become a symbol for people. This had been ordained by them as a travesty of a happy relationship. At about ten-thirty on New Year's Eve the door opened and a horde of ladies burst in, heading in no uncertain way towards Varela, their eyes thrown back and dragon-like. Glistening, blue and purple party dresses were slightly upheld from the floor. Nessan was ignored. Varela, never really modest, could only cringe at the shoulders as if to ward off some further weight of adulation. Soon the rooms were a sizzling bed of conversation. Pink and blue streamers drooped pathetically from the ceiling as if no one had bothered to determine them properly with tacks. Nessan, caught in conversation with an elderly professor of Egyptian studies from some point in California, lost sight of Varela until he made to go to the lavatory shortly before midnight. On opening the lavatory door he was confronted by a lady's funereal purple, frizzy hat kneeling in literary conversation before Varela's fly. There was no rousing welcome for the New Year that night, although one was attempted. Nessan's mood had permeated the crowd. Girls hoarsely raised their voices. When the crowd had dispersed, high heels still clanking on the

55

pavement outside, a bit of pink streamer snaking on the floor, the front window open at the bottom, Nessan huddled by himself in his mauve and blue lumber jacket in a corner. He stayed like that all night. In the morning he went for a walk by himself on Hobonken Waterfront and welcomed in the ships of the grey, mid-twenties' new year.

Inspired by the interest of women in him, Varela, in the next few months, began moving out, seeking tentative snatches of the heterosexual. The heterosexual could be gleaned as easily as the homosexual, often in edifices that adjoined those of the homosexual, houses with opposing interests brushing one another. A question turned over in his head but February weather and the look on Nessan's face braked it; maybe he was heterosexual after all. One day Nessan returned from a poetry writing session in a café, where men shifted chess pieces on small tables, to find him on the floor, on a much ruffled blanket, with a long-black-haired literary girl whose naked left arm evolved from her white slip, with her left hand clasping the floor in order to steady herself as unabashed she looked up at Nessan. 'We were having fun,' she said. That night Nessan began to holler like a pig in a tannery, seizing a bread-knife, waving it in the air like a Samurai warrior, expleting something, making for Varela, then summarily dropping the bread-knife. He'd surprised himself with his own capacity for hollering. Varela's plump and glowing genitalia were safe for the moment. Nessan sat on the floor by himself, again in a corner, and blubbered quietly, silent jets of red and blue tears eventually on stoic exhibition.

At Easter Nessan and Varela disturbed the pigeons on the steps of Saint Patrick's Cathedral, walking along side one another, a visible solicitude now in Nessan's attitude to Varela, a protective composure in his gait, the two of them with heads down, hands in their jackets, and the jackets nearly touching one another. Varela had a disease, a defect; heterosexuality had made inroads on him. The aura around his genitalia had changed, flecks of dust fighting around it like warring aeroplanes. This area was out of bounds for Nessan. Both of them seemed to be contemplating a disaster when they noticed at the same moment the fleck of a bride's white veil inside the church in the middle of a wedding ceremony and they both knew, that same moment, that Varela was going to go back to his own

56

country, that legend, and settle among the lemon ribbons of flowers, and take a bride from among the blossoms, seize a bride in the pattern of his father, marry her and settle into the effervescent, unquestioning continuity of the place, cinder-faced, bandage-white eyed madonnas, girls miniature waisted like Spanish dolls. The legend, the colours about to startle into life, or for Nessan the dream of Varela's leaving. In that knowledge they acquiesced to the steps of Saint Patrick's, bowing their heads further, and circulated their hands in their jackets' pockets – both at the same time. May was a time of re-acquainting themselves with one another, with the free-for-all May-bliss of Central Park. Nessan lifted Varela onto a white pony, their first physical contact for many weeks. Varela's limbs seemed longer, more gaunt, bonier, especially his arms. They seemed as innocent of conjugal love as a child's arms, those thin, resplendent arms. Varela's eye caught Nessan's eye gauchely and it said, 'Beware, I'll be gone sooner than you think.' There was a hesitation in Varela's body as his eye said this, his limbs and his muscles were momentarily arrested. Varela rode away on a white pony, among the laburnum of Central Park, into a country of continual, blossom sucking, mountain-swept wraiths. Varela was gone in September. He'd taken a jacket of Nessan's by mistake and left his own, hanging on the door, a cistern of all that lost carnal love in its shape.

Nessan abandoned New York when Varela left and went to Washington on another post in a solicitor's office. It was a temporary post and, as it was winter, the Potomac and the Washington Channel and Anacostia distributed fogs throughout the city, like postage stamps. The fogs were particularly thick at the sewage pumping station. Nessan had accommodation on North West Street. But his nightly strolls took him to Buzzard Point and around the Potomac Park. The lights in amber houses around the park, which were at first a lonely sight, invited him in when he made friends with a clique of army officers, civil servants, attorneys in the city. Early December they had a purple balloon party. A party in a room abounding in purple balloons. Pot-holed, parchment skinned old men let loose their arms on young men. The hands of those in jurisdiction on the nation tremored in the vicinity of young men's behinds. The dark brown wainscot with a peeping mouse hole in front of his head slithered into Nessan's view. He was on the floor on top of a young man. The string of wainscot fluctuated drunkenly before him. Nessan's mouth went to the sparse hair of a teenage boy's first moustache. Lobster pink lips ardently met his. An old man watched and scratched his thinly looped varicose backside, his trousers hauled down. In protest against love leaving his life Nessan was taking part in orgies in Washington. His penis dove into many backsides in the view of old men dithery with excitment. Some high ranking people in Washington had it in mind to recreate ancient Rome in their sitting rooms. At the purple balloon party the balloons strove over naked buttocks, like orbs of decay and death. The yellow ochre chandelier was partly garbed by a veil of purple balloons but that did not stop it from throwing out a rusted, exultant light on young buttocks. Nessan left a kiss on a teenage boy's buttocks. The parties spread like a disease and before long he was among bodies in the middle of a banqueting hall, an old man in Unionist civil war uniform looking on. The fields of Fredericksburg and Gettysburg were not too far away. In the middle of making love to a boy, Nessan remembered the train of a poem he intended to write. He got up. He walked the night in a dream of his poem. The fields of Fredericksburg and Gettysburg were full of bodies, but dead or wounded bodies, the bodies of young men. Young men wriggled in an orgy of pain, blood oozing between shades of blue uniform with the occasional shining, winter sky grey jacket thrown in, welds of navy running along almost parallel to welds of blood. Legs, shaking with pain, contaminated one another. Legs, throbbing with the last movements of death, made contact with one another. A buttock rested in a groin of blood, a buttock in pale blue trousers. In the middle of the heap was the boy with the sparse, freshly sprouted, prime moustache under his pale nostrils. Nessan, mentally, went to kiss him but found that around his neck, his collar pulled aside, was a silver cross. Christ was dying on a silver cross, a slender, emaciated-legged, bewigged European Christ. The following day Nessan went to confession in a church in Washington, as his mother had done, in another church, years before. The priest listened to the inexpert confessional routine and was alarmed, the electricity of his alarm igniting through the confessional. In soft mid-sentence Nessan left afraid it would become clear that he was not a proper Catholic and afraid the old priest might have a seizure listening to this epic confession. The path through the park was not lighted that night. It led to the Catholicism in Nessan and the sense of sin he'd never been given as a child but which he'd chosen as an instinctive Catholic. The arc-topped, mahogany-brown door of his accommodation let him into a dark and cold hallway that night. A woman from Tennessee moved in her room and listened to Nessan's incoming, presumably pulling a grey bed blanket around her as she always did, walking up and down the stairway, at this time of night. A cold, skull white sheeted bed waited for Nessan, a hollow in the middle of the highly elevated mattress as if waiting for Nessan to do acrobatics on. Nessan took off his jacket and jersey, peered at the encirclement of dark hairs around his navel and tossed himself into bed. Evangelical sleep and prayer in sleep taking over. In the morning he woke to the verdure of Fredericksburg and Gettysburg, winter sunshine on the slopes of his eiderdown.

At Christmas Nessan consumed oak and tortoise shaded brandy in long stemmed glasses which looked like champagne glasses, in the company of old men on the edges of parties. Now he was an onlooker at the antics of others. But before the image of debilitated perversion could be injected into his figure, slightly stooped now, in its inky dark jacket, his feet at a loss for a position to stand on, he fled the parties. There was a terror in his eyes at what was becoming of him. His hands were in his jacket pockets and you could just about see the merry triangle of lemon and lime patterns of a short sleeved jersey his mother had sent him, probably having picked it up at a store which smelled of teas and coffees, from an array of other imminent patterns. The blanch of the Washington frost and snow had alarmingly nuzzled into his features. He began writing again, ignoring the invitations to parties, but a chandelier which threw jaundiced or rose jewels in dim apparitions on the ceiling drove him out again. Second time around he was less committed at the parties and in spring he took courtly walks by himself through the parks, girls in pink hats swathed in pink, slender cream arms thrown out of pink Charleston dresses waving at him, or shining tree trunks, lolled by in open carriages. The capitol building was replenished by bucketfuls of sunshine. The poem was coming. The boys of last autumn had become boys on battlefields during the American Civil War. The trembling, faintly moustached lips were those of a boy dying in your arms. The sudden paleness of a boy's face was that of someone debilitated in action. But writing was not enough. There were the stubborn lusts of the genitalia to contend with and one night he slinked out from his writing bouts and stood in the fog which had assembled at Buzzard Point. Gradually a figure took form from distant dark elements of the fog. What first emerged was a nineteenth-century ballroom dress. The figure closed in on Nessan, a hand holding the right hand side of the dome of the dress. A face came close to Nessan's, long, dark hair, ringletted at the bottom, splotches of peach aghast on the cheeks, mascara around the eyes, hair on the hands, on the chin, around the scarlet lipsticked mouth. The man's face was long with gaps in the cheeks and his southern belle dress was pale blue. In the hand clutching the side of the dress was a sachet, pale blue too. Before Nessan could discover what perils lay in the sachet he fled, but having first paused, having had a momentary rapport with this man, this woman, having given a hesitant, slightly frightened salutation to a kindred spirit, Nessan's lilac and mauve jacket writhing in exchange with a movement from the pale blue dress, vulnerable clean masculinity to predatory pantomimic perversion, Nessan pausing before something which he was capable of becoming. The hair, which turned out to be black, wriggled, the mouth opened into a tobacco reeking smile and Nessan was off as if he'd just seen the ghost of his future.

Was it a wig or was it real black hair? I was a child on the coast of Andalusia. I had run away from my parents during a carnival. A carpet of anemones crossed rocks to the sea. In the distance was the sound of the carnival. My mother looked very young that day, too young, erect and broad-shouldered in a black dress which exposed those shoulders and a portion of her back. There was a little black hat plonked on the back of her head. I was not sure why I was running away. I wanted to run far away. Suddenly a monster rose from the crevices of the rocks. Long, black hair, ringletted at the bottom, a mouth and the cheeks scarlet, a dress – blushing pink. The creature held a handbag and the skin was painted white. It was the ungainly bones I noticed, the masculine arms and legs at odds with the dress and the legs spread out like a baby giraffe's. A hand slithered towards me, almost rippled towards me and the voice said 'Cher' or 'Cheri'. In saying this the mouth flamed into a furnace. The teeth had been sheathed by lipstick – there the lipstick looked like the traces of blood. Her, his hair was curled with profuse, almost unnoticeable beads, as well as being ringletted. Then I noticed them through pale silks. The genitalia of a man. Pubic hair trying to cover them over. I did not run away. I confronted him. I said, in my best Anglo-Irish, 'Who are you?' At which she shrieked and howled. 'Inglés. Joven inglés,' and ran away, across the rocks, down to the sea, as if she was a creature of the sea.

'Nessan.' Back in New York many people met him and talked to him on the street. 'Nessan, you've changed. You're different.' He'd paled, like a medieval saint or like an early Christian who had nearly been martyred, brushed by lions, scathed by gladiators' swords, but who had survived.

In Dublin once, as an adolescent, I visited a lavatory in a café and found a middle-aged man who had his penis exposed – like an elephant's trunk. He was holding it up as if it was part of a fire-fighting engine. I did not run away. I stayed, facing him, but one foot poised for movement. I was wearing my black school blazer, hair neatly combed, I must have looked like a schoolboy about to be sent on a message by a teacher. 'What do you think?' he asked in a Dublin, backstreet accent. I looked at the graffiti behind him. His long brown coat seemed to have been perforated by urine. I was vague. 'That I've come into the wrong place.' My Anglo-Irish accent was apparent in my voice. 'You're not one of the Gordon-Gillinghams by any chance,' the man said in a chatty fashion, interrupting the business of perversion for a bit of conversation. 'No,' I remarked. 'Well, you're every bit like one of them.' And then he resumed. My penis was small in his hand and disappointing and he let go of it. 'You should go out into the fields running. It'll make you bigger and stronger.' My head was bowed. In its effort to please my penis looked untouched and dun coloured and bereft. I put it in. I was the guilty one. Dazed I emerged onto a street teeming with hearse-like motor cars and with fascists, on which a fine, slightly writhing drizzle was falling, leaving the man to wait for the next entrant, an elderly country parish priest or a buxom suited clerk.

The letter arrived from his mother in early summer – she had separated from Mr. Muir. She had moved into her mother's house in the city. Nessan hesitated over the letter at his desk. Early summer sun had invaded this usually dark room. He wondered what sort of reply he should make. Now that his parents had been torn asunder he had to distribute himself anew. His hair, after a visit to the barber, stuck out like corn stubble. 'Bonnie dearest . . .' he wrote. His reaction was to make her into a first name persona.

Later he could see that on that wording a new relationship began with his mother, the mother-son relationship had been disbanded, they were friends now, confidants. And what a lot Bonnie Muir had to confide in him when he came to see her that summer.

Bonnie Muir had grown up in an avenue in a city but always had in her the sense of the imminence of cornfields, cornfields blond and stubborn. Buggys had sauntered along the roadway at the same pace as little girls sauntered along the pavement, isolated buggys. Little girls, hands behind their backs, sidled along in limestone coloured pinafores and wraiths of black dresses, often their heads down. The designs in those heads were great. Bonnie O'Dowd saw herself, from the beginning, as someone who would become an opera singer or an actress. Her mother had tutored her in tales from Shakespeare and in the stories of the operas. A wave of opera stories arrived in the street, anaemic and dying prostitutes, suicidal and incantatory nuns, syphilitically crazed young aristocrats, warring and barrel-voiced czars. Little girls were almost ephemeral on an evanescent street, little girls fading into an hallucinatory whirlwind of dreams. But life was corrective. Bonnie had two jealous older sisters. One in particular, Jonquil, displayed vitriolic and knitted-brow jealousy to her. There was a young brother to look after. But more than anything there were her mother's depressions, increasingly operatic, to cope with. Mrs. O'Dowd had created new worlds of depression. She sailed mentally to their borders, charting these boundaries. The passage was a vaporous one and her mind clotted and became mildewed with these depressions. Mrs. O'Dowd brought Bonnie with her to the outreaches of her pain. The other girls went, married, and Bonnie was left then, seated with mother. When Bethuel Muir came her way it wasn't just for escape from her mother she took him, but for the bull-like, intellectually untrammelled sexuality which flooded from him especially for her. She had never had a sexual experience with a man, saving sexuality up for constantly floodlit actors in New York, and when she married him she gave herself totally for a while to the pulse of that long, pig-faced mammal which protruded from him, herself in city lingerie and wisp-like tremors in her eyes by candlelight. Later, mental examination forced those conclusions on her about her motives for marriage. She had been seduced and unbridled by the emanation of his sexuality. She had behaved like a Turkish concubine, her body, neat like her mother's, and those buttocks that peered up from eiderdowns as if she were in an eighteenth-century French painting of a boudoir setting. Her movement towards Bethuel Muir had been a question mark after the word sexuality. There were no spiritual or intellectual questions. There was just an unloosing of a body. But time revoked this wonder. Her son came and with him renewed aspirations towards the stage, towards shaping her mouth in song to ensnare huge audiences in its circle. Nessan logically moved towards poetry and that was a triumph on the chessboard for her. Before these signs manifested themselves, she had loaned her svelte body to another man for the first time in a gesture of fatigue with and renunciation of her husband. This escapade had been followed by a number of other discreet acts. She found that infidelities, especially with young men, triggered off her artistic impulses and she gloated over this return of artistic ambition to her, by this devious and feline backroute. Her husband, the ignorant, sexually craving Methodist, could go and look after his own sexual needs. She tried to squash his advances but he came to her more frequently and then she became raucous and carping with him, a vengeful woman, vengeance being for the way she had imparted so much of herself to him. When Nessan prolonged his visits to Chicago she found herself becoming oddly jealous, there was a tingle of jealousy in her spine, a telepathic introduction from another woman; she salvaged her emotions towards Nessan's poetry and his life in a world of poetry from jealousy, she upbraided herself, but when Nessan went away finally, deserting the Mid-Western shores, she found that her sustenance, her witch's gaping toothed, smiling adrenalin was gone. Her husband now had a victory over her body. She could make no resistance, drained. He might as well be having a victory over a pillow for, in a terrible, metallically clanging moment, she realized that she meant nothing to him now, that she had withdrawn all her humanity in his eyes through an apparent millenium of wilfulness. He came and came to her, battering her unresisting, ragdoll-pliant body in sex; and the knowledge that she was a machine and a machine that could make no fight turned her hair grey and her shoulders frail. A much older woman, she dragged herself to Nessan in New York. But the sight of her son, this embodiment of a young poet, rejuvenated her and she found herself instantly losing years, although still in the guise of a grey-haired woman. Back in the Mid-West she foraged with a new strength. Bethuel Muir was drifting towards young girls and he publicly humiliated her, but she accepted his behaviour as God's punishment. There was her mother to flee to; her mother a steed in old age, a gauntlet against English tribulation vented on Ireland. Her husband finally took up with a young Jewish girl and her hold on the house and its wares was paralysed. She had to leave for the city, head down. All those times she had shouted at her husband and tried him, she with the stealthy upper hand, came back to her. He had not satisfied her as a husband and she'd punished him for her own stupidity in giving herself to him. She abandoned the house and the harp hanging from the tree and left for the city. Her husband announced to the world his Jewishness, always a trickle in his life, and when he had secured a divorce from Bonnie Muir, he declaimed widely, he'd marry the young Jewish girl in a Jewish ceremony in the house. The breeze would be banned from plucking Irish tunes on the harp. Jewish, multiple-pronged candlesticks and Stars of David would exorcise the avariciously gentile Mrs. Muir. But Mrs. Muir reacted to this newfound, lustrous Jewishness by imbiding some of its glamour into her own persona; she imagined the full features of a young Jewish girl in a suffusion of candlelight over and over again and partly annihilated them in her by channeling some of the innocence into her own presentation of herself. She dyed her hair black and curled it, leaving

64

two bolls of mouse grey by the ears, straightening herself up, her breasts protruding in white blouses again. And when Nessan arrived he found a woman waiting for him who stood like a suitor, Bonnie's mother muttering in the background about an unruly Englishman she'd bumped into once on a wharf in Boston, a white dray horse going by in the street outside where little girls in limestone coloured pinafores played hopscotch in the sun, Mrs. Muir's breasts making a heaving and satisfied movement in unison towards her son who stood still in a grey suit which indicated his angular limbs, with a red handkerchief poised like a broken carnation in his right hand.

Nessan's fair hair was incandesced by the summer sun, perhaps the first premonitions of baldness could be seen, bold red and blue streaks. Nessan strode with his mother through the summer streets. They stepped across urban railroad tracks. Bonnie's arm in his he pointed at the sites of her childhood, windows over whose yellow pansy boxes she'd leaned, looking into a new vista from a friend's second floor drawing-room. They sat in cafés and Nessan's white suit heralded a new life of leisure. His first book of poems was coming out in the spring.

When Bonnie had been a little girl there'd still been a rumour of Indians and Indian massacres. Indian massacres held you tight in your corsets. One afternoon Bonnie, with a friend, had sneaked into a clairvoyant from County Donegal, Madame Eilís MacPhearson. The clairvoyant took Bonnie's slender pale hand and informed her in her throaty County Donegal accent, Spanish saffron around her head, that love would come late into Bonnie's life, that the love in her life would be a strange one but it would lead her far. Her hand was stamped by the seal of love but a love she'd have to wait for, that would wear a strange disguise. Madame MacPhearson brushed a cobweb of grey hair from her black head and asked for money.

The bison on the far off prairies, the wild cherries by the railroad tracks, that would be Bonnie's life. The nomadic Indians, Mohicans going from one area to another. In Bonnie's tarot the devil was a Confederate general. She weaned her son on stories from the American Civil War and her mother weaned him on stories of Ireland. In Bonnie's childhood there'd been a father who'd had an accent thick and savoury as buttermilk which had spun tales in circles in the drawing-room air. When he'd died there'd still been the tracks of those tales in the air. Bonnie, in her pinafore, over toy railroad tracks would look up at the tracks in the air, in her pinafore, more interested in the imaginary tracks than the real ones. They were the communication offered by the dead. When she'd gawked at her tarot at seventeen the blond and grinning and robust cheeked sun had a peculiarly leprechaun face.

On the ocean corpses wrapped up, were thrown into the water, like crows, often some seeming to surface again. They were ultimately a mesmeric sight, corpses dappling the Atlantic. You wondered, everyone wondered – Páid looking absently at the ocean – if you would be the next to go, but the sense of absence in Páid's face really reflected his puzzlement at his good health. Páid crossed the Atlantic unscathed by ill-health. Boston received him, his wrappings. There the Famine Irish were encamped, whites of eyes, some with life in them, peering from the mouldering canopy of human beings. Páid tiptoed among the dying and offered prayers in thanksgiving for his safe arrival. Ireland now, the minion of death, was forgotten. Or had to be forgotten. But on certain days, days when December sunlight stole up on New England red brick, there'd been revivals of a gap in him, a chasm – the question. Why? Why had he to be torn from the place of his ancestry. Or more fundamentally – why had he to be separated from a jelly-wobbly blur on the Atlantic which was his home, knowing he could never go back, that he'd have to try to forget the thrushes' nests in the bushes and the small trees about his home, that he'd have to try to forget birds' residences in bare trees against winter skies. He would have to punish himself every time his imagination smarted at the thought of crossroad dances which revealed kneecaps as smudged red as cheeks on a winter's day, with their outlines a starched and snowy white. His going had not come out of a wish to leave – hadn't he got on well in the hurling team? – but out of a collective volition that he, the eldest boy of the family, should save himself and maybe later them, eyes craning after him from shawls, on top of an incline as glistening as the honey coloured hairs on an adolescent boy's legs when he bent to tend a wound in summer. America had led him outwards in a drunken maze of railroad tracks. He had worked for an indefinite period breaking stones in Boston and taking up stones from the ground in Albany, New York, his work punctuated only by snow, very, very white snow, snow that punished memory with its chill, or anemones and blue liverwort in a dell beside a white, spired church in spring. Snow splashed on New England stone like the wavering spirits of the dead. Snow came to tell him his family had passed away in Ireland, and anemones, in amber, struggling, Sunday-spring sunlight put the idea in his head that he was the only survivor of his generation. Tragic poetry, never really properly assimilated from a hedge schoolmaster, assembled in his mind. The lone hurler sat now like a Gaelic poet lamenting the passing of an aristocratic clan to whom he was attached. Páid O'Dowd had found a tragic mask. But each jab of the New World sunlight was a reminder that he had stolen life from others. Like a half-lunatic he traipsed across America. On the route he encountered many other travelling human wrecks. Men and women gibbering about their misfortunes and giddy under their weight. The voices and the languages of misfortune merging into one plaint. The urge to totally forget coming eventually, to leave behind. The gait quickening with that urge. During a long winter in Boston he'd forwarded pittances to Ireland, dollars he kept in an old sealskin shoe which made do as a purse, but received no reply, a few mocking snowflakes teetering on the grim, wet-black stone step of a courthouse confirming what he'd suspected, that his entire family had been obliterated. Nothing to do but eddy through the more voluminous attacks of snowflakes, down the street, sealskin shoe in hand, the laces wrapped around his shivering hand. As he moved forward the pace quickened as if in anticipation of a holy city. The sense of human wreckage lifted generally. Women walked more briskly, feet pattering. Sunsets sent ruddiness into pale and sunken cheeks and citadels of cloud threw shadows like spires over the multitudes at evening. A salmon colour entered a German woman's cheek, returning to her a little of her native robustness. A Russian Jew's face looked like a mouse coming out of a mousehole. Páid O'Dowd suddenly straightened up and remembered he was a young man. He braced himself like a tall sheaf of corn, the ear his blond curly hair. He imbibed a new smell. But only the demolition of memory in him could allow this reformation of his limbs. He strode with ease. There was almost a child-like chip in his lips, a corresponding one in his chin. He wore the same expression on his face as that of a landlord's son at home, that of languid, unchallenged innocence. At what seemed the outset of this journey, though he might have been travelling for months, having emerged from a city which held him in mental blankness, he stumbled on a woman dying, her body, from her feet up, being swept up in a swirl like a tornado. She wriggled then on the ground, a dark, inchoate, cone-shaped thing wrapped in dark rags, under conical, Western-pointing wrecks of grey clouds. 'Me son,' she said to Páid, 'Me son,' thinking him her son. She was Irish. The pink in her eyes was like that in a severely sick cat's. 'Me son.' Delicately she raised a mesmeric hand to him and died. Cabbages were skulls in fields. The light of grey clouds shone on their systematic pates. Páid went on to meet Jeremiah O'Driscoll, an Offaly man dressed like a lord mayor, who welcomed him to his patch of land with its hut. 'In the name of our dear little queen you're welcome.' He revealed large slabs of teeth, half shrouded in the brown of the Bog of Allen and essayed a forceful gust of cancerous breath. By evening he was playing the songs of the British army on an accordian, in the light of a log fire. He'd once had the privilege of opening a stopping point on a canal he lasciviously boasted, his chins moving simultaneously, drenching the pier in shamrock infested champagne to the bristle of brass instruments. By firelight Páid saw the madness in Jeremiah's eyes and by seeing it somehow dislodged some of his own. 'Me son.' He trod on now, convinced now he belonged to someone, but not to the family he'd left in Ireland. He was a child of the desperate. Having skirted the lakes and passed into the Mid-West he became part of a multitude or a would-be multitude who seemed to be about to converge on some evangelical city, heads raised to the pink vapours in the sky. Light caught mid-European throats. There was a hymn from the movement of feet. Huge paths were distilled by the density of people. Páid stopped in a Mid-West city or at least he was taken into it by a man carrying hay on a cart. When had he been last in a cart? He was left off at a farm on the outskirts of the city and the man driving the cart, having taken a liking to Páid's bleached, little boy's blue eyes and his strutting blond curls, passed on that fancy to the man of the farm, a giant with benevolent shoulders and a leprechaun, slouching smile, who steadied this apparent benevolence by carrying a ferocious thick black whip in his right hand and thundering it occasionally on the cobbles. The weight of Páid's blond curls got him included on the payroll. Páid also developed a kind of perpetual, clown's grin which kept the world and possible enemies at a distance. This grin turned somewhat solemn when he began working as a lumberer in the forest which stretched by the lake. The earnest-eyed solemnity impressed itself so much on those he worked with that he was given the most daring jobs. And maybe the acumen his forehead gained in his climbs to the tops of trees enabled him to reach the vistas he'd seen from those tree tops. Within a few years he'd started his own timber business by the lake, blood smeared flesh of pine logs from his forest lying about, dead spines of trees from the north, blond, raving chippings of wood in the sun. Páid had been bequeathed most of the forest by the man he'd worked for, an old rag-doll looking man who usually poked about in white suits. He'd taken Páid into his big log built house and left him the forest with one provision that Páid should bury his Irish wolfhounds there when they deceased. Through his ingratiation with an old pliant-looking, white suited man Páid now could walk on blond carpets of chippings in a dove brown suit. The new saw mill was sanctioned by a wooden, rippling sign over the gate, Páid's name in ribbony scarlet letters on it. People had presumed that the old man had taken Páid in as a son. But Nessan knew decades later that his grandfather had given his rodent skimpy buttocks to the old man in the house by the forest on winter nights when forest creatures came to peer at the small warmth of the fire in the house. Masculinity was exchanged for feminity in ancestral ante-rooms. Nessan, on nights, alone, in New York, saw that uncertain, giving crack in his grandfather's buttocks. When the last of the old man's wolfhounds had wheezed and curled up in death Páid O'Dowd met Bonnie's mother at a dance. It was a Norwegian dance held in the fields to the right side of the forest, by the lake, in midsummer. Girls in white seemed to have rushed out of the air, to a cataclysm of white. A melodian played, the melodianist seated on a stool and carbuncular. Despite his modest wealth Páid O'Dowd was still seen as a poor Irishman by the aristocracy of the town and it was as a poor

Irishman, his fingers trembling on her waist, that he danced with Bonnie's mother, her sharp face, eyebrows disturbed by the sunset, glinting at him mischievously. She felt insubstantial and inaccessible and flagrantly flirtatious in his arms. She slipped from his hands, like a fish hopping on the brim of the lake, and proceeded to dash into another dance, holding the snowy base of her dress. To woo her, Páid had to walk with his accounts to her father – her finger-nails were gnashed by the after-effects of varnish that day and it made him think of midsummer clouds, wounded things. When he married her, his wealth seemed to verify itself, he was granted the licence to be rich, but also he grew fat, as Bonnie's mother watched his balls swell up. 'He died from big balls,' she later cackled at Bonnie and it was true that before death Páid O'Dowd's stomach had rounded and become bulging, and that his scrotum had pumped up like a hot air balloon, an overall look about him that he was about to become a dot in a very ethereal sky as he stood by the window, waiting for death to come, not unlike a fat, amorphous, dazed eyed monk or a fat, half-idiot child, the first to go in a famine village in Ireland.

The woman and the man walked through the city. They walked for miles, mesmerised by their own topics of conversation. Nessan had to get back to New York. The ends of his straggling job had to be taken up again; he had to renew office work. The summer sun would pour in on him and bake him in his dark suit. The ends of a job increasingly difficult to hold on to were ribboned into an autumn when winter seemed to have come early and fogs trotted down streets in Greenwich Village which resembled an imagined aspect of London. Footsteps clanked like those of solitary night-time murderers. Poems frayed on the nerves, an ignition of chippings from them. Whereas before Nessan could unite poetry and a harridan lifestyle with the bountiful decorum expected of him at work now the fissures left by the poems and the nights of poetry showed through. The office he worked for had become part of a large company and he was dispatched at random to offices around New York, a point in the sky which unified the purpose of these offices. That point was seen by avaricious executives. It meant that their company wielded power in New York. Their company was part of the expansion of this city and this country and they were resolved into this expansion. Chests palpitated with serenity. Sherries were poised for ten minutes on end. There was a commercial silkiness in the voices of attorneys previously resolute and opening themselves to the impression of integrity. Nessan's pen scribbled faster in an office. But the poems and the lifestyle were now bare and visible to the world. There were warnings. About his hair, his demeanour. But, crossing New York, Nessan appreciated the new freedom these journeys gave him to see a puritan angel in the storybook blue sky over the East River. Going between small, sedately neat, amber and dun houses, houses tidied into their individual poses, Nessan realized that he was spending a lot of time travelling. He'd become an errand boy. He was being condemned to a vacuum. There was still a slither of ketchup-red Virginia creeper on one of the company houses when Nessan encountered a blond boy who looked like him. Blond hair was a stubble around a firm, translucent skinned face. Nessan was brought back to the exultant, bubbly voweled Norwegian harvests of his home. A truce was declared at work. He was the Mid-Western boy again. Not the poet. But poems dribbled down the skin of his face at work. He couldn't help it. A legal document became an excited ode. He was embracing a blond Dakota boy, tugging him towards him in regular laps. A Dakota boy wanted a bed in New York for a few weeks and left then, abandoning part of a deck of cards in Nessan's apartment. There was the winter to face again, the mountain of its fogs and darkness. But a prospective book of poems illuminated that darkness. And one long poem that was coming like a Mid-Western train, in fits, and starts.

Bonnie Muir had opened a clothes-shop in the city that autumn. Ethereal white clothes slid through the air, blue air that puffed in through the upper part of the window. Enthusiastically she displayed New York fashions to customers. The gestures of her arms were extravagant when her customers tried on her clothes. The shop was in a back street of the city. It was in one of the streets in which she had played as a child. Maybe this was another game. A divorce came through late in the autumn, nearer winter. There was a harrowed trio of lines over the bridge of Bonnie Muir's nose then, as she examined some garment, grey and white haired rain outside. The lipstick on her mouth looked as though it would throw itself off. But what did

71

throw itself off was her despondency. With spring she was a successful business woman wearing expansive white dresses. Her mother's voice called her in more frequently to a spacious, plucked, white room to hear tales of her life and of the great arc of Irish history. Her mother's throat now was like two chicken bones meeting, and sisters and brother came more frequently, suspecting that death was near, one sister, the eldest in the family, coming from the banks of one of the great lakes. This sister, Jonquil, fussed her way through the rooms, her face having grown narrow, like a mountain cat's. She was preparing the trail for death. Jonquil had in recent years turned to an audaciously Calvinistic God, there by the lakes, and she bellowed hymns to him. The only evidence of religion in her now was the blackness of her dress and the starvation of her quick limbs. The young brother came from nearer to hand while the other sister was practically a neighbour, living in a nearby town. But it was the eldest in the family who alarmed Bonnie. She insisted on marking the house with her blackness. But once she was gone Bonnie was extravagant again, carnival-light. Her husband was getting married in the spring and her son's first book of poems was coming out.

Preparation was under way for the book, for the marriage. The book would come first, nearer Easter. A white cover had been completed. Bonnie rushed for the lettering on the back. She felt proud, she felt exalted. She had a lot of money now, her own, some of her mother's, the divorce settlement. She could fly anywhere. Yes, she would attend the New York party for the book. By golly, she would. She lifted her dress and looked at a ladder in her stocking on her thigh. A child from outside peeped in. The little girl had a bonnet of black hair and seemingly unreproachful but curious eyes. And now for the New York decor. Bonnie Muir rummaged among the clothes in her shop for the right outfit for herself. Her mother had a seizure just before Bonnie was to leave but that did not deter Bonnie. She took a cab through the advertisements of the new part of town to the station.

The things that went into that book, little poems written since adolescence on bits of paper, which later curled up. Night-time

72

café jottings, Hobonken waterfront nocturnal meditations. Memories of childhood, of home; skin and heart corroding yearnings for departed lovers sublimated into portraits of ancestors: an Irish grandmother, gossamer waisted, bearing a parasol like one of the Confraternity solo banners at the funeral of the Liberator Daniel O'Connell. Nessan reclined and looked at this first copy. Many languages, had gone into this book, many utterances or attempted utterances. The first mouthings of a rudely fat-stomached little boy scampering about a slant of hill on which a harp hung. The mad yelps of a thrush bodied boy making erratic frog-leaps around the plains at evening, among a myriad, shyly silhouetted windmills, emulating the animal world because he fancifully thought he'd find companionship more easily there. The more sober, silent communications of a near adolescent boy on a hillside, claimed by mild, spring, Quaker sunshine, a broad brimmed, black Amish hat in his right hand and a white Amish shirt on him, black braces over it, both hat and shirt purchased for him by his mother from the Amish people. But, more than anything, parallel majestic rivers of ancestry ran into the book. Long, long ago, in one of these rivers, people were thrown out of Jerusalem, denied proximity to the wailing wall and, nostalgic for the city of the Bible, forced to assimilate the amber evening beads of a Central European city, where they ran around squares, little magic lantern men in black, bearing books weightier than themselves. Eventually they had to leave that city too, little boys hauling books, this time bigger than themselves, along roads spiked by puddles, black, twentieth-century hats punched on the little boys' heads. The centuries tended to be confused in this terrain. The little boys pattered along, an agreement between them that they would reach a place of safety. The covert and effulgent illustrations in the books they were carrying yielded to a grey and spindly spired city, a dark and murkily coloured tableau there. That too was abandoned. The trek was across the Atlantic this time, little boys in black with black hats on them holding their toes which were in black shining shoes. That was the journey made too by their blond counterpart. Páid O'Dowd left behind many exoduses – the exodus West during Cromwell's time, the exodus to O'Connell's meetings, the Famine exodus to the fields – to partake in the exodus across the Atlantic. He held his bare, famine sculptured toes. White with the skin coming off, like his face. In his journey to the Mid-West he met many ghosts. Many faces informed by whiteness. Motifs of a famine memory. But all strands of lineage began to contend in a boy in a white Amish shirt, one summer, his chest like a delicate cup in the shirt. Nessan reclined in his white Easter shirt, arms bare, sun-affronting hairs on his arms, dissatisfied with the book which lay in front of him, feeling it did not live up to the expectation of his ancestry. He rose and went for a walk, passing some preparation for Easter ceremonies at Saint Patrick's Cathedral, flowers laid out at the entrance, on top of the steps, waiting to be carried past the barrier of darkness. Back home, that evening, he began working on his long poem again, which centred on the meeting between two soldiers during the American Civil War, one from a Jewish European background, the other fresh from an Irish background, totting up more lines, but his wrist resisted the pen, the adrenalin gave up, and his mind fixated on a shirt.

At the end of a summer his mother had suddenly decided he needed a new shirt, put him in a buggy, drove him at top speed, the buggy slanting a lot, to the store in the village where the French church was, proceeded regally into the store, examined a casket of white boys' shirts which had been rumoured in her parts to have just arrived from New York, the rumour confirmed, and fished up a large shirt, white with dots of further white splayed on it, held it up against the light until the dots were accentuated and the arms hung as if from broad masculine shoulders.

The shirt didn't fit Nessan, of course. Maybe that was the idea. It hung on his ribs waiting adolescence. It was an exchange for a simple white Amish shirt. You could perceive Nessan's skin through the new shirt on hot days, especially at the beginning of his loins. He never did grow into it. It was always too big for him and when he would have been the size for it it had gone, marched off from a bush. Writing was like a new shirt, making things, making things better, attaining to things. Like his mother's new shirt, always too big for him and remote from him. At the end of a summer Nessan's loins had been the gold of corn through a white shirt. He slept on a couch cum bed in that memory and was sleeping like this when his mother knocked, all prepared for the day after.

*

'Yes, you go beyond what you're capable of now, to the day after, what you're capable of the day after . . .' the sentence broke off in his mind. His mother was here.

She talked avidly about the journey, about the clothes she was going to wear in New York, about the strange, cross-eyed people she'd met along the way. She dismantled her goods in a trail across the floor. She interrogated him as to who was going to be at the party. She talked so much she did not realize that he wasn't talking at all, just looking at her from the couch, still half lying there. In a sudden fit of laughter she went back to the journey and to a man in a bowler hat who had sour looking lips, who'd proposed to her in a Boston accent, and who watched her go, at a platform where she had to change trains, apparently sniffling over his tie with greengage shamrocks on it which he'd put on for her benefit. She was in what appeared like purple underwear now and she plucked a purple plume from her bag and raised it in the air, like a trophy. Her lips were smeared in red. Nessan could think of a place for her at a brothel.

She slept that night on the bed in the kitchen, he in the other room, facing the street. She lay on the bed, her face down, like a child nuzzling a sweet. He slept, looking up, one leg outstretched. Nessan, on the night before his book was published, dreamt of his next book, young soldiers in nursery blues on a field before battle. There was one tall young soldier who had dark hair, evenly curved at the front. Or was he a soldier? As Nessan's dreaming mind focussed on him, made him appear larger, Nessan realized he was a young man he'd been searching for for a long time, his chin unshaved and angular and a lost, chaotic but dreamily assured look on his face. Was he a young man Nessan had seen at a party?

Mr. and Mrs. Barrett had heard of Nessan on and off in the previous few years. They'd seen his poems make sporadic appearances, usually at long intervals, or else in one clutter of time, in various, highly varied, often unhinged magazines. Nessan's poems clutched at the edges of the literary world. But despite such temperamental appearances there was still the fact of them. They had to be reckoned with and more and more they stared one in the face, unblinking, until at last there was a glossed white book. Like something representative of a wedding. All one needed was the spray of confetti. But then that too came in the form of the people in their many coloured clothes, especially the girls, at the party. Mr. and Mrs. Barrett received an invitation and decided to go. Nessan was someone they'd partly put out of mind. He'd been a fad of theirs. Irish reneguing of the once-loved one is the worst. There's meant to be no going back on it and a determined curse to boot on it. But, moved by the sight of the book and dented by the appearance of the many poems, a literary couple, older now, more establishment, more invested with the immobility of an institution, made their staid but unbridled way to a third floor literary bacchanal. Once there, in a room which strongly smelled of the port and the ancestry of the house, an early nineteenth-century storing house for goods come from the sea, they remained alongside one another at the edge of the party, accepting the odd overspilling glass of white wine and silently observing. The crowd towards the centre blocked them off, and the other odd particles of people at the side, from being noticed, for a while.

A few years before, four years exactly, Mr. and Mrs. Barrett almost returned to Ireland. They had travelled to Paris. But the civil war had been at its height in Dublin and that previously remote fact had been integrated at the last moment as a buffer against going back. But stronger, when it drew near the moment when they'd planned to go, was the realization that they'd created a myth, they'd absconded from Ireland with a myth, and they could not return to Ireland, especially to Dublin, for fear of damaging that myth. So they contented themselves with dispatches from Dublin. They arranged meetings with new arrivals from that city, arrivals who spoke salaciously of its street names. 'Ah sure, bullets are going up Merrion Row in greyhound races,' said one. The mosaic of Dublin, the slabs of grey and dun, were slyly conceived of by Mrs. Barrett. In a way she was in tune with change in that city and she saw prostitutes going down gander-grey streets, heads down. In a way she was a prostitute now herself. Or at least she'd prostituted her country in order that she be acclaimed. Her husband and she herself lived off acclaim now from their country's many wrongs and many and highly elevated transcendences of wrongs. For the first time, in Paris, she and her husband capitulated to their own share of guilt in their exploitation of Ireland, but they circumvented that guilt, ultimately, by quickly reneguing on the idea of returning to Ireland, pretending they had never had it. The golden articles of twilights, either mischievous or of manifest integrity, were not then interfered with. Instead they indulged in Paris literary life and were fêted as Irish Americans, protectors of young artists and survivors of obscurantism.

First to be noticed was a middle-aged woman with obviously falsely black hair, who was circled by purple – her impressive bum best manifesting the funereal nature of the purple – at the centre of the party, a twitching, pale, fan-type object in her hand, her black hair too circled by purple – was she acting as though someone had crowned her? – a lustfully and unapologetically bloody smear of lipstick on her mouth. That red lipstick gave great smiles. The smiles were often in response to the abashment of frail and porcelain men in shirts with patterns of Japanese cherry and apple blossoms on them, who were fixated at the centre of the floor as those who represented power in the world of literary opinion. One man with hair like sporadic cotton manna looked particularly repelled by her. Their verdicts, on Nessan's poems, to be discerned by the acrobatics of their upper-lips, were obviously negative.

Nessan in a white shirt, the achieved cleanness of which he was obviously proud, stood a little way away from the centre. He'd changed, grown much older looking, statuesque, raw dabs of colour in his face, desperate flames in the whites of his eyes, an irregularity about the waves of his hair, the breadth of his shoulders giving a military concentration to his body, the concentration of a recruit from the wilds of Arkansas or the low and murky pastures of Kansas itself. For someone whose party it was, Nessan was clearly not getting very much attention. He was surrounded by cartoon ladies, leaning forward, hair athletically bobbed and, in one girl's case, hair that looked like black spider's feet thrust into the air. Near the edge of the crowd there was a quieter effulgence, lacrymose stoles of smoked-salmon pink draped on ladies' shoulders, kipper-red hair gnashed on one or two demure older ladies. A mackerel-grey mantle disposed itself to a literary question. Late arriving was a stout lady who wore a hat that looked like a lobster, curling in mayhem over her face and whose nails were decorated with Eastern Europe stamp edges, a scrap of Lenin's head vying with a shade of Polish or Bulgarian lilac. Her dress was simple and white, showing arms that were podgy and emerged from the dress in embarrassment at their own podginess but with a bold determination to reveal themselves. They were at least attractively baby-like. Once this lady had been expected to come to parties with coal skuttles, children's seaside buckets on her head, with earrings of ancient English silver teaspoons, even with vermilion messages like rashes across her face, so familiar was the sight of her with this apparel, but more recently the tone of her appearance had become subdued, since a boy from Rio de Janeiro, her lover, had apparently crawled out of her bed, showing his antelope buttocks to her on her mildly green bedspread for the last time. With the lover went the coal skuttle and as someone said 'the coal'. She'd been known to distribute galaxies of money sums to young, especially male, artists and her presence was imperative at literary parties. Now she was here, but virginal, without the money. There was a languor surrounding her presence whereas previously there would have been a teeming excitement of youths. Nevertheless, the congregation welcomed her presence and semi-cloaked her in the spirit of the party, that spirit which was apparently wilfully leaving out now a slightly distracted looking Nessan.

In spite of having just published a book, Nessan found his poems were not generally approved. True, by reason of their profusion and their unabated though desperate persistence, they found their way into a book of their own, they forced their way into a book which was a surprise even to those who published it, almost as if those people had published it without knowing what exactly they were doing. But the word was: Nessan was uneven. Nessan was lousy. Nessan was self-indulgent. Nessan was, in his poems, as a peeved child who not only showed no signs that he would ever grow up but demonstrated genes that would make him incapable of ever going beyond a plastic lyricism. Content with the status quo of this knowledge old men turned away from him at his own party. So Nessan had to shoulder disdain at the party for his own book. But he did not allow himself to believe that the poems had been rejected. Instead he obsessively believed, and obsessively demanded of those who were close to him to believe, that he had been acclaimed by the people who mattered. This was not the case. Nessan's talent was disputed in the most intimate circles of New

York literary life. People who were silkily familiar with him over Bourbon scoffed at him behind his back. In the outreaches of American literary talent there were those who admired him. But for the moment he was alone, almost ignored at his own party, brave though in his predominant aloneness, but fragmentary reds and blues flushed into his face. His mother though did not receive tidings of these quavers. She continued acting as though she was the mother of a messiah, raising her leg so high in the direction of one delicate sprig of a white haired old man she nearly kicked him in his hollow felt crotch. She'd taken to raising her leg in order to reinforce points of her conversation. On a later occasion she fell back because she raised her leg so high, being caught by a very unwilling woman, to judge by the expression on her face, who in her dress, purple like Mrs. Muir's, had blown out like an unruly balloon.

When Mrs. Muir finally became noticeably obstreperous to everyone present, their heads turning in her direction, her Mid-Western accent shrill and shrieking, Nessan, visibly, at last, took note of her, removing himself from his solitude and pacing towards her. Then the ballet began. She caught his waist and flung back her head, laughing. This time Nessan was not drunk. Sober, solemnly sober, he clenched her wrist and sobriety seemed to come to her too. People turned back to their drinks and their conversations. Mrs. Barrett remembered for a moment that there was a time when Nessan's poems seemed to come out all in one piece in one particular magazine. For a moment she approved of Nessan. But when Mrs. Muir's witch-like laughter rose again from the long pipe of her throat she and her husband abandoned the party, sure now that Nessan, who was holding his mother like a lover, his arms around her shoulder, would come to a bad end.

Yes, there had been continuity and approval for Nessan once and that approval seemed to return after the party. By surviving rejection he'd gained friends. By holding out against disapproval he'd found himself, by a change of whim, being heaped with approval and minor decorations. He'd done a test. Attitudes to his work changed in a matter of weeks. Millionaires, vaguely sighted at his party, popped up in proximity to him all of a sudden and Nessan begged funds from one half-caste millionaire whose white shirts luxuriantly

79

gleamed against the New York night and against his skin colour, particularly the collars standing out in cabs, daring contours of brushed fabric, and was conceded enough to enable him to throw in his work with the legal company, discard offices at last, and become solely a poet and nuisance to all other literary people. That was the point at which Nessan began to drink in earnest and also the transition period when he took his sexuality with a vengeance, usually after much drink, into the hovels and dens that lined the waterfront and looked with desperate hope of expiation to the lights of Brooklyn Heights. Nessan, his back bent from his pursuits, felt himself to have graduated as a dissolute.

His father's wedding took place in May. He packed a small, cinder-black suitcase and took a train West, bringing the aura of his new-found freedom with him and stretching his new-found funds to a sizeable degree for the first time, exercising his capacity to spend. The reviews had been coming out slowly, most making jabs at him. For those who were aware of them, there were wide blanks in certain magazines where his book had been pointedly ignored. But the fact remained, disapproval was sliding from under the collective reaction and there were one or two organs of literary statement which made manifest gestures of approval towards Nessan's book, presenting solid columns of print about it to the literary world. This counted more for Nessan in the long run, the fact that some people rather than all had taken trouble over him, the suggestion, implicit in his head, that the ripple would build up to an enduring impression. So, with the excitement of this anticipation, he journeyed West, chaotically reaching for the bars as he stood by a train window, his suitcase alongside him, a perilous thing. The sun fell in a yellow, cowslip colour on the licks of his hair. He'd be bypassing his mother, going to see his father first. The last few weeks had made him younger looking. He'd reverted to a boyish rakishness of appearance, the tussled hair, the virtual lemon colour of it. Cows of the Mid-West slid by without any rapport with him, but an ease about his perception of them, the image of them transformed by the success he'd left behind in the bank in New York. One particular cow nuzzled in the grass near the train, unafraid of it. The cows of the Mid-West were of a different calibre. Homesteads built by Manichean hands revealed themselves, isolated homesteads, women going through the gestures of cleaning, of emptying water, of fetching water. One little boy with an upturned cupful of momentarily albino white hair pierced the train with a look. A rocking-chair was adjacent to him on a porch, adjacent to his white disconnected shirt. Nessan was going home to the porch which had harboured a saucer of milk for a cat for an interlude in childhood, the milk puncturing the darkness of the porch. But the house would have changed now. Its matron had gone. It waited for him, solidly and transparently in turns. Nessan trekked up the hill, case looking dainty in his hand. It had greyed with the journey. A woman waited. Her face dark as a dun frog's. Suspicion and amber ignition in her eyes. The table inside was set. It was a different table, larger, darker. Its edges snapped at you from under the white cloth. She glided her hand over the display on the table. Fruits – oranges crowding together in a bowl – a salad or two, cucumbers, mushrooms swimming in a dark oil; a cake which rose up in ruffles of white icing. She had introduced herself. Mr. Muir would be back soon. 'Poetry,' she said, 'You're a poet.' Nessan did not have to present his book. They already had it. She was not living with his father, she had come to make preparations for his visit. The young woman with the long dark hair in a ponytail moved around the far side of the table, Nessan on the side nearest the door, his suitcase still cramped on the floor, the young woman's back almost to Nessan as she authoritatively supplied him with details of the bed he'd be sleeping in, her presence all the time captivating Nessan. She was young. Her foreign accent was strangely knotted. She was young enough to be a sister close in years to him. She already exercised rights over the house and predisposed herself to have authority over Nessan. He was not going to cause his notorious disarray in her life and in her marriage to Mr. Muir. With this almost ceremonial inception Nessan was then given freedom to leave, to spend time in the washroom, to prepare himself for the meal. He emerged from his toilet in an immaculate white shirt, buttoned at the cuffs. She already had poured wine for him. He was fiddling with a button at the left cuff as he approached.

The wedding took place a few days after his arrival, almost exactly in mid-May. Crowds congregated on the hill after the indoor ceremony to witness the bride and groom. The indoor ceremony had consisted of a rabbi's prayers and plantation of the long, dark drawing-room table with tall, burning candles. There was also a stray tall candle on a flower stand. The rabbi was one mustered up from an outlying colony of houses and he had an appropriate wardrobe of garments. As he emerged from the house, a Greek lady, old, in black, her skin falling about her face in snail-like patterns, thought she was having a vision of a patriarch of the Greek Orthodox church. Candles and words shifted in the ceremony. Nessan stood by, the granite-shouldered son, those shoulders drooping a little in the course of the ceremony, his arms folded for want of something better to do with them. As Nessan's head dipped his gaze became entangled with a bunch of crimson roses placed for some reason there on the floor, caught together in an object which, though painted gold, Nessan knew to have once been used as a chamber pot by his mother.

From the darkness and mustiness of a room they emerged onto a hill which was packed on both sides by curious, papier mâché faced Jewish people in black, their pallor and curiosity suggesting that they rarely let themselves out in this Mid-Western clime; by runaway Amish people, they too in black; by more pacific Mennonites, but mainly by baffled but respectful local farming people, more than one woman in a dress of shining grey material, and more than one man in a grey, loose, gangly city-type suit, young, manly-shouldered factory hands awkward and crouched up as if awaiting a camera to shatter on them. There was a fact about the factory which they did not know yet but which Nessan was privy to. His father was selling it and moving to the village where the French church was, if his prospective purchase of the general store there came off. He wished to retire with his new wife to a restrained business status. There was no ready indication of this intention now and if there was it was subverted by Mr. Muir's toothy gratified smile which went out in different directions as he led his new wife who was in white, her dark face surrounded by a hesitant shower of white, her eyes darting outwards and sideways and upwards from her face, coy, unsure, but still sly and knowing, this impression of slyness and knowingness confirmed by the almost rancorous twists of her smiles. These twists particularly juggled in her smiles at Nessan. She was led forward to a table where food was rounded up and where sodas and orange juices

82

and lemonades waited. You suddenly remembered at the imminence of this celebration that there'd been Prohibition in the United States for seven years. The luxurious bottle of wine sneaked in on the trail from Canada or Mexico was left deep in the pantry. The reality of Prohibition in New York was negligible but it did have side effects; you sometimes found yourself consuming wine which had shamrocks on the bottle as if designating Irish origin. There were Polish, Jewish, Italian, Russian, Hungarian, Irish, Swedish, Norwegian alcohol entrepreneurs. Alcohol came in processions from Canada, Mexico, across the Atlantic and in some of the dingier dens around Hobonken Waterfront it was in fact, as someone declared 'jumped up diesel oil'. Prohibition had the effect in New York of making you drunker or, at literary parties in upper floor apartments on Houston Street or Charlton Street or Debrosses Street, of giving an exotic glow to the bottles, an exoticism which caused competition among literary hostesses, Mandarin faces appearing on the labels, Bolsheviks, druids. A literary lady whose house was splayed by a flag of carmine Virginia creeper in autumn, recently had her party invaded by the police whereupon a fat older lady in a long dress, striped as if made from the same material as beach chairs, approached the officer in charge reciting a poem she'd composed in the bath the previous night and waving a glass of white wine at him. He, being from a part of Lithuania where maledictory incantations are taken seriously, fled with his battalion. It was probably the badness of the poetry, the hoarseness of her voice, and the ruffled seediness of her appearance which put fright into him too. Generally literary New York was left alone. Speakeasies had become as common as skyscrapers, often speakeasies at the base of the skyscrapers, and then there were the myriad night-time saloons around the water front whose decrepitude and inertia warded off any viable intrusion. But here, in the Mid-West, the spirit of the Amendment had helped to create a mostly parched people, members of whom sidled up to the table now and started to pick up legs of chicken weighted with curd cheese, almond eyes in the cheese. One old lady seized a whole baby capon by a leg, knocking guts of stuffing from the dead creature. She squealed with this event. The white table-cloth had been damaged for the first time but people went on munching into chicken, right into the bones. Bones with the imprint of curves of frail teeth were put down, soon piling up. A young man, typically broad shouldered, who looked as though he might have a nervous disorder, asked Nessan what New York was like, if it was possible to find a suitable wife there. Nessan said no, all the possible wives were Italian and were already half rotted. The young man smiled at Nessan and abruptly turned his face into a hillock of chicken leg flesh. To these questions were added questions about Nessan's 'station', in the words of one squeaky voiced old lady, as a poet. 'What station?' Nessan quipped, 'Pennsylvania Station?' 'What are your work hours?' 'Do you know . . .?' 'Is it true literary ladies wear rose coloured transparent underwear so as to make the seduction of young poets easier, revealing their pubic parts before a state of total undress–' was the paraphrase of a question of one young man who had in fact been drinking 'moonshine', which had seemed to come up from under the table.

A cake was cut, the lowest of its three tiers. Songs were sung. In the evening it was Poland and twilight came, stealthily, over that doomed land to this brigade of revellers. Nessan was drunk on 'moonshine', lying in the grass, one leg over the other as he stared at the night. His father had not spoken to him for hours after their first encounter; the poems, he'd read the poems. He'd understood little of them but he had gathered, funnily enough, Nessan's leanings towards descriptions of the male breast, his wrestle with an ambivalent ancestry and his making in that ancestry sexually ambivalent personages. Nessan's father had spat into a whiskey, 'Are you queer or something?'

Of course it was only a joke, only meant as a superficially scathing remark. But Nessan had jolted up straight, his visibly but subtly thinning hair, neatly groomed now, standing up straight. That moment remained with him years later. There was no danger, as it turned out, his father knew. He could relax. But there had been a waspish statement. Nessan was left with a reference to something his father could never have truly conceived of as having connection with his only child and son at that.

That son lingered after the wedding, hovered around the locale. He stood upright, captivated girls' hearts, wore ties, half white, half lime. He was a unit of beauty. Being loved by women from

84

afar Nessan could cope with. They could not have him. He even enjoyed the pose, stealthily and uprightly moving across the fields, measuring his steps, his jacket off and his hair burning right to the razed flecks around his ears. He bore his jacket on his shoulder with aplomb. There was time to think in this space between him and others and time, oddly enough, to be masculine, to be the son. The new wife was one of the first to pick up the pose and took it as a kind of challenge to her. She became more taunting towards him, back turned on him as she pressed forward with an errand in the fields. She had a honeymoon of two nights in a hotel called The Plaza in a town which boasted an artificial spa. Men and women waded through water in front of the hotel. 'More a drinking trough for horses,' Nessan's father gulped later. The artificial spa was an excuse for frilly hats and white clothes. Men and women met in the spirit of courtship here, the last post for many rich Mid-Westerners, but it was more a ditching ground for voluminous buttocked spinsters whose orangeade and white colours clung to the saucers of those buttocks. The fierce and multifarious buttocks of middle-aged ladies gave stupendous scope for conversation to Mr. and Mrs. Muir on their return. She, the new Mrs. Muir, was particularly carnal and lascivious in conversation over these attributes. Always in the presence of Nessan it seemed. Her rash-scarlet tongue rolled on the words. Was she inviting Nessan to a confrontation with her. But then she'd laugh after making lewd conversation and go and empty water from a large, white, blue rimmed dish into the struggling and knotted clover. Nessan found himself sitting with her a lot and joking. She was near his age, younger than him in fact, he remembered again. She wore her hair in different ways, ponytail, pigtails joined together with the juncture expressed by a scarlet ribbon. She had an almost grey olive skin texture at times, her face particularly, and handsome and large white teeth broke out in embarrassingly large smiles. Her face held onto these smiles for minutes at a time. She'd soon perfected a way of dealing with Nessan, of taming him, of holding him in obeisance to her as he waited to see what her mood was. She'd laugh, throw out laughter, at points when he was beginning to get worried and determine another reaction to her. At moments there was concentration, silence between them. She was his sister. A sister with a lizard ponytail which she flaunted as she crossed an emerald incline in the direction of chickens. Nessan, away from New York, was finding peace strangely brought about by the raucous cries of hens running over earth squiggled with turgid droppings. But even as his nose, peeling with bruisings from the sun, having become an overall pale in an interior, began to pick up the redolence of smells from their droppings and from the underground and from mud bottomed chickens he knew he had to return to New York to attend to his book, his career. Millionaires awaited him. Parties awaited him. The pear shaped bunches of lime grapes on stalls outside shops on Washington Street and a gleaming contagion of oyster shells on a stall beside a maverick Chinese owner outside such a shop. The invitations had been sent. He had to go back to a summer of edibles and sex.

On the train back he thought of his mother whom he did not have time to see. His head dropped guiltily as he contemplated her going about her chores, smoothing a bridal white dress in the air, talking to the dummy on which the dress was put. There was a snowdrop paleness about his face despite the tan he carried from his father's home – the interior light made it so – there was the little languid leaning of a snowdrop in his face, all abashment. His brows took on a blanch and became thick and surprised railroad tracks. There was surprise too in his blue eyes at his own remitting of a visit to his mother. Lips parted, a child's lips. Pale, he fell asleep, taking himself out of guilt.

His blue check shirt with its blood scratches of pink had nuzzled to his chin when he woke up. He'd grown a half day's beard. New York was coming up. And now for oblivion, he thought.

Her body tremored in the bed. Not just her mind was remembering something but her body was too. Her body had tremored of a sudden. She groaned. She'd fallen asleep with me all the time sitting by her. Even silently at times, so these silences could warrant sleep if you liked. A handsome face adjacent to her, my face, a stripe of dark hair adjacent to my forehead. Diving over it with a near somersault at the end. Narcissistic upturned divisions at the end of the stripe. I was silent, fixated in my silence, as she slept. Fixated by the fact she'd come to trust me so much and upholding that trust in a silence that hardly twitched for fear it would disturb that trust, however she'd come by it anyway, and she'd go into questions about it.

Even in that silence and stillness there were truculent copy books on my lap, waiting for the notes. She knew what I was up to and accepted it. I had a very young face, she'd said, a very innocent face. 'Sure you're from the green land,' she'd said, like any mind-frayed older American lady. Green land, I'd concur; green of Trinity's cricket fields. Once I'd taken a boy into the showers there, a white armoured cricket boy with pads shooting up over his knees, a Unionist from County Fermanagh as it turned out, and there, in an aperture, regardless for a few moments of the world, a single jet of a shower going, emblazoned by the Dublin evening sun, mustard coloured as in part of the stained glass in a pub, fiddled with the most cumbersome part of his garb until I found his rock hard Unionist buttocks which he eagerly yielded to me. They were very white and I wasn't sure what I was supposed to be doing with them but when I decided, unloosening my fly in order to put my penis in the stain between his buttocks, it was too late. Two level, male voices were heard approaching and presently two black jackets came. I retired with the boy to a bank of green in the early summer capsizing twilight, listened to the finish of his autobiography. But an adolescent fantasy had not been acted out and he went with more decorum, alone, into the changing room, and I never saw him again, being left with an image of a momentary generosity, two taciturn buttocks sloping uselessly towards me, and a catalogue of fantasies spelt out on the edge of the cricket field, iron hard penises entering his anus, fingers groping for that part of him, tongues. But all in all, despite these fantasies and the hush and reverberation of his voice as he'd spoken, he'd been, unlike me, a very masculine boy.

Bonnie was worried that summer. She could not curtail her worry as she smoothed a gown suspended from a dummy. Nessan had not been to see her. He'd evaded her. And, apart from that, she knew that he'd given up his job. He was silent now. No word from him. What was he up to? Writing more poetry? Maybe. But something strove against her, some image of him that had dissolved into a blur, recognisable to her only by the fear which closeness to it in her mind avalanched through her. A boy's hair clasped the brightness on the street, golden hair, honey-coloured you might say. A bonnet of honey-coloured, amber threaded hair. An attractiveness about the boy. A girlishness about him. Yes, in that evenly curved thickness of hair, protruding at the back of his neck. An oval shaped thickness of hair. Its perimeter at his forehead reaching up to the neutral coloured, sectioned, multi-floored business façades, some higher than others, like grimacing heads. It was the curveture of his bottom as his head reached up she noticed the most though, that head, those bulbous piglet nostrils savouring the air, that hair, which had swiftly turned to a dun acorn colour, thrown back, a bottom proud of itself, in flannel trousers, a bottom which asked to be a sculpture. Bonnie was thwarted. Why did that boy and the rhythm of his movements put her in mind of Nessan? Why did a white shirt and flannel trousers on a Mid-West, sun-baked street make her think of her son? Some notion about Nessan had been wriggling in and out of her mind for years. But the boy and the abandonment of his movements defied any mental concept. He had purchased a cornet, had seized it from the outdoor ice-cream man and she followed him and found she was following the path of her own desires. She passed a gaggle of rouge balloons. Prayers came back to her, her mother's prayers, as they always did when she was trepidating with sexual expectations. 'Mother, mercy.' The boy merrily crossed a meadow. Mrs. Muir tripped after him. It was as if he was aware of the pursuit, or at least his bottom was. It taunted her. Down there among his underwear she imagined an embroidered name. Years since she'd made love, she was surprised now at the frolicsomeness of her breasts. His bottom, the protruding defiance of it, steered a defiant course for her rippling breasts. They hurried, competing with one another. Their points dipped. She remembered how a farmhand had once taken the swarm of pink in those breasts, plunged it into his mouth. Her own bottom felt giddy with excitement. O dear, she twittered, the actress in her, how could I be thinking these things? But there they were. She never caught up with the boy. He disappeared around the corner of a block. She never meant herself to catch up with the boy. His form slithered around a corner. At the point of his disappearance she saw that he was not only taller and more gangly, standing straight, but that he was younger than she'd first perceived. Maybe fourteen, fifteen. He was a child who might still play with toys. Bereft, stranded, she stood a while and then, walking home, treated herself to a panoramic fantasy. The boy she'd first seen, first imagined him to be, a seventeen, eighteen-year-old, but still tall, the tallness of her final image of him, took her into a room in one of those multi-storey buildings, laid her on a bed, and bent the curveture of his naked bottom over her. Caging her. His hair stung her, stripes of it. The curveture of the lower part of him was narrow, ribboned even. He remained kneeling over her, caging her, until, in a park, her nose ran into a child's bubble. Semen ran all over her, pearly, white sequined semen. It had been so long since her skin had run with semen, her knobbly skin. O dear, I should not be thinking these things. And yet there they were. She had that bottom in her mind, its white plastic curveture when her mother's voice shouted at her. 'Bonnie, I think it's a good day for dying.' Then she hurriedly dressed the boy, allocated a toy to him – a wooden tram – and a blue and white striped blouse, and dispatched him to the city streets. In her room, taking off her clothes, examined the scars on her tawny pubic parts. She wanted the boy to be innocent again, she wanted to redress the violation. But the limbs kept coming towards her, kneeling over her, a protective platonic animal's limbs. Nakedness, she decided then, was innocent. Having changed her clothes she faced her mother again, first noting the blackness of the dye in her hair and deciding her skin was not quite so gnawed as she had imagined. There was an implosion of physical well-being and control in the skin. Her narrow hand skimmed the top of a bannister. She was aware of the contact between the bannister and her hand. What she needed was more contact, more abrasion of skin on her skin. She was not a rubber duck yet, she told herself. Then she saw Nessan again, and wondered at the point of her reverie, why it had begun from contemplation of him and his disturbed and his slightly stooped figure fleeting around the labyrinthine and drowned New York pavements.

Her mother elaborated on her reasons for it being a good day for dying over afternoon tea. Bonnie was in a white dress, tied up to her neck, frilled there, almost Edwardian. Her pose was severe, attentive to the dress, her back straight. She listened, cup stranded in the air – one of her mother's English, galleon-like cups – to her mother enumerate for her reasons for thinking it was a good day for dying. She listened now as if she was hearing an outline of a diplomatic mission. The cup, creamy with little waves of pink in it, was deadly still. Her mother considered it both pleasant and jovial to pass away in summer, when skies were ethereal blue and lifted high over little girls with skipping ropes on the streets. One would escape, in a drugged way, from the raucous cries of little boys and the antici-pation of evening, when dew alighted on the apples. Mrs. O'Dowd was slightly hysterical today. She was old. Her time was done. Time recollected was knifing her. She wanted to sublimate herself. She wanted to escape into the painless blue overshroud of a sky. But little things were holding her back. Like the wrangling nasturtiums she had to tend in the backgarden. Like the delicate and hoarse ritual of afternoon tea. She'd spoken so long about dying that now this topic had a confectionary quality. But Bonnie remembered when it was not so. When conversation about it was not so gossamer-like around the edges. There had been a time when Mrs. O'Dowd's sole purpose in life seemed to be to die. She'd wander about the house like an automobile off target. She claimed harassment by life, by fate. That she'd been prevented from fulfilling her destiny by her meeting with 'an onion faced' Irishman, that worlds had waited for her, cloud carpeted worlds, the fluffy white clouds as in the ramparts for the delicate, urchin-girl feet of the Virgin Mary in pious cards. The exact location of these worlds was difficult to ascertain as, before she married, the only men who surrounded her life were quack, dithery-kneed, white suited, cane tripping artists. Maybe those artists saw lavish prospects for themselves on the East coast, for it was there it seemed Mrs. O'Dowd felt she'd missed out. Mentally, she hugged little shards of the craggy Eastern perimeter of the map of America to her, her lost hopes, this scroll edge. It was more likely she felt she'd be abducted by a rich man, one of a battalion of rich men who were camped on the Eastern perimeter, young, dashing – yes, dashing – rich men. Dashing because they had sweeps of hair over their mauve or pale, inky-blue eyes. But a young Irishman sauntered through the early summer heat of a street and vaguely looked at her – or did she meet him at an open air dance? Either way, his look swept her off her feet – was it

under the sign for Moggridge's cigar and general grocery store?
– or did it occur later when the palms of his hands – which she
noticed were long and feminine – took her waist. Though the
rest of his skin was dark she'd noticed this part of him still
purveyed whiteness and fleshy pinks. A memorial. A mindful-
ness. For what? Pain. Famine. Starvation. The majestic, sky
seeking canopy of Irish history. And in the terms of Irish
history they wed. They wed their different sense of Irish
history, their varying receptiveness for Irish history. Irish
history had made the sapphire ring on one of the fingers on her
right hand. Irish history created the vacuity in the slight and
occasional stoop in his back; it conjured a pale smoke of horror
to his facial features. He was closer to it. The Famine and the
landscape of the Famine was just behind him. His mind's eyes
still toured the skeletons and the grossly intermingled corpses
on the low, English caricature green hills. The caricature green
was true in this: it highlighted the fallen, the outstretched
limbs, the fingers that flowered on a skeleton's arms. The
difference in their receptivities for Irish history created an
enlivening, an imagination stimulating tension on their
wedding day, especially as they stood beside one another before
the altar rails, that stoop on Páid O'Dowd's broad shoulders but
in his eyes anger, hope, anguish, conquest. An interim
conquest. For her too, Irish history, despite its bravado with
her, was soul debilitating. This did not emerge for a year or two
after her marriage. Certainly there were stories you could get
your tongue around but there was also once a point where time
and possibility stood still in the Finuacane family. No end of
literary replenishment would undermine that fact. Out there in
the landscape of the Finuacane family there was a numbness, a
petrification in the air, an annihilation of life in the trees, a
charred deadness in the clay, a vacuously swinging pendulum of
madness in a woman, a forbear of Mrs. O'Dowd, who inhabited
that terrain. That woman walked into Mrs. O'Dowd's dreams,
creating a continuity of all-out madness between seventeenth-
century Ireland and late nineteenth-go-gettingness of Mid-
Western America. It wasn't until years after her husband's
death that this mysterious, occasionally writhing madness
asserted itself properly. It asserted itself in a kind of sleep-
walking quest for suicide; somewhere inside Mrs. O'Dowd was
a mainly dormant bed of acidic quagmire, the repercussion of

all that history; but when it spat and trembled the manifestations infested the house with deathly circles. Bonnie's two sisters left and abandoned Bonnie to her mother's tirades against self and life. Mrs. O'Dowd was disturbed by a vision she had within: a vision of a world where hope and animation had stopped but a new life had begun, the life, the thriving, the long side teeth of death. Black, varicose leaves whispered. Trees themselves and bushes were shell-shocked. A woman walked this terrain. It was Mrs. O'Dowd, searching for a way to oblivionise the coming armies of madness.

Her first suggestions for ways of killing herself were ludicrous, eating white mice – on a night of madness – hanging herself from a balloon, but then came the more logical plans, that she'd spill pills that looked like white beans into herself, that she'd rummage her heart with the bread-knife. Never did she ever bring herself to do these things but she spoke so long about them that eventually it seemed as if the tirade was focussed on Bonnie; it was, in short, a revenge for Bonnie's youth and that creamy, freckled beauty.

On leaving the house to marry Bethuel Muir, Bonnie was sure that all the time the madness had been feigned; it had been an attempt to subvert Bonnie, to weaken her and debilitate her and make her mad too, make her a tissue of madness, of debilitation so she wouldn't reach – New York, the stage, what? In middle years Bonnie knew she'd reach it though. Her son, Nessan, the poet, his adventures, were her insurance.

So she could poise her cup of tea with certainty and even the decorum of madness in front of her mother.

But even as words came from her mother's throat over tea, words about death, a sexual panorama addled Bonnie's mind again, an adolescent making love to her, or at least kneeling over her and she wondered again why this flirtation with fantasies, to the extent of following a boy, had commenced from contemplation of her son, why uneasy thoughts of Nessan had driven her into a charade. But maybe her body needed more real charades. There were a lot of adolescents in her dreams that night, like horses on wallpaper of flying horse patterns. Next morning she woke to her shop and the banana colour of the wainscot there from which mischievous eyed and cheeky mice peeped at her or from which she imagined a cast of mice to peep at her, before the start of the working day, dresses taken down then and smoothed before the eyes of local matrons planning visits to relatives on the East coast, white, reasonably narrow dresses for women whose breasts, stomachs and bottoms would be lumpy and rebellious and contradictory in them.

'My dear Nessan . . .'

Bonnie did not write her fears that day to Nessan, at morning-break when the door was briefly shut and the blind evanescent over the window wares, but addressed profuse salutations to him, and a stream of language influenced by his mardi gras poetry.

Bonnie was right to be worried about Nessan that summer. He'd returned to New York to indulge in sex, as much sex as he could. That intention, a small, unadmitted particle in his mind, grew to immeasurable proportions as the train neared New York. From the springboard of a small literary success, with limited financial independence he intended to leap into a world of untrammelled sexual indulgence, to foster his sexual tastes as never before, unchecked by a finger on the back of his lilac and blue jacket. But on the station platform as he walked away from the train something touched his shoulder. A cowslip shaft of sun through the ceiling above. He was walking away from the pastures of the Mid-West and the abrupt occurrences of spring flowers. Knapsack on his back, a knapsack he'd purchased in the Mid-West, leaving his suitcase there, he marched towards the folly of New York and the Salvation Army band's summoning of sins. He was walking towards his thirst, the thirst he'd always had, for things of the flesh. He was walking towards drink. He was walking towards something in order to walk back to a time, to nights of loneliness when mystic, early adolescent pubic hair appeared before him, and to make up for that time and those nights. He walked hurriedly in order to be on time for his sins. He declared an all out landscape of sin in his life.

The colours of sin were apricot and peach, the shirts of a boy he fondled, having found the boy in a gutter on Hobonken Water-front. The boy had been thrown up by a South American country, he was a visitor to this city, a drunken and drugged one. Nessan's mouth welcomed the nub of his penis. His penis refused a full erection so Nessan had to suck something, as if it was a plum. But it still refused an erection. Eventually Nessan got fed up. 'What do you theenk I am?' the boy said when Nessan shouted at him, 'Quier?'

But the boy kept coming back while he was in New York, the liquorice, neatly waved, oil scintillating hair of him, revealing his array of shirts. When all the colours of his shirts had been exhausted for exhibition he returned to South America or else to a gutter where he was invisible to Nessan. Nessan drove on, his nose smelling out sleeping boys and men.

Matt was a sailor. He took off his trousers for Nessan, stood over him as Nessan lay on his narrow bed; the hairs on Matt's legs, the many hairs on them, were a reminder. Nessan all his life had wanted a brother, a mate, someone stronger than him. Matt did not make love to Nessan. Or he would not allow Nessan to make love to him. He was a Catholic and went instead that night to pray under a picture of Our Lady of Dolours. But Matt too came back. He came back for conversation, cigarettes, bourbon, and the occasional mouthful of brandy. They slept separately and Nessan counted his snores, his own heart throbbing audibly, waiting for the moment Matt would join him. But Matt did not join him in bed. He prayed, drank bourbon, and asked Nessan to talk to him and to recite his poetry. But he did sometimes stand over Nessan and show his genital area to Nessan – as a gift – Nessan lay there, a child with blond eyelashes and daunted, fragile eyes. Matt put Nessan to sleep one night with a tea cosy beside his head.

The people you pick up, usually not penises, but lonelinesses, stories. Most of them not queer. But lonely. Searching. Open. Vulnerable. Those treading the earth with vulnerability. Nessan saw many men through his life that summer. Mainly men rummaged out of gutters, provoked, in bars, into going home with him for further conversation. Hobonken Waterfront was the scene of most of these meetings. Little sex happened. And at the end of the summer it became more noticeable that the men were becoming dirtier and dirtier, smellier and smellier. A rank, sourceless smell hung in Nessan's apartment. He opened windows to let it fly out, but it stayed. In autumn he purchased many carnations to drive the smell away.

Vagabonds, destitutes and broken sailors, sailors enmeshed in alcohol and remorse, had put down their, very often almost square, heads here. But at the end of the summer, coming towards amber glint time on the façade outside, the real sex happened, the real putrification.

Cheri was blond. Streaks of almost salmon pink in his hair. A mark of scavengery, a hint of blood, as phosphorus of some disease. Though male his name was near a female's. But, despite the blond, even, dripping hair, his face had an upshoot of something very masculine in it, scars, dishevelment, a purple and pink colour. The masculinity ended at the full carmine female lips. Cheri too was picked up in a gutter. He'd posed in a gutter rather than lain in a gutter. In a way he looked extremely like Nessan. He was a reflection of Nessan. A shadow of him. But the lips were more feminine. His buttocks, pearly ones, had addressed the bodies of millionaires. Bored of millionaires he was in a gutter. A banner, a brocade of cigarette smoke over him. Cheri was a disease. He insinuated himself in terms of ambivalence. He insinuated himself in terms of a shadow. His full, carmine lips curled towards Nessan, the purple of a street lamp reflected on them, on an autumn night. Nessan got a disease from the autumn and became very ill and nearly died. But life and January light offered him quarter again and he won a prize and had money and could go where he liked, could choose where to go to. But first he stalked the fog and the winter again to find a boy, a friend, a hand, a large, masculine hand, intricated by life and promising a magnanimity and a lack of judgement learned from waterside or pier bars, and cheap, gut-tearing red wind, from sailors' brawls and round the table, sacramental, sailors' confidences. Night was a lonely tide which brought Nessan to a shore of red lights, sailors' brawls and the grasping of hands on a table in combat. But the noise of a water-side bar receded as Nessan moved away, unrewarded by flesh or enactment of fantasy that flesh would give. Only a red light remaining, telling the way for the next soul, searching through the fog for perdition. Nessan was torn between the search for a boy, buttocks more minute than his, and for that of someone bigger and stronger and more enveloping than him. But most of the time the search ended up with only the sound of his own footsteps, echoing into the months of non-creativeness and nonword-construction, no slabs on the railroad line. He had to take a way out, towards creativity again. But the red light gathered into a fog and faded out, with no obligations to poetry or creativity or to the search of a young man for fellows. On such nights, looking for a mellifluous alternative, Nessan recalled the Irish origin of his name.

The red neon, the barnacles of light around the skeletal letters; I moved off, I nudged off rather, reluctantly, leaving this space to the early summer fog, the space around the light, the space of pavement and fog under neon. I'd been unsuccessful tonight. It was earlier this summer and the paces of my feet were uncertain. They hung halfway between staying and not wanting to be here in the first place, uncertain about the validity of this entire mission. There was a further element of uncertainty, uncertainty even as to my sexual proclivities and, even if certain about them, if this was the right, the moral, the specious place to bring them. My figure wavered off, aware of a black leather jacket on grey flesh. I had meandered back to my old ways after Phineas died. But the structure, the ready acceptability of old ways had crumbled. The paces of my feet were addled with uncertainty, with moral doubt. Although it was summer, my black leather jacket closed in on my shoulders. I folded my arms, the fists night-blanched. What had I been thinking of in that space: confession, the soul, the mischances of a life?

When I returned from the United States in the early summer of 1949 I brought not just the pages of a potential book with me but the giddiness of a relationship with a woman, Gerry. I had met Gerry in the spring of 1949, after taking a bus which had slanted into Massachussets. It had been Easter. I'd had a fragment or two to pick up about Nessan; a visit he'd made to Boston. I'd met Gerry. She had reddish-gold hair which attempted to form a dome over the back of her head; it rose bewilderingly from her forehead and fell like an avalanche at the back. It anticipated a hair-style of the late fifties and early sixties. There was something crooked about her, her nose, her bones, her stance as she sat over a table. Over a table we met. A white cardigan drooping from her shoulders, a few white, virginal college books on the white tablecloth in front of her. The random cloak of a cardigan was a mascot. A student mascot. She was fiddling with being a student for a while. It was a role, a protection. Something she could hide in. She came from a rich family, a very rich family as their houses and palatial bathrooms were to reveal to me. But for the moment she was a slab of red lipstick and a subsequent smile. 'Hi. Who's the clever, sturgeon-faced guy on the cover?' Gerry was referring to Nessan's portrait on the cover of one of my books, one of the books I'd virtually thrown on the table in front of her, Nessan looking particularly inflamed in the black and white picture. I had to explain. 'And he's wearing a new shirt.' At the inkling of his shoulders and space under his chin could be divined a Central American type shirt, a bird or two with upward, fussy tails in it. I was not sure if the shirt was new or not; it was a novel idea. I paused over it. True the slight hint of the shirt and its pattern had an affirmativeness which challenged and in turn affirmed the downward looking chin. Gerry's fingers rippled towards her lemonade. 'I like his face.' She had not heard of the poet. But she was open to and interested in him. Her ignorance was not an embarrassment to her. She'd already put him in the plain of the obscure but still saleable. Nessan was ripe for revival at our table. Her finger now choking him at his shirt, had followed him to Central America. That was where she'd placed him in the Boston, vaguely accentuated, spring sunshine, among the fads and bloated lunged mysticisms of Central America in the 1920s and 30s. 'And what do you do?' 'I'm writing a book about this man.' A pause, a long pause; Gerry pondered on the information as if it was something overwhelmingly salient. 'You're an author.' The 'author' was dragged out in a New England drawl. It led to the next question. 'An Irish author?' I nodded affirmatively. That surrender of information was the cause of a great deal, a visible cascading of cognition. Gerry's head drew back. 'You're an Irishman.' Heartened at the correctness of the statement she went on then into a dissertation on her and her family's love of Ireland. That love had not been substantiated by a visit to Ireland of any member of her family but they did know the country of Irish America, plenteous green lawns, the studs of golf holes which carried the eye over those lawns, the country of Irish America. But Gerry did have clues about Irish literature. She was a student after all. We turned to that topic – her studies. She'd been a student for three years, thinking now of a change.

The change she told me with a gesture of her arm, her arm outstretched for a moment, would be a journey, a different country, the ameliorating influence of another country. Tired now of America, tired of lethargic fortunes, she wanted Paris, the wide liberating pavements there, Berlin, the laurel trees there annotated in American literary works. She got Dublin. By dabbling in lunch with me, a flag of half blond lettuce sticking up from a prostrate and lapsed limbed shrimp, she ended up spending the greater part of her life in Dublin. Gerry Kirstein chose to follow me a year or so after my return. She'd already packed up her life in America, shuffling the papers of a vague academic project together, riveted inside by the emotion activated by her mother's suicide, an emotion which clung most closely to the hallstand mirror in which her mother had last looked at herself and which Gerry departed from, leaving the wisteria on the hallstand, the clonk of a runaway tennis ball on the darkened, cloud-aggravated verdure outside.

Her mother had killed herself because the stack of cards of the rich man had fallen in upon her, cards with seared scarlet hearts in them. That was the image Gerry took with her to Ireland. She'd decided to have done with her family's riches, to have done with the mesmeric fortunes, and in order to devote herself to poverty she thought of me. I was the card she'd resurrected. We'd had an affair. She wanted to renew it. On a hot June day she packed herself into a fur coat and left an emerald estate, with the intention of ending up in Ireland. I was waiting for her on a pier. She'd taken a boat from Holyhead. It was July, stroppily hot, and we were close to my parents' new home. I took her there and presented her, for want of a better description, as a spouse.

The years between America and Ireland; the gulf of the fifties. Gerry was the wife of an antiquarian bookseller, a Dublin hostess. Hair, grown much darker, in a bed-like bun, a generous downfall of a bun, she served to guests platters of tarted up anchovies, anchovies with mysterious dabs of pink in them. She'd been divested of wealth all right marrying me and I, marrying her, had been divested of my book. Bit by bit, pigmentation of red and blue face scars upon pigmentation of red and blue face scars, folded out of my life; my father's business was gone, I'd opened my own business. I possessed a small, slim, usually rain wrapt, grey Georgian house. Gerry was my wife. I had a status in Dublin. But the more I entered into social life and social status the further away the book went. It was left in the hands of the young man I'd been in New York in the early months of 1949.

Bonnie Muir was chirpy that Christmas, sitting up, laughing. A blue cracker snapped out of her frail, surprised, almost disappeared hat. The smile came then, in response to the act, slowly. I was standing in front of her, two even sweeps of dark hair punishing my forehead and earlobes. Bonnie's smile teetered on a laugh. 'You're a grand fellow. You'll make a good book out of us. Me and my son.' A nun scooped up some fallen, dried, yellow flowers on a tray, the flowers apparently showering down from the effects of a cracker or two. 'You'll write this book, won't you?' She beseeched. 'It'll be good. It is important. Nessan was . . . is important. Nessan must live.'

A young man in New York, all the possibilities in the world. Christmas, New Year, January I danced along. 'So long Ireland.' But Ireland was all the time pulling me back, my mother dropping snatches to me about her illnesses. 'I don't want to go back there. I'll go to Spain, Portugal, anywhere.' I did go back to Ireland in late May. But first I unwebbed the story of Nessan further. I disentangled it until it seemed that I was Nessan. One evening leaving Bonnie I caught sight of a woman letting herself out of a top window of the home, by way of ghostly, shining white sheets tied together. I let escapees and night gnomes be and walked in the direction of the subway station.

Gerry was tortured almost from the moment she arrived in Ireland. She looked tortured and that was what, in a way, attracted me to her. You could be totally absorbed by her appearance and think of nothing else. Gerry immediately set about attacking Trinity College, attempting a course there. We married as my parents completed the papers on their new home in Dalkey. Enough had been left of the business to buy me the Georgian house and help me set up a business. I really took over the bookshop from someone else. A friend of my father's and an inmate now of Dundrum mental hospital. Gerry thought she was marrying her way out of the memory of suicide, but the wedding photographs display a bewildered anxiety about a world which drives ice maiden blonde-haired old ladies to suicide, ladies with their smooth nests of hair emblazoned with a brand of peroxide.

It had not been just the natural stages of fatigue with the place which had finally driven Gerry out of America but the darkness of her mother's suicide. She'd left in a trance and arrived in a trance. She'd thought I'd be a suitable habitat for her, the 'auothor'. But a meditation on suicide and death, and particularly on her mother's death, informed our marriage and our years together. It lay under the surface of every dinner party. And then history, that untrustworthy thing, changed around us and threw us up in a gaudier age, an age which revealed the lack of connecting forces between us. We'd been hiding for years behind the card of her mother's death, a card with at least one seared scarlet heart in it.

Gerry admitted to me, the morning I met her, that she was bored with her studies, she was bored with academic life. So she decided to pursue our meeting into a lunch; she did not wish to return that afternoon to her college. She asked me instead, she lavished questions on me about Nessan. Where he was from? Why had he committed suicide? An arm, freckled, big drops of rash-like freckles on it, crept towards me, her fingers ending up in my fingers, after having retreated once. The tiny hairs on the crest of her arm managed to dart me with their electricity at one point. These hairs, a contingent of practically invisible ones, on the edges of her fingers, were blandished by sun. 'Nessan Muir', the words rotated in her mouth. At the sound of them she invited me to her home in Boston, prior to my departure.

Nessan Muir walked the nights before leaving New York, looking, looking for something despite his resolution to change, and the putting into practice of that resolution by his purchase of a travel ticket. A boy turned up then, in the fog, a late adolescent, the kind of face he'd always been looking for, vague; thick, charcoal hair around it, pendant charcoal eyes in the pale of that face. There was no doubt what was meant by the language between them. There was hesitation in the gestures of their faces at a distance from one another, but the outcome was that a boy straddled home with Nessan. But when it came to the bed Nessan found he did not want to sleep with the boy. There was the innocence of lush Latin madonna about that face. Nessan put the boy into bed, taking off his black jacket, and himself rested in another bed, the boy grateful for the sleep. Maybe that's all he really wanted to go home with Nessan for.

The Irish element of Nessan, the landscape which went with him on waterfront streets, was the one, at its most exhibitionistic, I introduced Gerry to shortly after her arrival in Ireland. An old Ford brought us to the West coast. White tops of waves threw themselves in the air. Rocks sprayed their way to the sea, often aprons thrown under round tower type buildings or castles. The waves lifted off their hats for Gerry, seal-like emergent bosoms on them. Gerry was impressed as she was supposed to be. What connected us was sex. My body in the United States had been liberated into a world of sex. It was a subterranean world. There were outward signs, outward notes of anxiety, but all that was real for us happened in the covert world of bodies.

Easter 1949 my penis was particularly filled with alacrity; the United States had not only replenished it with life but gave it a new wizardly animation. Heterosexuality was a newly discovered country for me; it had breezed through my body, and my body, my genitalia had taken on a life of their own. At times the rest of my body was disconnected from genitalia. They decided my schedule, my genitalia. So in Boston I abandoned Nessan for Gerry. But Gerry was only one of many. Gerry stuck. My penis in her hand had a knob the colour of an unshelled garden snail. In the arteries of those colours were many stories. The surface of that knob withdrew slightly with the torture of Gerry's fingers examining it. But it was a pleasant torture. More pleasant than the torture meted out by the kings of Spain.

My last summer in Spain, 1934, we journeyed from Andalusia to Castile. I was the intendent college boy there, a dark blazer on me, white defiant trousers as I strode over the evening and summer burnished fields. A strange light had grasped Castile, a light which grappled within itself. Many colours in it, a tumult of blues and oranges and pugnacious reds. The colours stated not just the political climate but the advent of change in me. Alone in the fields I was already a solitary adult. Old rubbery male Spaniards rose like snakes from their seats in my direction. Bishops implored me to caress their rings. One evening I walked and walked. A few days beforehand an opera-singer-looking, middle-aged Spanish lady had approached me with her cleavage as if she wanted me to be swallowed in it; she was obviously taunted by me. I knew I had a power in me, it was a power vested upon me by the kings of Spain, my ancestors.

There was an aristocratic, spacious erectness to my shoulders, a pouting irregular thrust to my lips. My mother had filled me with ideas. But Ireland took back the levelness of my shoulders, it filled me with tumours and tortures. By the end of the 1930s I was a rather weasely, upper middle-class student misplaced in the environs of University College, Dublin.

At University College there were one or two affairs, sperm in the off-centre of girls' pubic parts as their school reunion or college society ball dresses were fluffed around them, one girl's pubic parts sticking out from a lot of meringue clothing, bewildered. Sex was in a way as repugnant to me as it was to her. But it was not until Portugal that my sexuality moved on, that I and my lonely nature were taken by the hand and jolted forward. And in this jolting my body burgeoned and grew graceful and my chest filled with delicacy. On this wave of delicacy many memories returned.

I'd noticed the young man sitting around cafés in Lisbon, the heavy haunches of him in flannel trousers. It was his solitary bigness which I'd picked out and the debonair and almost joking way he used a fork. The motif of him recurred from café to café until he became an unavoidable and passive object of my vision. It was my second spring in Lisbon. What had started as a stupendous, imagination-gasping adventure had become a routine, a ghetto, a mind oblivionizing burial. I clung to my small basement premises. Lisbon had become grey with routine. Spies, prostitutes, international adventurers, a large number of them ladies, had become grey. We were all enveloped and numbed by war. War held a fog over our senses

102

and even the most exotic preambles of fashion had the daring taken out of them. Many excitements took place under this fog: sex, card games, seances, but they had the intended excitement clipped from them. In Lisbon, during the war, the apparel of exoticism was just not exotic. There was danger, mortality there and, more than anything, incarceration. Incarceration showed up on the brain after a while. I was doing an office job. I had many friends who were redundant spies. They turned to alcohol. Atrophy and fixation spread across their faces in cafés. Their eyeballs were dead or unawakened cannon balls by Lisbon harbour. There were no memories. Just the ghost of a city. But in my second spring there the cherry blossoms and the almond blossoms cluttered the city like a military occupation of their own. Little bolls of trees vied with one another to fête the new air of jubilation. People could leave more easily now and now that they could they did not wish to. The business of intrigue took up again. Spies put on ridiculous antiquated dark glasses and glamour was allowed to make gestures in clothes,in the one stricken, sidelong crease in a girl's navy skirt, in the volcanic tuft of a young man's orange handkerchief in the breast pocket of his white jacket. Lisbon became what it aspired to be throughout the war. It was difficult to know what made it be like this, a premonition about, a general agreement on the end of the war. In fact it did not become easier to get out until the beginning of the summer, but in my mind that spring and early summer is all one. It was the lifting of a darkness off a city which was an ultimate phosphorescence, a defiant pot-pourri of nationalities and intrigues and the habitats of millionaire and mysticism-crazed Jews. It was the last bit of night life left in Europe. And this night life contained some of the practices of Berlin of the twenties: singalongs, striptease, seances – more than anything seances, communication with the dead. Seared, mattress-haired, tall, male Jewish mystics straggled along. The streets were narrow here and led back to streets in Berlin in the twenties where mysticism was an expensive and binding aroma.

In this station-platform-crowd sway of suggestions I met the young Jewish man from Romania. His image rebelled against its own passivity. Suddenly the young man whose figure was a motif in cafés began to become disordered; he began coming alive by making combative gestures with forks or by throwing his back backwards erratically as if he'd had a seizure. From being a submerged part of the spring he became not just noticeable but a central point of attention. He suddenly thought of and became obsessed by something and the impact of his thoughts were there for everybody to see. He stared at a high ceiling, framed by a moulding of little pale blue, Portuguese Cupids and little flowers, from a pale pink shirt, his jacket off, with Old Testament prophet eyes. The whites of those eyes were burning, old man curdled and febrile. They were what attracted sufficiently my attention so that I made a movement towards him and as I moved towards him he turned to me as if he'd been expecting me. We spoke, in a café, about the weather, and arranged to meet again.

The weather was not just an idle point of conversation in Lisbon that spring. It was a confusion between displays of blossom in petrifying brilliance and little cantankerous showers which sent the bolls of blossom into flurries and smashed sunshine on them at intervals. After some of the ferocious showers the nakedness of the ground was miraculously and densely covered for miles with blossom. Squares, boulevards, broad pavements were dismayed by blossom. On top of that streaks of lightning appeared in the air, momentary, exhibitionistic, lop-sided dragons. In the middle of these confusions I met the young man from Romania whose nose, above all his physical attributes, fascinated me, a big, mountainous nose, and started having rendezvous with him, fluid rendezvous, rendezvous that reminded him of his lost family and me of my search for a brother, for male companionship, for someone stronger and more male than me. His presence bathed me in a sucrose feeling of physical serenity.

We trod through the fallen blossoms, always a distance between us, talking quietly, he mainly doing the talking, obsessed as he was by a family who had fallen to the Germans and a past which had moved out of Romania into Yugoslavia. He was heir to a mansion in Yugoslavia, one his family had taken over when they'd left Romania, a move they'd made when he'd been five or six, and if it was still there after the war he'd reclaim it, but in the meantime he'd brought some of his family's wealth here to distribute it among the frolicsome maritime dots of sunshine while the mansion was seeped by the rain of the mountains which rose suddenly from the plains at its rear, surveyed by Nazis or attended by cranes. It was the Celtic touch which partly bound us, the rain the young man had generously created to envelope the mansion like cellophane. But there was much more to hold us together, a willingness to discuss high and consuming topics, to float our conversations over Lisbon, to pivot them on a point in an unblemished blue sky above wide promenades through parks, promenades with generous flanks of trees. The young man looked to the point of contact between his cane and the pavement, a born aristocrat. I beside him, had diminished in size, had become a cerebral-limbed and rubbery-skinned Dublin student. My back had manoeuvred itself into subjection to this role. I listened to everything he had to say, even put glasses on for some of our meetings. I was his audience. Heartened at his interest in me I wanted to demean myself, to diminish myself in size and physical prowess for his sake. But the effect that had on him was to make him more academic too. We both walked about Lisbon, at a safe distance from one another, the two of us diminishing through our talk of philosophy into candidates for the priesthood, to fussy and cerebral-physiqued young men. I suppose our conversations, the level they were pitched on, put Europe into the background. What amazed me about the young man was the depths of philosophical interest he could conjure, the knowledge he could confidently unfold. But philosophical knowledge ruthfully turned into conversations about brothers, brothers he'd grown up with in a dank house near overseeing mountains, sweaty and long limbed brothers piled into beds big enough for the fornication of emperors and empresses, brothers always with their faces to the pillows on which they could turn one ear to the wind from the mountains. The lament for things butchered caused us to shed the sublimated apparel of the physique and become solid and certain young men again. But the journey through the remembering mind was a perilous and involved one and created strange contacts between us; we were at one on certain points of experience. Those points were elabo-rated by him but I kept my knowledge of them secret; they were for me the landscape which ran into the Irish sea, the dirty and weather tawdry lawns which almost capsized into the desultory and dish-water sea. The Irish sea, the margin of it, held my adolescence. That adolescence made me listen to the young man and hold on to every word he spoke about his family and his murdered heritage. But grief and remorse, remorse for having

105

escaped, alternated with debonair airs and guffawing, macho voiced jokes. The language we spoke was English, his learnt in Budapest. He'd spun around Eastern Europe. His voice was heavy, leaden when he joked and when it was like that it tended to make my voice feeble. But my voice recovered sufficiently to make myself attractive to him and I shed my glasses permanently. But we stumbled around, like two youth hostellers from two different countries who'd encountered in a foreign city and clung to one another for company, seeing the sights, the museums, the castles together. There was too the atmosphere, and the innocence, of a school expedition about our walks. For the moment. But the more I was with the young man the more I became aware of my sexual subjugation to him, a sexual subjugation invoked myself, and my own need to identify with the sexuality of someone bigger and broader than me. Something had happened to me growing up in Ireland. I'd become a miserable, peripheral thing. I became more aware, in the young man's company, of broad, quirky, unapologetic shoulders, of the placement of his genitalia. I at once wanted to make myself into a shadow beside him and yet had to present something appealing about myself to hold on to his companionship and to vie, secretively, with his masculinity and to balance it.

The walks led us on down straight throughfares and the more we walked and the more aware I was of the tacit sexuality of his broad hips, the more Dublin unfolded inside me, unprovoked: my adolescence, corners of it previously considered of not much importance, edges of experience, the whip of a tree of almond blossom against the sky in the garden of the house of a friend of my mother's in Rathmines. A disused bathtub there, tadpoles at the bottom of it. The anxious face of my mother's friend above me as I looked into the bathtub, her anxious eyes – all of middle years in them, above her carmine, tied out chiffon scarf – on the place my pubescent, bare legs disappeared into my short trousers. A travel poster showing Chartres Cathedral, apple blossom beside it, at the corner of Westmoreland Street and D'Olier Street. A place I alighted from a tram on my flights into town from school. The subterranean café lavatory in which I presented my penis to an unimpressed tramp. The streets in which fascists marched, politicians paraded, fumbling with their umbrellas, bishops, red pear cheeked and dimpled, holding catatonic prayer books to them while they smiled. The furore of the sky. The sexual humiliation at the school. My penis was too small and people christened me 'breasty' because they claimed I had nascent female breasts. The room in the school in which I was caught, otherwise naked, wearing pink, woman's knickers. The court martial. The rocky cove where men swam where I went, already in a knowing long mac, to survey them emerging naked from the sea. The white underwear with apple blossom ensignia on them, lambs' wool, my mother purchased for me in Brown Thomas', her long, red varnished nails delicately and swiftly scraping the ensignia, an adroit game of hers on the shop counter before the gleaming items were wrapped up. My mother precociously walking up Grafton Street, underwear under her arm, her little liquorice curls darting out from a pugnaciously placed little hat. The splutter of semen on the waist, gleaming under the navel, the first real sexual encounter, the shame, the wetness and the vulnerability of the body, the shabby retraction of the genitalia, the cold, the sea, the boat coming in from England. College, then university, the ladies in apple blossom dresses. My father grinning into a half raised phial of brandy. He knew everything. His cardigan half open on him at the dinner table. Those Protestant deceitful eyes of his fixed on nothing in particular. A big haul of mixed flowers on the table: anemones, tulips, gypsum, irises, fiery, orange irises – my mother's favourites – all the flowers from the garden outside, which sloped a little, had secret valleys and panoramic stretches of landscape of its own. His bemusement at certain things. The inefficiency which followed me when I started going to the Catholic university, my shirt tails always hanging out, my shoulders slouching. 'You won't make an industrialist.' He'd taken to art and flower arrangements. He purchased many paintings at art exhibitions and put them up in the disused stables. In Lisbon, with the young man, these stables came back, where as a youth I went to query the sunlight and try to recreate there a childhood or early adolescent imaginary companion, Manuel, having a need again for him but an updated representation of him, his body and his genitalia having grown bigger, his chest broader, firmer and a jaundiced, receptive colour. And instead of sexual adventure games we now had intellectual disserations, conversations about the clerical collared philosophers. The late summer seas off Killiney, County Dublin, where my uncle lived, had subsumed this boy once, the blue. Now he returned. He was more even, bigger, but even in the middle of the most intellectual discussions nearly always half-naked. I spoke in a stable to a wraith. I was going mad. Tawdry bits of apple blossom crowded in on the stables. I had adapted one of the figures in the paintings purchased by my father, the fantasies of Dublin Protestant spinsters, Adonis from 1920s London art schools. He was my revenge on hearses and fascist marches. But the revenge took strange forms, multiple shaped and profuse stains on underwear which hung from my body in a runny lump. There were renewed profusions of stains on my underwear in Lisbon. I woke in a basement bed to be shut in by the shadows of blossoms, by the darkness of the room itself and to be surrounded by the smell of body leakage, of a chamber pot with giant marigolds on it, of the dampness and mustiness of the room and of chaotically blowing, inviting blossoms outside. I was in a yard bordered by frail, lichen covered boughs, an army overlooking the walls, the stable roofs, wondering whether to go in and to trespass on a figment of my imagination. But figments of imagination gave way to intense studies and acquittal at university. I was then on the loose, free from fantasy until I met the young man in Lisbon. He bound me again to a primordial need to be subjected to, to be overwhelmed by, to be oblivionized by someone of my own sex. I was a Spanish-Irish boy in glittering black shoes walking alongside someone who made up for an inadequacy, an aberration in his dual inheritance, Spanish and Irish, and combined Irish Protestantism and Catholicism. The Protestant-Catholic conflict of my inheritance was hidden in buds breaking into blossom outside walls of a yard in County Wicklow, in which I stood and trembled on the brink of consummation with a shadow in a stable.

My clothes became very dandified in the young man's company, not that they weren't dandified already, but pink shirts and rudely polka dotted ties came out from a year or so of disuse or hanging, dusty death and draped me. I walked as if I had a cane in my left hand but I had not one though I looked to the ground in the strains of someone bearing a cane. It was around my neck that my clothes fulminated, reds, oranges, patterned pinks of shirts. I strode in a modulated way, head very often as that of a pony, going up and down to a rhythm, listening. The dashing dress made us noticeable, even in Lisbon that spring, and we took to walking at nights. The fireworks in the sky were as red as the shirts at my neck, Sevillana red shirts, tentative reminders of my ancestral, assured sexuality, of the part of me which had wanted to revisit Spain but ended up in this dreaming, ocean-precipiced city.

To our surprise, in the wartime city, there were celebrations of spring or some spring event, dancers on a platform in front of us one night, fireworks in the sky above them, dancers rushed in from some mountain-side region with the clothes of that region, spinning about, hands on one another's shoulders, a topsy-turvy orbit of colours, hands, smiles, backsides. The young man had led me to the point of consummation with the real. Around us were men with red handkerchiefs like balloons in their breast pockets, pudgy, lop-sided bellied, middle-aged men, straining to hear our, or other people's, conversation, as they pretended to have their ears glued to the lilting songs about the Primavera coming from the stage. I was aware of the young man's prospective genitalia beside me. So as to be more aware of them we walked through a twisting path made by oleander bushes the following morning, past a group who seemed to be holding an open-air seance in a white baked yard, to the river bank where I made myself into a woman for the young man. The immediate reaction was one of mutual shame. I held a sticky and contaminated breast pocket orange handkerchief to my pubic parts as if trying to obliterate them. It was his handkerchief. His haunches on the ground were a generous sculpture. But afterwards I realized I'd been a slithery armed, slightly jaundiced-skinned brother for him. I had invoked an annihilated inheritance for him and, before leaving Lisbon, I learnt that the young man, who had become distant from me, had dropped off a clifftop on a hazy day, whether it was an accident or whether he had thrown himself off I'd never know but I did know that the haze on the ocean had thrown up Atlantis-like shapes that day, conjectures of the imagination of some old Jewish palmist in her dark and ornament-cluttered, ship-like, Lisbon apartment.

With Gerry there was no doubt about my masculinity – for a few years. In fact it was partly for my masculinity she'd followed me to Ireland. In the newspapers I was the Spanish-Irish heir. I was in fact heir to nothing as my parents' fortune was gone but I was an antiquarian bookstore owner and I participated in Dublin's social life. Dublin's social life received us enthusiastically. We glided into parties, as a couple a byword in Dublin. The fifties sent out their lethargic smog in Ireland, thread-like bishops hurried around in limousines. But Gerry and I were going the opposite way as was a whole coterie in Dublin. This coterie kept itself to itself and refused admission to almost everybody except those with the closest connections to those already part of the coterie. Gerry didn't need my connections to get her in, however. From the beginning she took over. She exerted influence, riches, education behind her, beauty with her that adapted to the Irish air by taking on sploshes of freckles on her face and a redness in her hair, disarming old men in long coats, waveringly prepared for rain against the gigantic skies Merrion Row cut open onto. In Dublin old men swam against skies. It was mainly sky. The brown and antique doors of Baggot Street were all hospitable to Gerry and counted in her itineraries. She gave Dublin an image of itself and in this way allowed a portion of Ireland to transcend itself in these years. Boys on cricket fields in Trinity, arms back, about to throw balls, doors, previously vacuous and bald, were all grateful to her. She gave Dublin an imminence of something else and artists and sons of rich men alike flocked into her presence, cigarettes very often triggered off in their mouths. But, as if by all the work Gerry put into entertaining and paying attention to these people and as if by the familiarity which sneaks on a person, the auburn and the cheeky, startled red patches of her hair were overwhelmed by darkness, a soft but not mediocre brown which fell into a placid bun behind. The bun was always intact for parties and parties were the order of the day, Gerry with platters of anchovies, transfixed for diplomats, artists, millionares and – traitors. Dublin is a city full of traitors as we were to discover.

My homosexuality crept on me in 1956. It had always been there, an unstated part of my bond with Gerry. What had brought me to her sexually had been my own new-found admiration for my own body in the United States. That body had grown more masculine of its own accord in the United States, the muscles of my chest accentuated, my chest, pale from its recent lack of sun, billowing outwards proudly and unapologetically. I was what Ireland had never prepared me to

110

be, the male. I'd wanted to vent this new-found sense of masculinity on the nearest possible female and in Boston Gerry had been the one. But sexual extravagances lead to complications as they did in the case of Gerry and me, with Gerry, in a petrified coat of mourning, following me to Ireland, thinking she was in love with me and me at the other end taking her word for it, renewing the sexual activity with her until our bodies were drained of a need for such activity, until the high water-mark of sexuality had ebbed from us. That left cement, men's bathing huts on grey mornings, deserted but for one old fat swimmer undressing under the summer delinquents' graffiti. There was a mouldered wreck of a trawler on the edge of the sand. A schoolteacher strolled up the pier, in from viewing the sea, a spaniel beside him. Lessons were soon beginning. The whiskey coloured spaniel suddenly ran on ahead. The schoolteacher nodded to me. Behind those spectacles he knew, his lightly wizened face knew, he'd seen me somewhere before.

In 1956 I began walking along the Liffey, my figure very tiny in competition with the gasworks opposite, static doldrums of cloud in the sky, cloud that had been static for a long time, my figure knowing its way to the point where nymph skinned boys emerged from the wastes, a whole contagion of these pale-featured denizens of the dockland topography of citadel and shed. There were moments to be had with those boys, kisses to be placed on foreheads, venereal, like the zone of themselves fingers were placed on by them, splashes of pale blond curls on those foreheads that would have done a slum boy chorister at the Pro-Cathedral proud. Kisses moved from lips to lips, an ever-quickening rota. But the purse of the boys' lips as they kissed always seemed the same and the odour of their pubic parts was as one, poverty, strangled semen mingling with the smells of mud and hemmed-in canals surfaced with paraffin. They were sacramental, the kisses, had the air and the self-conciousness of sacraments. A whole coterie of Dublin males came here to partake in a heretical but respectful sacrament. Caps, coats came here rather than men. I always went there with the hope that there'd be a special boy, but there was only a uniformity, a lack of distinction of boys' kisses. Eventually, confused, I became a bit mad and settled for quick sex, easy sex, unclean rectum smelling sex. My life with Gerry went on. We had submerged into a pattern and in this pattern there was a lot of dark, Hades. Gerry had lost the first fervour of being in Dublin, courses at Trinity, young men's attention. Her face was bewitched by depression and meditation on depression. Gerry and I continued like that, red, single decker buses trailing through the foothills of the Dublin mountains, taking her to a seminary where she lectured, taking her to a hospital where she saw a therapist, until our lives clashed and we saw one another, not as partners, but as two people who'd skulked in a house together for years, virtually unaware or uncaring about one another's activities. Gerry had become the typical Dublin wife, with a husband who dragged himself along by the Liffey, in a black plastic anorak, looking for boys, and she didn't know or want to know. A persona which indulged in all kinds of social activity until that activity in the late 1960s questioned itself and poured cataclysms, which were more than just academic, on Gerry. That's when she packed her suitcases, those left of her coming to Ireland, and deciding she was in love with a young, pugnaciously short haired visiting American scholar, followed her to America. The 'being in love with' was a tease. It was adopting a jargon as a suitable way of escape. A way of escape that was bound to leave literary anecdotes after it. That was what Dublin was all about. The pursuit of things so they'd leave an anecdote or two. Gerry had found out about me, of course, and in her finding out we were reminded of the child who was nearly born to us.

The landscape by the Liffey had branched out, had taken in spacious islands of cement outside public lavatories, had taken in sites under Victorian lamp-posts, had taken in points by gates and, again, venues of cement outside certain bars in Dublin. The search for boys became more frenetic and yet more silent. Not a stone hit the bottom of the water. People practising in these rites were so much in fear that they, generally, did not dare speak about someone else. Famous clerics' faces looked from over collars and under kaftans, Soviet-spy grimaces on their faces under their heavy spectacles. But there was more to it than all of that. The baby Gerry had carried in her womb had died in the eighth month and after that she was neurotically fearful of being surprised in pregnancy again, never wishing to go through such disappointment again. And she blamed me, in a way, invoking a famished, impoverished side to my sexuality she'd guessed to have been there once, fixating it on me so I

112

would not come near her again with gluttonous, prodigious sexual appetites. What kept us together then? Rain, art, Dublin, a combined social image, and a friendliness to do with all manic depressive matters. I still made love to her, I made love to her throughout all our years together, but with a penis that was pale, sheepish and didn't get up to its work at times when she risked pregnancy. But all the time I was implicitly the sexual failure for her, the man in the anorak with slightly stooped back, and genitalia eaten away. So I took that beaten sexuality into a world where it could have new, untrammelled fantasies about itself and where it could perform, in brief, subversive moments, with a new, unwatched prowess. And perhaps the baby had just been a cataclysm, it was mainly forgotten, remembered only as the point at which our enthusiastic and untrammelled sexuality for one another ebbed, that is until Gerry discovered that I'd had a backlog of hundreds of lovers and blamed that fact for the child which went from her womb. But the ultimate betrayal was that when we'd made friendship out of potential enmity a young man came to her and told her how I'd supplied guns to young I.R.A. men for sex.

Being of the class I was from, with the connections I had, it was easy for me to avail myself of a supply of guns a few years after the Northern troubles started up, to plummet a cache of arms, to have secretly supplied to a new breed of young men who infested the grey wastes of the dockland, young men who were a sturdy and controlled and sure collection of arms, legs, torsos. They came out of the history of their country and were giving sex for guns to jaunt away with and shoot soldiers. It was the military air of these young men that drew me, the military cognizance, the preversion which they indulged in, sex for sale and guns for the chalk Virgin with plastic lilies at her feet in Belfast. These young men were the most lost people of all, erect and automaton-still figures against the waste peripheries of the landscape. I gave them guns when it was still fashionable among the Dublin middle classes to parade loyalties for the Nationalist cause, before the bombs, when the odour of guns in Belfast, sent by the Dublin middle classes, was mixed with that of Bloody Marys in Torremolinos. The fashion stopped, but the story stayed and reached Gerry's ears. That was after a noxious bomb in Belfast. It was with these funereal odours, as when she came, that she left.

*

Gerry was a plain girl, a plain girl in some ways, with rich auburn to red hair with a benevolent streak of blond on its front when she came. She had dapples of rustic freckles on her arms which she liked to show, freckles which authenticated her claim to be simple. She had a smile on her face a lot, an uneasy smile albeit, wine coloured, hesitant, waiting to disappear into her cheekbones, always a fear on the edge of those cheekbones. The smile very often disappeared into her cheekbones, into her eyes, into a memory of her mother's suicide. She wanted to escape America but Ireland made her depressive, made her moribund and she ended by escaping Ireland, the jolliness of an escaped convict on her face the day she left, surprising ramifications of good health – gold-course flushes on her cheeks – and relief. She'd been my wife for over twenty years and from the day she left Ireland I hardly heard from her again. She went back to her family, their estates, and their belated pardon. Recently, I heard, she wrote a long article in a literary journal about an American poet called Nessan Muir.

The bright colours, the jerseys of primrose and of cheeky vermilion, then the succession of mauves, of discreet purples, this was the world I entered, briefly, after Phineas' death this year. I was going into the makeshift caverns of modern Irish homosexuality, homosexuality a new discovery. Straub lights caught the intendent pederast's face, some dithery middle-aged celibate up from the country, made an apple of rouge on his startled features and like a mad and frolicsome poltergeist then deftly slid away from him, leaving this stooped backed man more confused than before about his sexuality. Coffee was offered in cups with geisha girls running around the rims. Red wine was borne in by young men with their legs in black leotards and the top part of them mostly in amorphous white, the wine in fat, overspilling glasses or sometimes in its bottle, white tissue between the neck of the bottle and the young men's fingers as if the bottle was after a strenuous massage, the young men's legs going lightly, delicately, like those of women in high heels in 1940s' movies. 1940s' Dublin female decor was brought out here: necklaces, bracelets, stoles, the heads of particularly

114

Irish-russet foxes looking as if they were about to bark in their drooping state. The clamour of recently released femininity was here, high pitched Mayo and Cork accents yapping to one another, nimble chests, previously restrained – flames of black hair very often spiralling on pale flesh in the chosen apertures at the neck – making writhing gestures of communication to one another from stools. But generally here the air was one of masculinity, of steadiness. Young men in lemon or vermilion T-shirts, facing one another on bar stools, had no need to affect stridency in their voices. Members of the army, of the police, rugby players, soccer players, mechanics, house painters, labourers enlisted for these clubs. In advertisements for Dublin saunas and gyms, lemon skinned, sturdy young men stood upright. Dublin was agog with the flesh and into these clubs, into these saunas, into these gyms I went after Phineas' death, at Eastertime, Dublin a resurrection of colour and vibrant bodies, beads of water pouring off the tanned orb of an arm muscle in a sauna where I went looking for the ghost of Phineas but found only penises, pinks of penis tops and pinks of male lips, the lips of a young man sitting Buddha-like in a sauna. I entered, less and less wary, into the clubs and arrived in one club on a night young men were giving one another Easter eggs, feeding the crumpled chocolate pieces onto one another's tongues, robin-food morsels. I trespassed on a world I was too old for. The Buddha-like young man in the sauna, naked, looked at me, from the corner of his eye, and then looked away. Later I was told he was composing a long poem in Gaelic. His lips had been carmine, contemplative, as for an advertisement and there were snowy lilies on the towel, thrown beside him, which might have been in his poem if he was true to the Gaelic historical associa-tions of this time, the 1916 rising, lilies outside Patrick Pearse's school in Rathfarnham, walls of white hawthorn blossom leading to it. Soldiers marched with Easter and Christ-like young men preened themselves to advertise gyms. The young men in the advertisements looked many ways, up, down, solicitously, coquettishly, chins over shoulders. But the message was the same. The body was an admissible property in Dublin, if not in Ireland generally. I walked into the caverns, remembering the shades and inflections of clubs in cities Nessan had travelled to, the purples, the morgue blacks, the buttock pinks, the iodine odours, the waiting, crouching eyes,

115

eyes of women or boys, whichever, landmarks under the curtains, figures crouching on the floor. But always at the end of the perspective I was confronted by two quite ordinary young men, facing one another on bar stools, talking, leaving me out.

After Gerry had left in the early seventies I took to going to the homosexual pubs of Dublin, parking myself in the back lounge of one pub in particular, this secluded area lit by rouge shaded wall lamps which gave just about enough discreet light to the faces rearing above the trough of darkness, of seated figures, of philosophically outstretched shining black shoes, of torsos. There was anxiety to glean the prizes that were there but also notable politeness about these endeavours and time enough between the audits of the eyes to have conversations about what play was on in the Gaiety and what the wife and kids would be doing in the forthcoming summer. Whatever the wife and kids would be doing in the forthcoming summer there was no doubt what they would be doing, part of the time anyway. In the summer pubs they'd be hunting boys, amalgamating that part of their lives with middle-class veneers – cars, wives, children, loud, easy, professional smiles, synthetic smiles. Many of these men had come from the slums of Dublin to the middle classes and now they went back to the slums for boys; well, indirectly, meeting the slum boys in this pub. The slum boys came here, prettified, pasteurised, seating themselves. I had taken my homosexuality out of the wastes of Dublin to the middle-class, deodorized points for it. And in making it public, at least surreptitiously, particularly in the pub with the rouge lampshades in it, I had also made it into an anaemic thing. My homosexuality grappled with other people's homosexuality. It fought for survival. But by the end of the seventies there was little left of it except the ghost of a man with a domed forehead who had sold his house, his business, and after his parents' death went to live in their bungalow, still dealing in antique books from that place, playing two-in-the-morning card games with youths he'd brought home and whom he would not sleep with, exercising his nudity at the men's bathing place on the Vico Road and, occasionally, as a new neon sign was added to the Dublin skyline, remembering who he was, a man from Castile, a boy walking through the Castilian sunset, knowing that he'd always be drawn back to the south for doses of his own integrity. In short I was a well-known Dublin nonentity. Heterosexuality (marriage), had been good for my homosexuality; they had challenged one another. My wife gone, I could only give into a country of many other shadows and non-statements, non-lives, non-vocabularies. I had lost my speech and, I suppose, my soul, until I met Phineas.

I'd frequented the precincts outside homosexual pubs in Dublin during my years with Gerry; on occasions I'd even stood inside the doors but only with the intention of being outside after hours. That space outside a homosexual pub after hours commanded mystery for me, commanded the sublime; at any moment a living soul could take form out of, a boy could present himself from the summer night fog or the winter dazed light, a series of features, an anorak, a mask of a face. There was religion in the stance, sublimity. The boy was sacrificing himself. There was often a black scarf around his neck. The black scarf was twisted and knotted as if in anticipation of some future penitence. But when I met Phineas I realized that black scarf could stand for something else. The obsession with, the devotion I had to Phineas was of a familial nature while my relationship with him lasted; it was only when it ended that I remembered how I first saw him, sitting naked next to the sea, and how I was attracted to the area around his neck, vulnerable, shivering white, the white of penitence, of poverty.

Phineas Ward had taken a bus to the sea so he could have a swim. He'd had money enough to get the bus that day because he'd been on the game a few nights previously. But perhaps the motivation of having a swim had got addled by the desire to pose because when I saw him he was sitting pensively on a rock, loose blond curls about his face, a sadness, a distraction about him. Nothing would have prepared me, when I spoke to him, for the knife in his bag, for the pocket gun I later discovered he had in a locked drawer under a statue of the Sacred Heart, the Sacred Heart gallantly pointing out his heart, in Phineas' room in his parents' flat in a block of dingy, dried blood looking flats near a lump of a road bridge in the area collectively known as the North Wall. Phineas Ward had sat like a maiden from an Irish pound note that morning, contemplating the fate of Ireland. The rhetoric of flatland political orators had prepared him for this stance, the destitution and the scarcity to which he was

117

accustomed had spruced him up for an amoral life. There was no reason for self-doubt as he crossed a yard decorated with broken bottles and with slabs of rocks, amid the yowls of children and pinched looking cats. The debris of the yard was the debris of life for him. He'd never really known anything else until he joined the ranks of Dublin male prostitutes, assuming primrose shirts and Irish flag orange shirts, but keeping this, a basic, devouring sense of poverty and vengeance for poverty. There was a little crucifix around his neck which insisted on a belief in God while he lectured me on the Nationalist cause. That contradiction was Phineas, two people, the soldier – the military man – and the boy prostitute – the maiden with the cowslip hair who led men to their doom. He was mad probably. But I kept him, I held on to him as a woman whose first child was a mongoloid would hold on to that child. I listened to his garbage because sometimes in the middle of that garbage was a poetry that reminded me of Nessan, of my youth, of faith, of madness, of miracles, of risk – of trust.

That morning I asked him if there was something wrong, presuming maybe that he was an idle, local, middle-class youth on drugs, but he wouldn't answer at first, disdaining answers, and then he turned to me and said he had a queasy stomach and was waiting until it got better before he entered the water again. A troupe of jaundiced bottomed old men, scarlet caps on their heads, entered the water. I should have gone away but, fascinated, I stopped and asked, maybe because I'd recognised the proletariat depths of his accent, why he was sitting there like that if he was ill, wouldn't he get cold? He looked cold. Automatically he trained a large towel on him, disappearing into it, all of his body except his head, as into a tent. Was this an act? The profusion of curls emerged from the tent and the eyes looked away from me. The onus was again on me to summon up some more conversation. I was sure he wanted communication now but was waiting on a long and unpredictable route to get it.

After a few moments of standing and virtually studying the form of Phineas in the towel, at a loss at first, I suddenly said, 'Maybe you'd be better off having a cup of coffee to recuperate. I live nearby.'

His face turned towards me, almost threateningly, and his lips quivered as a prelude to saying something. 'Do you have the percolated stuff? I don't like the instant any more.'

118

There was a dumb, almost wondrous pause, on my part, before I noticed the monkeyly grinning face, the sudden visibility of constellations of freckles, and a ship slowly nudging in behind Phineas. Yes, there was, I said, coffee I could percolate, at home, and I had in the meantime, very quickly, worked out where Phineas had acquired his tastes.

On the way back, after he'd dressed, he'd told me his name and I told him mine and he added the stipulation to the coffee that he hoped there'd be continental biscuits.

'You know, the ones that taste like straw in your teeth.'

Phineas Ward had been nourishing himself on a lot of continental biscuits lately, in the mornings, after rising from an effete smelling, spick and span sheeted double bed in one of the posher regions of Dublin, his work for the night done, and his arse staring at some Dublin bachelor as he made, with fascination, to the coffee percolator, that's if the Dublin bachelor wasn't already percolating the coffee. Phineas never really managed to work the percolator, different percolators presenting different kinds of difficulty, so it always ended up that his bed-mate rose, in his candy-floss pink dressing-gown maybe, and got the percolator working. Then Phineas sat down to, as he'd say, 'a nice breakfast'.

Nice breakfasts had been in short supply where he'd come from. So Phineas accustomed himself to immaculately laundered white sheets, weird, raspberry coloured body oils which were applied into the reluctantly yielding crack between his buttocks, all kinds of talcums, shampoos, citadels of talcums and shampoos on dressing-tables, razors, bathrobes, dressing-gowns, plastic bath curtains always open, Dublin bachelors preening themselves under showers in baths, exhibiting the nubs of their penises to him.

Phineas accustomed himself to hair on the chest, hair around the genitalia, tufts and matts of hair around the navels, hair on the legs and the armpits, thinning, breakaway crests of hair on the head, near baldness, like Dublin mountain showers on the suntanned pates.

For money, Phineas gobbled genitalia, was sodomized, or simply cherished, like a convent girlfriend. His least favourite was this position, being in someone's arms as if he was their sweetheart. For about fifty per cent of his clients liked doing this to him, his blond curls and his pale, childishly disgruntled face inviting it. Phineas often made off after a night of sex to count his money in Donnybrook church.

On top of his sexual committments there was the layer of Phineas' political life, his political propagations. He stood with a man outside flats in the North Wall, lecturing on the iniquity of partition in Ireland. Young, dingy kids came to hear him. The graffiti from the walls seemed to disentangle themselves and come and hear him.

Phineas made a good platform orator, an impressive figure, in summer that pale face darkened and his tiny crucifix stood out in the aperture of his shirt and his blond hair scintillated above the sun streaks of red and the conflagrations of bronze on his face. His anorak drooped with the story of Ireland; little mottos on it, insignia, the tricolour, Easter lilies. Young girls came, in particular, to watch him and one long-black-haired girl, from nearby Sheriff Street, proposed marriage to him on the spot so taken was she, not only by his oratory but by his ultimate sense of lostness. Phineas Ward made a new and vote-catching style of demagogue. With the same breath as he'd launch out about the crimes perpetrated by British soldiers in the North of Ireland – the Six Counties to him – Phineas accepted penises in his mouth for an Irish fifty pound note, though very often the price was much higher. Phineas had been trained in prostitution by a tall, lanky boy – his hands at the end of his long arms looking dislocated in his pockets – called Parsnip O'Callaghan. That lad had always dressed in inky blue outfits – the colour of autumn night shade, he said, the best time for business – and he'd led Phineas by a waterfront by which rats sidled, at night, silently, ushering Phineas as though to a sacred covenant, the way fraught with danger and the possibility of being discovered. On his performance there, Phineas had quickly graduated to the boudoir quarters of pubs, the backroom, pink lit quarters. There he'd made a good student, quickly ensnaring the men to his livid attractions, if not to his conversation, conversation about slum characters and alcoholics remembered from childhood. Phineas became famous for his literary turn of phrase, his turn of phrase was second to none and people came as much to hear his verbal outpourings as in the expectation of taking him home. In Dublin, literature and sex made common-place bedfellows, sweatily and noisily sleeping with one another, manoeuvring their bodies over one another. Phineas achieved a literary reputation without people knowing the other side of his literary ability, the exploitation of words to inspire young, stooped backed, Dublin adolescents to join the I.R.A. and go and place devices so they'd go off under the noses of R.U.C. men in the North of Ireland.

When I met Phineas he'd not so much being going through a crisis about his prostitution as his stamina for it had waned for unknown reasons; even the attraction of money wasn't enough and he'd often found himself broke in the previous weeks, only half-heartedly going to pubs again. At the same time his political activities were increasing, his speeches outside flats became more vocal and louder from his body which looked pale and anaemic again from the strain of hunger. Maybe that's why his enthusiasm for prostitution had suffered, because his two worlds were catching up on one another, because there'd been close skirmishes with revelation. So he'd had to prove his patriotism all the more, which was not difficult. Phineas Ward bellowed about his martyred H Block compatriots but all the time his mind was haunted, as much by cells with florets and stars of excrement on the walls, as by figures in orange and yellow shirts, tall, elastic figures, dancing on a wide floor in a flat in Donnybrook or near the sea. The shadow of a male dancer fell across H Block walls.

'So you're not from these parts.'

'No.'

I waited to hear where he was from. After a pause of about four minutes he obliged me.

'I come from inner Dublin. A treat it is.'

'What?'

'Inner Dublin. It's different from here.' He looked around at prim, carrot-coloured bungalows fronted with blushing bushes of obscurantist, white-eyed purple and red, suburban bees laconically buzzing, flower heads, old ladies coming to doors in sudden apprehension as if smelling him. Phineas developed a rhythmic, sure, almost laughing gait as we walked.

'You know I was thinking this morning of Jerusalem.' We passed a bungalow called 'Jerusalem' with its own old lady standing at its doorstep and a bit of circular stained glass above her head. 'I like this area,' Phineas told me. Back in my house, after I made coffee, he took off all his clothes, except his under-

121

pants, and lay on a draped mattress on the floor as if sun-bathing. Although the mattress, one I carted out into the sun, was used by me to sun-bathe, there was no possibility of sun-bathing in the drawing-room. That set the tone of our relation-ship. I did not jump on those white legs and arms. I left them alone. They had a defiant purity that kept me away and an almost embarrassing whiteness that put me in mind of cathecism promises of Heavenly beings. Phineas had not seen much of the sun that summer. But he saw more of it as he came to stay with me, sitting outside my drawing-room on the porch, admiring the sea, admiring his own legs, more tanned now, and talking politics. I could write his biography he said. He gave me the details of his life.

The sea came to us like the Mediterranean for parts of that summer; nasturtiums crept into Gerry's old, black kettle and bloomed. Phineas, in shorts, looked at the sea, legs widely apart, approved of what he saw and went through the chapters of his life, suspecting I was a writer at heart and that I had the ability to immortalize him. He had an odd, distanced, wondering sense of his own schizophrenia as of some rare nugget of of psycho-demonstration. Phineas warmed sometimes to his own muddlement and his face broke into a freckled laughter at some of his own ideas. But just as swiftly it reorganized its iron composure and Phineas expressed some fanatical curses, some genocidal wishes. His face resolved itself into a look in which I saw male, grey hordes marching in wide columns between dense, eagerly looking crowds in Nazi Germany. The emblems were unfurled, the hall-marks were emblazoned, the notification of the future given. The grey rigidity in the sky augured what sort of future that would be. The echoes of the cheers of the crowds resounded in groups of birds who broke up with disconnected motion high in the sky. My imagination was brought back to Phineas' face. It had changed again, quietened, leaving no traces of fanatical emotion. The only difference was that, after one of these outbursts, after one of these wild commotions, it would have drained itself of colour, leaving one in no doubt that it would come again, an overwhelming, a catatonic, a precipitated outburst, and next time it would be worse than before. Phineas chained together his outbursts in sequence. It was autumn and the sea was hurling itself at the foot of my yard and Phineas came to stay with me.

Phineas Ward packed up his socks, his T-shirts, a book or two, a childhood jigsaw puzzle in an old technicolored box, his gun, his knife in a sand coloured rucksack of flimsy, unhealthy material and vacated his room with its overseeing crucifixes, a ghost of a crucifix beside the window looking on to another block of flats, an inquisitive ghost of a crucifix. Something had given him a fright. Something had pushed him into leaving in a hurry. I did not question the cataclysm. I did not know it. But I knew it was there. A rumble at the bottom of his life. And despite the trepidations I knew he was feeling we both relaxed into a pose of two bachelors, sitting up late at night, drinking red wine, as though readying ourselves – especially Phineas – to take part in a TV advertisement. Phineas had heard the clonk of a gun readying itself for action. Or he'd been dismayed by something. An irregularity in his own philosophy. But he was, in October, living with me, the child I'd never had, the son he was now. He had his room. His bed. A double bed. And I had my bed nearby. The only sexual involvement was the sound of him pissing at night. The satisfaction of imagining the immaculately white bowl being abashed by his urine.

By November, after some weeks of isolation, we both felt we were under siege here. The darkness, the November evenings brought out the storyteller in Phineas. Still very often in shorts in the centrally heated room he'd tug out some story from his childhood, a bottle of wine by his side. His hair less curly, it dropped in a more straight and matter of fact way. The freckles on his face almost had the nonchalance and the attempted benignness of an American teenage television star. His shorts were white. The edges of Phineas' legs razed in gold hairs. But often in the middle of a lengthy yarn I was startled and wondered, facing Phineas, how this boy came to be here. The last months were ethereal, insubstantial; they'd entranced the mind. And then one night facing Phineas I found I had my fingers on my notes for Nessan. Phineas had jumped out of a would-be book and presented himself as a real person. Phineas was Nessan, was my youth, was articulation – words as opposed to silence. And how articulate he was.

But the night outside was daunting and eerie with sounds and we both realized we were inhabiting a political climate not favourable to poets.

123

'Ah sure, that fella's a swindler.' We were discussing a politician friend of mine one night. Everbody had to be twisted for Phineas, at his best; and at his worst they were criminals, murderers, thiefs, sadists, traitors. At worst that was Phineas' favourite word. Traitor.

Phineas Ward was in fact at his best and his most relaxed now, late at night, his legs apart, his hair that unkempt American TV margarine colour and also that American TV length, the gap in his legs challenging me. I was Phineas's only audience.

Despite our isolation we imported luxuries from the city: wine, cigars, chocolate. There seemed to be a caravan trail to us. But maybe someone malevolent would find that trail too.

There was so much to haunt the mind, so much that quarried the mind, haunting it with little edges, little sideline nuggets of fear. Phineas' fears stood out sometimes, mesmerically, in his eyes. His very eyes stood out and mesmerised, polarizing themselves from the rest of his body. The whites of his eyes seemed outrageously clear at times and at one remove from his body, suspended things. It was as if they'd popped out of his sockets on children's cartoon wriggles of wire. But the image of wriggles of wire was sinister in its own way. It reminded one of bombs, killing devices. The inside of a clockwork soldier was the inside of a bomb. A clockwork soldier strode across a famished carpet in Phineas' home. A bomb ticked in a shed near the County Dublin coast. A trial ticking. Outside were marshes, signs sinking into marshes. Disconnected voices entreated one another. The look of remembrance on Phineas' face caught my look. I was hearing dogs, the sea, the circumference of my life, Gerry's voice. There were fears about being old and homosexual. No progeny. No child. No bearer of your name. 'Have a sweet, Phineas. Have a sweet.' Phineas' fingers reached for a sweet and then he stripped it of its wrapping in his pale, ewe-white fingers.

'There, there was the one . . .' The stories went on and on. Outside the sea, a vicious slap of a huge wave and simultaneously an affirmation that we were both in fear of something. The political climate. A city in which children ran around with little knotted plastic bags full of snowy heroin. Phineas' schizophrenia. The other side of which was catching up on him. There was an armed man in his mind who was catching up on the Botticelli boy who'd given his bum to Dublin art gallery owners and who regretted that now, having become a kind of house-boy, the resident story-teller, a collection of health and random bone structures. The door blew open one night and a shadow got in. Phineas was watching TV and turned, challenging the shadow. He saw a man who'd come to tell him what mission he was to do in compensation for his months of culpable absence. I was not at home. There was assent between Phineas and the shadow. I'm not sure if the shadow was real or imaginary, but I gathered from Phineas' behaviour that someone had come, a piece of his mind, or a real person. There was an echo of a Roscommon twang in the air.

Phineas went off to the city for a few days and came back with bruises around his waist. He'd been having strange sex. Sex in which his body was punished. The bruises were blue and red, like markings on a sheep, stripes. He brought back more than that: the taint of a city; the giant unseasonal strawberry slipping into whipped cream at the top of a tall, tapering glass of assorted ice-cream; the neon lights over the cold Liffey, their rhythmically rippling reflections having their rhythm addled by snow which speared slant-wise over the black water; the substances which sheltered you from the black surface of the Liffey being to'd and fro'd past the Liffey parapets; the syringes, like church spires, whose needles entered your veins; the threshold of a flat's door on which you sat and waited, your young, emaciated arm out, not feeling the cold; the fetishes of the night, the old men's fantasies; the gym door on which the advertising cartoon of a male had an erection drawn onto him and an armalite drawn into his hand and the motto of a swastika drawn above his head.

Phineas was subdued and I was silent; I left him to contemplate this breach. In the meantime I went back to papers I had not bothered much with for thirty-five years. I was thinking of writing my book on Nessan despite all the books written about him since my visit to the United States. But the more I reacquainted myself with his poetry, boats coming in and going out over the skyline, I realized how out of touch I was with Nessan, how I'd betrayed him, that lavender shirt he'd worn around New York in the spring of 1928.

While I mulled over Nessan and came to the conclusion I was making an allegory out of his life, not a book, Phineas was darning double, triple and quadruple coloured socks. He'd given up sex. And renounced his old life. Repented in Whitefriar Street Church before Our Lady of Dublin, the black lady. Phineas had presented himself in a blue denim suit to her. Beside him market women, standing, audibly articulated their prayers. There was only one defilement on his denim jacket, a little piece of literature at the bottom right hand side of it which said, contradictorily, that sex was good for you. None of the old ladies noticed it though. An old man with a cap on his head stared at Phineas from among the seats, the old man, too, standing. Phineas prayed as he was taught to do as a child. The gap in Phineas' buttocks was very pronounced. Afterwards the old man among the seats went and hid in an empty confessional and wet himself, then waited outside for a priest to arrive in the confessional box so he could confess his sin.

In preparation for Christmas Phineas lost himself among the Christmas shoppers. He never left the house until it was already nearly dark and he arrived home when it was still the early evening. Sometimes floundering pile-ups of packages came with him, in his arms. Where he got the money for the presents or who they were intended for I wasn't sure. But I did know that they were directed at Christmas. Phineas intended to go home for Christmas. At least he voiced that intention. But when it came near he found he was stuck here and, anyway, things were plentiful here. There was a wine-red carpet to collapse into, in his blue denim suit, the jacket of which he kept on for a while after coming in and then removed. Those gangly limbs had never seen better days. That tussled hair had never been more mirthful. But occasionally a shadow of his former life crossed his face. It was a doubly schizoid shadow now. You weren't sure if it was to do with his prostitution or his political life. Or you weren't sure if it was to do with a sense of his own madness now that sanity had ensnared him. But I could see that he was haunted by clean modern partitions between drawing-rooms and kitchens in modern flats, in the mornings, after a night of giving himself, when the formica on the top of the cabinet type partition was glazed with the Donnybrook sun. Phineas had a deft but distanced inclination for all kinds of luxuries. He'd been atoning for those lacking at the flats. Now his proclivity to luxuries had been consummated for him. He was on a floor, in a blue denim suit, giving forth, a bottle of red wine beside him, laughter in his eyes, but an unsuspected halo of loss around him. Previously he'd run his fingers over the formica, uniting two or more spots of coffee, before leaving a flat, after giving his pale backside in service. It had been hit and run. There'd been a division between him and his surroundings. Now that that division was gone the luxuries had lost something of their mysticism. There was no price to pay. There were no demands. So Phineas placed it upon himself to pay a price. He'd launch into some long, foolish, verbose story in the manner of a veteran stage actor he'd frequently made love to, standing, wandering around the room in a sudden, unctuous upper middle class way. I'd try to stop him. And then he'd get vicious and obscene, talking about sores on his rectum. The night he first did this I made the connection. He'd met someone or something in the city that day. There had been a flurry in his movements before he'd started talking. There was a stumbling. Phineas had confronted a dark, inky blob in the city.

'Now there was this lad called The Rock – his real name was Peter – who'd sit among rubble, a dandelion to his lips, staring. He was hypnotized. He'd always looked hypnotized. Something had happened to him and then he became more like a girl and his hair became more and more like dandelion petals and he became more and more worried-looking. You'd ask him "Rock, what are ye worried about?" Then he'd bite a bit off a dandelion and say, "The Morahans." The Morahans were a family upstairs who'd all learnt Irish dancing in one go and would go tap-dancing well into the small hours to trumped out ceilidh music.'

'There was this girl called Sheila who was mongoloid . . .'

Phineas had encountered a shadow on the street one evening. He was walking along Aungier Street, near where it hit South Great George's Street, not far from Whitefriar Street church – on the opposite side of the street – a little way down, the neon sign advertising cures for baldness, a toupee jumping up and down on a bald head and all this in scarlet, when he bumped into his stringy overseer. That day the man had been belted in a coat, like the young De Valera. There was acumen in his voice. Urgency. The Roscommon accent more pronounced. The accent more rural even. The English more reminiscent of national school Gaelic in vowel sound. Phineas was to do something. But Phineas had changed. A woman dashed by them, a long, black rosary by her side, the beads buxom and fresh from being massaged in prayer. Phineas twiddled on his toes. 'Right,' he said, 'Right.' The working class reasserting itself with mandatory nasal sounds. He had his arms clutched in front of him when the man disappeared and Phineas was left standing, passers-by to presume that he was a youngster with ears glued to the cheap imitation-Jamaican music being barraged from a record shop opposite, coming out under festoonings saying 'Happy Christmas' in Gaelic.

When he said 'How are ye?' now, when he greeted you as he entered the door with 'How are ye?' it sounded like an anachronism. That evening, the evening he'd met the man, Phineas entered with his customary 'How are ye?' but what followed was a polite middle-class accent. The young man had assimilated a lot of Dalkey and, when the new nervousness wore off, there was a young man there, just in time for Christmas, who was polite, who was my son, who had stepped into the shoes of a spectre who'd been there all these years, growing. Phineas inherited not just the pensive face and the groomed head of a ghost but his parent's memories, his parent's obsessions, the landscapes of Spain, of Portugal, of America. In a jumper with a diamond pattern on the front of it he'd borrowed from me, Phineas, in a hallucination, as he sat on the drawing-room floor, envisaged the fields of Andalusia in the early 1930s, with poppies skirting them, a ragged, deflated battalion of poppies, forewarning one of the war under a sky which was grey and racing and low with dramatic whites in it like bird droppings. The pensive face of Phineas on the floor just before Christmas, his hair cut and groomed, his pensive eyes under a painting by a deranged woman who had tried to capture a flock of wild geese over a bog in the West of Ireland, summoned up a landscape which was mutual now and assuaged and cathartic for that. Phineas Ward had momentarily grasped worlds beyond those that an emaciated, haphazardly and vacuously put together old body might suggest. He had seen another me and was reverential because of it. I had been a wild, affirmative, purposeful young man once. There was a young man connecting Phineas and me.

The depth of the wonder in Phineas' face lasted over Christmas. A letter arrived from Gerry just before Christmas, her first for a long time, a card with it. Phineas was wandering around the house, different now, subdued. He had collided with a person who was my imaginary son. He had taken over from him. There was distraction, uncertainty, but willingness to fit the shoes. Phineas had a kindness on his face which had not been there before, a hesitance, volumes of hesitance around him. He wandered around the house as if continually picking up clues to an enigma. The old man hid a young man and he also hid dreams, landscapes of many countries and specifically an encounter with a young man who was not personally known to him, whose identity was to be known from his poems, through the biographical data people who knew him threw up and the places he knew revealed. Inside an old dithery man in Dalkey was what for Phineas was a consummation of personal identity and pain into those of another person who was standing, a silhouette, against a tornado of spring cloud in the Mid-West. In the darkness of the silhouette only the fringes of a very brazen skirt could be seen, white with blue pock marks on it, quite like false teeth that jumped out of someone's mouth.

Phineas' face remained in that state for much of Christmas, his lips wondering, the features of his face generally in a trance. I served the Christmas meals. When I called Phineas to them I was disturbing him from contemplation of another part of the century and wonder at it, a part which I'd made up, bold colours, bold, doomed by instructive lives. Phineas had equipped himself with part of Nessan, for the final phase of his life.

After Christmas there was home and a mother he hadn't seen for a while. He'd dumped his Christmas gifts on another member of his family in a café. 'Phineas, you cur.' His mother was holding a packet of durex. Phineas had just taken the durex from someone with the intention of using them as decorations if he ever got a place of his own. 'Communion. You need communion. The host in your soul.' As if she didn't know he had been a prostitute. She'd been one herself. Was one to his father. A little woman with a climbing vegetation of straw dry black hair on her head, a navy pinafore on her fat bosom that someone accused her of robbing from a war bride so old-fashioned it looked. On his days home Phineas was marched to Sheriff Street church and made go and pray in another church in Dublin, especially beloved by his deceased grandmother, under a mosaic depicting Our Lady's Assumption into heaven, dating from the Holy Year of 1950, the bottom of the mosaic, the clouds on which Our Lady and her cortège of angels were standing, porter coloured and most of the rest of it, the sky, Irish cream liqueur coloured. Sheriff Street church where he'd been designated to go to mass was Jansenistic spired, that spire very often black with rain, like spires of small Irish towns, in contrast to the other church which rose, a brown mistake, out of its environs, the whisking sound of planes leaving the near-by Dublin airport a constant drone, the proximity to the airport a part of the evangelical plan, the planes, glittering in low flight, suggesting, in those times the church was built, holy ghosts in contrast to the dirty, subsumed, already tired suburbia which lay below them, the flashing bodies of planes still retaining a pentecostal glamour in contrast to those even dirtier suburbs as they struggled to get out of reach of them and their churches.

Phineas' hair was unkempt when he returned, his face with that guilty look, fragmented into different patches of pale. He entered the house almost slyly. He looked younger and also more impish. I noticed the dark lemon of the hallway behind his almost lime anorak. I decided I must adjust that colour soon because it was getting dirty. He crept in in a circumvent way. There was no need for him to sidle up to the wall to come in. There was a roughened remark thrown out in the kitchen, over the table. 'I hope I'm not too late.' He'd rung to say he'd be here much earlier than this. 'No, you're not too late for dinner,' I said. A few stray, decimated pieces of celery lay about to tell that the evening meal had just been made. Phineas' anorak was still on. He shrugged. 'Sorry I'm late,' he said. His face had colours in it like the radish colour at the top of his tongue, as if his skin had become disturbed by a manifestation of a disease in his days away. The old life, the old ways were signposted in a pair of soiled underpants he'd neglectfully left on a chair before striding naked to bed, long after I'd gone. He'd sat up in the light, closely and studiously examining the pop column in an evening newspaper. The next day he told me, 'Bórd Bainne was found dead in the Liffey.' Bórd Bainne had been a fellow male prostitute, with hair the colour of milk, that of an albino, thus the Gaelic name which was that of the Irish Milk Board. Board had become Bórd lately and he had been found dead, face up, in the Liffey, face red, gnashed, albino-type, on a grey sky desolate January morning. That piece of news was supposed to be an apologia for his sullenness and for the return of an all out,

130

guttural Dublin accent. There were about three, big, shining, blond hairs over Phineas' upper-lip that morning, as if complimenting that image. But those three hairs became a battalion of hairs in that place, a defiant trademark of a cult. Phineas was aiming at being like his martyred comrades, hair all over his face and this successful gathering of hair was the first serious assertion of this aim. Then of course there was a sexual element in the ragged curveture of his moustache and the overall haggard appearance of him. The sexual renegade's face was avenging itself on that supposed to be modelled on the martyred young heroes. It was borrowing something from that look.

Along with the hair over the upper lip came a jaundiced colour as a background to the hairs as though Phineas had caught the disease of some medieval Christ on the cross, a flushed, mustard skin colour that was suitable for someone who espoused the cause of Ireland, connecting him with the shades in those suffering medieval Christs. That yellow colour over his upper lip also gave him an alienated look, as though he had developed it, had forced it on himself so as to alienate himself from me, to distance his image from me. In his days away from me, Phineas, like an alleycat, had dived out through a side entrance from the direction his life was going. He'd made a quick exit from my life and the issues of my life. That fact gradually made itself known through the welter of Phineas' disguises and the fronts he put up. Something was over and Phineas was using my place.

The yellow over his upper lip built up into other shades on his face, a fresco, culminating around his blue eyes until those eyes looked out from different shades, spied out, those of a demon. They were looking out to see what he should do next. Phineas' shoulders skulked a little. There was 'divilment' in them as my occasional charlady would say; there were plans and schedules rotating in his head. Phineas rebelled against my place. Some irascible madness returned to his brain; he could only go so far, stretch development so far before coming up against a genetic wall. Phineas looked over that wall now and saw what was for him the landscape of Ireland, children squawking and wandering among the rubble of flatland, mosaics of the heroes on the walls, painted, giant Easter lilies, the posters for Sinn Féin, young men's faces set among those posters, the huge, clamorous graffiti announcing solidarity between Dublin

131

blocks of flats and Long Kesh, the refuse of syringes, of durex, as offerings, under these festoonings, the Virgin cased in glass who looked as though she wanted to lift her skirts and escape.

Hair all over his face, Phineas at the end of January, shirt off, chest naked, before going to bed, mumbled. 'You're a bourgeois pervert.'

Bórd Bainne had been buried in his mind; Phineas hadn't gone to his funeral; the young flesh so much defiled, in a blue denim suit – at least in Phineas' mind – had been lowered into Glasnevin Cemetery. So too, down went the nights, the neon, the aphrodisiacs, the oils, the odours of the Dublin male bourgeoisie: detergents in the bathroom, opium smelling after-shaves.

Phineas was connecting again prostitution and revolution and about to make a gesture that would amalgamate both. There were rendezvous in the city, interims of a few days when he did not return. He became mysterious, fugitive, insulting, brash, the owner of my house. He sat like a little Neptune against the sea, surveying me. You're pathetic, his eyes said. Or wanted to say. But he knew too much about me and there were the landscapes of my past which he had entered and been seared by. The fields of Andalusia towards summer evenings, the wide, endless fields of central Spain, the alleyways of Lisbon, the frescoes of backstreet buildings of New York had the effect of debilitating his purpose, of thwarting it. He'd been emeshed in my past and could not escape it.

When he tried to build himself up, to summon his body together to be insulting, there were poppies before his eyes like slow drops of blood, a few vagrant flowers in a field in Andalusia. Those poppies were wounds in his face, one, two, three wounds. They stalled him and created a seriousness in him and made him my offspring again. They punctured him with my personality.

But before I could reach him in this moment of tenderness he'd retreat again and I was left alone, to walk the house and put things unsettled back in their places.

The seriousness, the vulnerability, the openness in Phineas' face, these moments lingered though to create, to capture a sense for me of what my child might have been like, this imaginary child, and to delineate again, for the umpteenth time, his imaginary life, a life and a development that had

132

accompanied me through the previous thirty or so years. My son had ensnared something of the history of his country. He had been with me particularly on visits to big houses in small towns in the country in the 1950s, big houses with views of gardens outside, pastoral, soft shaded sheds, corrugated roofs occasionally russet colour, trees, a river maybe, stone, crumbling walls wending their way alongside the sheds, beyond the river a different kind of stone wall, lower, undulating through the fields, the big house enjoying the imperial view of these recesses of the town and the landscape beyond it. My son, the kind of son I wanted him to be, was indigenous to the gardens of these houses. He'd have liked them, playing among the green and the ivy that fell lavishly from the walls. He'd have kicked a football near the more voluminous shields of ivy. Those shields sprang out unexpectedly from the walls, maybe at the back, to the left hand side of the garden. They were landmarks in a particular garden, berries associated with them and covert, dusty smells, the smells of spiders' homes and maybe darker, more dust laden depths. My son had auburn hair at this time, swept into a flux of different side shades, gold, brown, mouse grey. There was a generous crest of hair on his head and a pale, inquisitive tilt to his nose. In reality he would have been no more than a baby at this time but in my imagination he had sprung up, had already taken on all the possibilities of a five-year-old. He was a child of country town back gardens, the gardens of lawyers' houses. He had already accosted the world, in a backgarden, a football in his hand, a little, meticulously made sweater on him, dun with a pattern of a lime coloured tree on the front of it.

From the windows of these houses I'd look out on that child, Gerry's voice raucously asking me what I was looking at, vestiges of travelling show actors who'd visited the premises still in the air of those drawing-rooms. By 1963 that child was watching television in our drawing-room, his legs packed up in front of the television set. The country town gardens were almost forgotten in this fog of city living; the television, the swimming pool, palm trees thrown up over freezing outdoor swimming pools in the summer, by the sea, my son paddling along by the white side of the pool, black oversize swimming togs on his shivering, pale, almost guilty body. I was solicitous to him, standing over him, I also in black oversize togs which

garbed an overlarge part of my body, my head looking down on
him, my face pale and untouched by sun, like the rest of my
body. I wanted to remove the guilt from him. Occasionally a
ball other children were playing with plopped over the
swimming pool wall into the severe grey sea. The sound of a ball
splashing into the sea, rather than making me look towards the
drama of it, caused my head to dip towards the labyrinth of
black hair winding down from my navel into my black togs, that
is after I'd swum and the togs would have lowered themselves.
The child in the late sixties had to deal with politics, revolution
and change, a television revolution, B Specials, looking like old
brain-damaged hounds, batoning away on the heads of innocent
Catholic politicians. He'd be attending a Protestant
comprehensive. He'd have many records, L.P.s under his arm.
His gait would be sure in narrow, Aegean sea blue jeans. The
child had gone from me. He had girlfriends. Holidays in
Greece. In the early 1970s he'd taken off to a remote part of the
world where stodgy camels still greeted sandstorms with the
same indifference as they had three thousand years before. The
child had gone in a lime anorak with a cravat around his neck,
white with a pattern of scarlet yachts on it. That was his motif.
Boats. The sea. Change. He'd left me until I encountered
Phineas.

Phineas had become more erratic and more snapping by the
end of February; he was crunched up in his jacket, his hair had
grown longer, his body, especially his waist, had become snake-
like, wizened, mean. That amber shirt he had on, straight from
Johnson Court off Grafton Street, looked incongruous. It
seemed a rash day when I'd given him the money for it. But the
shirt and the colour clung. It seemed an odd shirt for someone
who was mouthing spleen about the Nationalist and the
working-class cause, combining both. But I thought the colour
was that of the orange in the tricolour, the orange of the
Northern Protestant. A Chinese vase behind him, Phineas
lectured me on the ills imposed on the Irish Nationalists and the
Irish working class – Dublin working-class people rallying to
common cause with Northern Nationalists – working-class or
not – by people like me. 'Bourgeois,' he spat, 'You're bourgeois
sh. . .' Phineas had no hesitation now in denouncing me. His
mouth in trying to pronounce a word gnarled up in a circle. It
still had a feminine pink colour, that belied the venom and

issued a plea for help as did the eyes, navy irises now almost lost in the dismay and chaos of the whites.

Phineas sometimes retreated from the moment of his argument – and the scene of it – like a dog after an outburst of barking, Phineas tired of the outburst, dishevelled by it, looking mangy after it. He'd make his way to the bathroom where behind a locked door the toilet bowl was the same colour as the whites in Phineas' eyes. I'd hear the mahogany coloured lid going up and down. Phineas was retching or Phineas was suffering from diarrhoea. He had the same thin, starved, creased skinned look as his comrades in H Block or as Sinn Féin militants on the dole, a fanatical zeal about his shaken frame.

But more often than not Phineas just stood there after one of his outbursts, teetering, making a pause, leaving an acute space, as if expecting me to reprimand him or even slap him in this pause and space, his face inclined up to me as if in a vigil for a slap and his eyes, those sullied whites, almost begging reproach, or words from me that would be constructed in such a way as to divert him from the machinations of his own words and borrowed verbiage. The pale in Phineas' cheeks had a girlish quality, in defiance of the attempted machismo. In fact these vindictive sorties on me had the effect of making him more girlish and almost, for moments, removed the emaciated, mean, closed-off look. They made him vulnerable, they instituted vulnerability for a few moments. In those moments there was a tide from my body which he could feel but I always held back. I wanted to save him. But something in me stopped it. Sternness. Puritanism. Jealousy.

The tide was almost a tangible thing, a current, a stream of sympathetic energy. But it never got very far from my body, it stopped, flagged and retreated and we both looked at one another, awkward strangers.

Phineas would falter away from me then, but I'd be left with the memory of the pink, the desperate pink in the whites of his eyes, that last minute inflammation, crying in the eyes of a woman in front of the ghetto Madonna in the glass case outside the block of flats, a sort of lingering plea on the lips after you know the Madonna has rebuffed your request.

By March occasion for alarm had come. Not only would Phineas disappear for up to a week, but when he did return he'd wander around the house at night, still in his clothes, blabbering to himself. On his own onetime confession Phineas was mad. He had generations of ancestors that had been kept in an asylum near a tannery but now he was an eighteenth-century, waif-like Dublin lunatic meandering about, talking to himself, discussing things with himself. Sun in the eighteenth century hit on a gentle fronted, terracotta building which housed human beings who squealed like pigs in the nearby tannery and walked about like pigs' entrails thrown into circular orbit, the house on the inside worse than any tannery, full of excrement and urine and blood and vomit and the tardy smells that come from the sins of the flesh and the sin of alcoholism. Phineas was speaking from an ancestral voice that remembered giblets of black excrement thrown about corridors and an overall blackness which always drew convergent, spectral women back into it no matter how much they seemed to converge on you, a wavering orchestration of howls accompanying these motions and echoing in Phineas' mind. 'Sure we're all a bit looney,' his mother had once boasted over a tin of peas she was opening, in her pinafore, on the kitchen table. She was proud of the family madness as if it entitled them to an honoured place among the archaic rabble of the Dublin working class. But Phineas' madness accelerated until he seemed possessed by a manipulative influence, a Northern accent coming out in his voltage of words, and until he was beyond any harkening to me. The last night in my house he talked and talked, his anorak grimy, his body shaking – he'd just come in – and his words, though incomprehensible, were directed at another presence in the room, a presence in front of him. Phineas nodded his head vigorously towards the presence and there was acumen in his eyes as he looked at the presence and fear of not being understood by it. There was a confrontation of some kind between Phineas and the presence, a showdown.

In his room about five in the morning, sauntering around in circles, still talking to himself and arguing, though now the argument seemed to have funnelled into himself, he made a particular point of not being touched by me, of not accepting my physical gesture, a hand on the shoulder, to reach to him and to steady him and to assuage him. The pink lined pillow case was still uncreased in the morning when he had gone, after I'd fallen into a slumber on top of the bedclothes on my bed, in

136

my dun, raspberry sherbet corded dressing gown, my face down on the bedclothes.

I went looking for Phineas after a few weeks when he did not return. I didn't dare knock on his family flat door and instead wandered around the grounds of the flats, hunched up in a nondescript anorak usually worn by me on summer walks to ward the rain off. But I still smelt of affluence, and children, especially little girls, stood, looking mesmerized at me, one short black-haired little girl with a surprise of big lips in her olive face, had stopped her skipping to stare at me, the temporarily redundant skipping rope in her hand. An election was imminent and posters for Sinn Féin were everywhere, a young man's face inset in them, a seductive young man, a young man with a moustache. His eyes were the most appealing and seductive part of him as if they were melting the voters into acquiesence. The poster repeated itself long after I'd left the grounds of the flats, it had climbed electric poles, it stood on the side of big pub houses. But outside the flats, I remembered, it had vied with graffiti, long, explicit graffiti about the advantages of buggering girlish, little boys.

After Phineas had been blown up with his own bomb near the Cavan-Fermanagh border, I found this scrap of paper in my place.

'23 March 1984. Went to the Liffey tonight and met a boy and went home with him. He asked me if I'd stay with him for ever. He was from Loughrea. His breath smelt and his fat pudgy toes smelt but he had a nice face and he had a clout his father gave him still on his backside, blue and red. I kissed him there, on his fat, creamy white buttock, and he said no one had ever done something so beautiful to him; would I stay with him for ever. I said I would. He said, "Stay with me as long as there are stars." I said I would. He was a medical student. He said he tried to write poetry in his spare time. He said the stars he was thinking of were over fields in East Galway, low, farming fields, unkind fields. I said I would stay with him for ever. He kept an arm around me as if I'd slip away and he stared at the ceiling and he said in his funny Galway accent, "I was the captain of the hurling team." I left in the morning before he woke. I left a note saying the city and the country can never meet, we're poles apart. Before I left I saw the place he kept the five pound notes he got from home. In a round tin box. Beside it a pencil and a

137

poem. Beside the poem was a dispatch about some victory for a Galway hurling team. A lad's face on it and underneath, written by pencil, "Padge Finnerty, love me until I die. Remember the Mecca ballroom, January 19, 1984. I put the red rose from my jacket inside your trousers in the loo." He'd go back to his girlfriend outside the loo though. Goodbye now, goodnight, there's no girlfriend outside the loo for me, no hope. I'm looney and always was looney. That's what me ma said. Goodnight. Goodbye. Adios. Au revoir. So long. Please, please love me. Please, don't, no . . . O.K. Phineas.'

In less than two weeks after writing this Phineas was blown to bits with a bomb he'd been carrying, like a new television, about seventy to a hundred miles from the city.

Goodnight, goodbye, Phineas.

Nessan in the spring of 1928, after his illness, after recovery, handled his round trip ticket for many weeks before leaving, succeeding in having the date for departure brought further into the spring, twice, rubbing the ticket vacantly between his fingers as if in confirmation of a miracle while his eyes stared ahead like those of a mad Bolshevik sailor in New York dreaming of the revolution back home and the new mystic frontiers of the revolution. And all the time he lingered, almost glued to his habitat, the rooms, the square, the pigeons, the lazy, angular backstreet buildings of Greenwich Village, he knew he was trying to prolong something of a city, something of an idea he would never return to. He was trying to stretch out the city of his youth before it was tested and challenged by other realities. He was trying to prolong a childish dream. Before he left, his hands palpitated, large, masculine hands; they'd grown larger and more masculine, almost elephantine. In fact his whole body had become sterner and more masculine, his head larger and hair thrust on the top of it, lemon, gold even, in contrast to the dark hair of the rest of his head and more voluminous at that, a tuft, a throne, an affirmation of hair growth before balding. He'd seat himself in dark places as if posing for a portrait, sun coming through windows, a solitary, laden beam of it mainly, illuminating that tuft of lemon to gold hair, his hands like awkward animals, face down, covering his knees and his kneecaps urging uncertainly forward. Nessan was meditating on something, the strains of his white shirt in the darks and lights adding a complexity to the visuals of him at these moments, visuals he was keenly aware of. He was posing for an imaginary photographer before taking off from the city and breaking the spell and the fixation, that brought both good and bad, of his stay there. Brooklyn Bridge was the colour of Greek temples in the early morning light or at least a version Nessan had of it while he was still lying in bed. A gull charged slowly towards it, a gull that had made a long pilgrimage to see it, coming all the way across the Atlantic, maybe, to see it, having heard of its magic from his fellows. Before going Nessan realized he did not really want to leave. He'd have stayed in a dark room with the sun coming in in a solitary beam, in the city, for ever. The city was his place. It had been his first real plaything; his first real companion.

In the weeks after Phineas' death I toured Dublin for him, the nights with the lights spread out in silent processions. I went to the outer margins of these processions. There were gold and green and white lights beside slim, skeletal Georgian buildings with domes on them, their fronts a watching tissue of white. He'd been a city boy but I thought of the boys who'd come from the country to the city, of the city people who attained to a more universal city, of my own yearnings as a young man for the archetypal, all fulfilling, universal city. But I just had Dublin now, a diet of sparse, riverside lights. I was old. The boy had been sublimated into the sparse but still carnival-like orange and white of the riverside lights which promised more subterranean things in the city: clubs, brothels, harems, dances, jukeboxes, couplings of all kinds, couplings outside chip shops, in clubs, or by the river under disused cranes. Phineas had died and a city not only went on living but seemed to be undergoing a revival.

Nessan stayed there in that position, seated, his whole life coming to him, recollected. He wanted to hold on to this tide of past doings, this incessantly flowing tide of past doings as a kind of drug. He wanted to make his position on a chair in a dark room permanent. But slabs of blanched early morning April light called through the window. A boat was waiting for him. Before he stirred though, the past regrouped itself around his seated figure into an order which gave meaning and benediction

139

to his posture. There was gratification about being seated there, a knowledge of how comely he must look, there among the struggling lights and darks, white shirt with its creases and his chin, his newly attained masculine, square chin, groping pontifically forward. There were many thoughts in the young man's head, many pictures, masts in the last century lying in dock in New York and peering through your bedroom window at you – like craning ganders. There were no masts now but a mesh of their memory at the harbour as Nessan approached a boat, luggage in one hand, and left New York behind.

Footballers ran across a field in Dublin in a game of Gaelic football, blue and white striped jerseys on them. It was a few Sundays after Phineas' death. I huddled around Dublin, in an anorak, hands encased in the anorak, a pervert again. 'For here we have no lasting city . . .' What did those words bring me back to? O yes, a story I made up a long time ago, a story in child's colours about a man who'd remained a child all his life.

The country boys and girls returned to the city in jammed trains on Sunday evenings in May, the gold, exuberant, Dublin evening sun optimistically greeting them. They disgorged themselves onto the streets, walked up by Westland Row church to their various isolated bedsitters in Rathmines and around the South Circular Road. Each one had satellites of others around them, their heads down and their thoughts buried. Old men popped up in the gardens of Merrion Square to watch them, hands in their pockets, among the borders of primulas and mentally went home with them and went to bed with them, lying their heads alongside the young people's heads on pillows in narrow, kipper-tin rooms.

'For here we have no lasting city . . .' The lights of Dublin in May, started up in a carnival way along by the river, blues, golds, reds in them, took off on a journey. A story was coming back, not just a story I'd made up but one which embroiled your own life and youth. There was no stopping its flow now among the profusely intermingled, fanatical, wet blossoms of Dublin.

A boat glided through azure, outer fields of May water. Nessan standing in the bow, still in the lilac and purple and blood veined lumber-type jacket of the northern climes, his frame passive in it, shoulders frigidly hunched, hands in his pockets. He was still immune to the heat and the friendly brightness. He was going to a house, legendary in his family, visited once by his father, which belonged to a New York aunt of Nessan's father whom Nessan never met, like the relative from whom he rented his rooms. Nessan imagined it to be chocolate coloured but that was only because of a childhood fancy and association with the West Indies. The colour of punitively dark and somewhat dangerous looking New York Easter eggs and of negro faces had escaped into it, making it into a kind of melting chocolate mansion surrounded by a forest periphery of vivid lime, scissors-spliced edged leaves bearing shamelessly orange coloured fruit, with frequent, subdued but expansive blushes of warm pink on them.

The house it turned out was a kind of meringue coloured villa, almost lop-sided in its stance or at very least wobbling like jelly on its feet and definitely squint-eyed; inside full of layers and layers of cobwebs like veils put over invisible, often levitated-looking furniture to protect it. The cobwebs were huge, spindly – and balletic in their pattern of being. A black woman opened the hall door for Nessan and declared that she did not go there often because there were ghosts.

The ghosts were of a mythic family of New York brothers, Jewish looking, who came to this island during the American Civil War, in cricket type clothes, even cricket caps on them, fierce and smouldering boulders of whiskers under the caps, and threw up this house in the style of generous New York suburban accommodation and then played cricket, these pirates in cricket gear, and bowled on the pacified, scintillating lawns until there was blood spilt, one of their tongues cut out under the cricket caps because of an insinuation that a chapel, built beside the house, with Abraham Lincoln's portrait on the wall inside, his vulnerable Adam's apple, the New·England, leaping simplicity of its white tower and the simplicity of its squat, white body, were a sacrilege against an older religion that their ancestry had emerged from, and against the beaverish, pitch-black mutterings of the magicians of that religion. The chapel, having provoked blood, was judged irredeemably unholy and razed, and a lodge house built near the gates. The house was sporadically visited by an old New York lady, bent over in black, and it remembered severe, gold coin haired

141

young men in bible black materials striding across the lawns in the mid 1880s.

Nessan stayed in the house until mid-November. The cobwebs were brusquely brushed away. Room to move and breathe was therefore given to Nessan, a sober, greyish-black, hefty contraption of a typewriter was plonked in the sea haze of the drawing-room. A young man in a red check shirt, sleeves rolled up, attacked it. The ghostly demeanour of the house was put aside and the negro woman, fearing the ghosts no longer, acted as though she'd given them the order to be banished or at least vacate the premises and find new lodging for the moment. She acted in a brave, new, business-like manner. Her attentions to Nessan went as far as washing and pressing that red check shirt so that its tiny fibres of black were always immaculate and muscularly neat. The young man to whom she was assigned she watched; she skulked about, was mesmerized by his engrossment in his work. In a hot climate his forehead was pale with work and the front of his hair ghostly and blanched with interior light. Nessan was writing profusely for the first time in years.

Away from city, away from past and all relics of past, his life was renewing itself. He was among a luxuriance, a thick and undulating carpet of growth. There were lilies to greet him, many kinds of lilies, mainly white ones, chalices of white lilies, white lilies with gold specks inside them, clustered, intimate, like the specks on anonymous birds' eggs he'd meandered on in the grassy plains, as a child, white lilies with bold emerald dabs thrown inside them, like shamrocks on a handkerchief of his grandmother, white lilies with sequins of red and gold inside them, white lilies with a vaginal pink inside them, white lilies which threw their heads in many directions as if having conversations with one another and answering questions to one another or denying statements made by other lilies. There was a circus of lilies and white lilies became pink, blue, lavender, Chinese lantern orange. At their most affirmative they were orange. There were other flowers, some easy to identify, others difficult to identify; freesia, violets, pansies, white irises, geraniums, feverfew, candytuft; segregated from the profusion were the heliotrope, gardenias, mignonette. The white, red, purple of the candytuft were his favourite one day, the next the purple heliotrope beckoning to the sun. Gardenias stayed in the hands of coy, bridal island madonnas who had Spanish eyebrows and Chinese lips, scarlet lips; madonnas that were placed in shrines among the rage, the driving forest fires of diffuse flowers. Nasturtiums entangled on the white beach, like pulsating veins, come September, and with the nasturtiums something did a somersault inside Nessan while he was on the beach; his world was turning over. A black man's face became bluish in the sun and a scarlet cardinal bird swept through the freesias, towards its destination with a message. Places, cafés, streets were leaving Nessan; catacombs in the city; rooms; café tables on which he'd distributed cards from a pack; the tiredness of the soul; the bleat, the multiple languages of traffic; the fog horns; the race across water by boats; the fog that consumed hope and put icicles on aspiration; the menopause of the mornings; the days he couldn't work; the days, nights, months, years when he could not forget, when he was strangled by memory; the days, nights, months, years he could not find love, maybe because of paralysis from memory, maybe because of feelings of inferiority, maybe for trying too hard. The admission came that love is not a prick, love is not a freckled prick, that love is not a hefty sailor, exiled from the farming sealessness of Kansas facing you in a waterfront bar, that hope and escape were in making oneself commensurate with possibility, were in being brave. You had to be brave. You had to be brave. As the subway lavatory walls suggested, all hope would collapse into gibbering chaos if you were not brave, always brave, held yourself in bravery. You had to march into the menopause of life with bravery, in order to attract life. You had to transcend yourself, be born again, resurrect yourself. You had to die and bludgeon yourself into birth again, remembering the oppressed of the world, the negro women in cafés on Broadway, the wisp of grass chewing squatters by railroad lines in the Mid-West – lemon, one-eyed birds in cages on verandas in wooden towns. You had to love all these things and try to find their cousins in other cultures, in more outreaching climes. The cross of Christ faced Nessan in a West Indian church, a Spanish cross. Christ drooped from his long, starved, outstretched arms as if in acknowledgement of the confrontation. An inevitable destiny was meted out to Nessan in a Spanish church as he sheltered from the heat of the noon, faltering because of his change of outlook, of philosophy.

143

The negro woman guarded him, she was solicitous to him; he formed a relationship with her. There were picnics they had together, a roll of crêpe thrown on the beach: often an effort involving both of them to get it down because of the breezes, the narrow roll of crêpe writhing, the body of it, between both their pairs of hands. She dressed as though she was hiding from something he said, all in long clothes, a strawberry, white speckled apron on her, a turban on her head. Her face only reluctantly emerged from the clothes and a babyish face at that, with no evidence of hair or even eyebrows, the whites of the eyes surprised in the face and the mouth a gaping volcano. She encouraged Nessan to surrender all chores to her. It was as if she understood his mission, the importance of it. There was something psychic on this island and when the tornadoes came and tortured palm trees, turning them round and round in wide circles, blowing a wooden house on stilts into a flurry of annihilation, it was as if the voodoo of the island noticed the turbulence in Nessan's soul; headless birds that were probably geese were found in the morning in a pile under a scarlet totem pole, like tired out dancers. Deranged things were happening inside Nessan. He was scribbling himself to death. The ghosts, the demons of Ireland, of other places, were after him, the void of his ancestry. They didn't wish that he'd draw things into a pattern of lucidity, of meaning. It would be an embarrassment to history, to them. These ghosts, these demons wanted to remain an amorphous, screaming commotion in the ancestral memory. They did not want to give way to clarity. But after storms there was clarity, a clarity so tangible it was intoxicating. The driven bric-à-brac, the debris were part of the landscape of crescendo inside Nessan. There was a grin on his face like that of a groping idiot, a sudden, smacked pale had come to his face. He had finished his poem. He wrapped it in cellophane in which the negro woman had given him candied scones for the journey. There were two scones in his hand as he looked back from the boat. A woman was walking on the pier, her almost ankle-length rosary by her side, little flags of scarlet on that rosary. The texture of the scones crumbled, the two of them merging into one lump in his hand.

But with all the peace on the island there was also sexual disturbance, the nights of storm when his penis stood up like an electrified boulder, all the vintage of his desires in it. He wanted to appease this thing, this machine. But only boys would do it and there were no boys here so he masturbated, thinking of boys with backsides white as yucca flowers.

Gerald was thirty-six when I met him early in 1949. He was an ex-heroin addict and had all the graduation marks of the one time addict, he was huddled into a sandy coat that flapped on him because of the thinness of him and he was querulously stooped as if he was slightly deformed or had been bearing heavy weights all his life. The locks of black hair that straddled that head told of an extreme beauty once, and at thirty-six, he was still arrestingly, almost explosively handsome. That body and that hair seemed almost a fulminating phosphorescence. There was something inexact, dynamic, voltage-charged about him. His face was an awkward crust suitable for the look that was just becoming fashionable in the cinema, but his brain and his words were paradoxically gibbering. In him Nessan had almost achieved the idiot that he was so adept at describing in his poems.

I met him in a house in one of those streets that plunge into the confusing depths of Greenwich village and he immediately insisted on exercising himself and his coat on that street; he must have known that he cut an impressive and cogent figure under the glacier houses, warehouses and sky, cogent because he summed up the distress and the philosophy of that time, jazz, heroin – 'horse' – and marijuana, in that on-moving, insistant fugue of a figure.

Nessan had first met Gerald the night of the party for his first book; in a dim restaurant, in a cloistered corner of that restaurant; Gerald was his first publisher's son, just turned fifteen. He was a boy whose face emerged from the dark of his clothes, pale, ostrich pale and vivid, a doubtful look on that face, regression fighting with approach. The boy's vivid blurred eyes and the almost clown-like rashes of rouge on his cheeks were obviously very impressed with Nessan.

Bonnie at that stage had arms like a rubber doll's; they went out in many directions simultaneously as if she was conducting music with both hands, because of the plenitude of alcohol in her.

She picked on Gerald as the most likely candidate to give her attention and he seemed piqued by her attention to him, smiling

145

in a slow, adult way. But his eyes were on Nessan. Gerald's night dreams at the time had been of muscular European weight-lifters in gyms in New York. His eyes were green, sullen, in fact like emerald suddenly and exhilaratingly sighted through murky sea water. Bonnie, dipping her neck, in the flexible way of an inquisitive farmyard goose, across the table, was quick to applaud him for having eyes the colour of her inherited Sunday afternoon idea of Ireland. But the boy's mind was still on the line of serious and more sober adults, the retinue of them, the wonder of this literary gathering, and most particularly on Bonnie's son. He was the kind of poet, squat, gymnast-muscular, that Gerald could take into fantasied baseball matches as he lay in bed at night, young men running on one another from all directions, ancient Greeks from an art book reproduction in baseball clothing.

Gerald did not meet Nessan again after that night until Nessan returned to New York from the island. Then it was a casual encounter on a winter street, February 1929, Nessan bumped into a boy against the blanched rimmed skyscrapers and trees, whose face was a foil to the vapid pale of New York, stooping shoulders, a face dark, angular, unshaven, hair that was Jewish, shining, eyes that were emerald and held a host of brown spots.

This was Gerald whom time turned so I met him in January 1949 when he did not look much different, stoop there, definitely, but metallic, formal streaks of grey in his hair – aeroplane grey – on the front sides of it and hollows in his face like holes blasted in dirty earth from mines.

The troublesome thing about Gerald Kerensky's life was that he shot into adulthood at an inordinately early age and at an inordinately specific point of that early age; just after his sixteenth birthday he had a masked, unshaven look on most of his face which, in relation to this phenomenon gave his eyes a perpetual querying intensity and left the part of his face, not covered by small hairs, like full-blown masts of pale on the sides and around the eyes, and the forehead wondering looking, frail, damaged. Those eyes were pocketed by the dark of his brows. At sixteen Gerald was thrown out of home for pursuing his sexual fantasies with no reticence; the hairy, black apotheosis of basketball players' and swimmers' and gym users' backsides. In sexual terms Gerald was a tart and gave himself generously.

When I met him, Gerald still had that daunted look on his face, a slanted curve of uncertainty. Since Nessan had rejected him, Gerald's life had become a sheaf of waste paper twisted round and round at its middle so it would be a kind of work of art born out of boredom before being thrown away. There'd been essays at life during the 1930s: little jobs picked up here and there, jobs in publishing, in art houses. But Gerald never lasted long at them and moved on, a vagrant. During the 1930s he literally did become a vagrant, trailing across the United States in a coat too long for him, on foot, a haphazard, straight-ahead look on his face, birds gathering for autumn flight on electric wires in the Mid-West becoming familiar to him, the mustard coloured, summer drained fields, the calf nosed trucks abandoned for wearing out while carrying refugees from the economy. The journey was an aesthetic one for him at the time, one for the New York literary and artistic albums because he had money left him by a rich aunt. But as he moved, as his head, more erect from remembrance, pointed forwards, he was consumed by thoughts of Nessan and the loss of Nessan, and of the sheaf of white paper, delicately twisted at its centre, twirling into the waste-paper basket. Tornadoes twirled over cornfields here. Black birds took off. Once or twice big, mangy looking, black birds stopped on electric wires to look at him and to examine with their eyes his torment. Those gold beads of eyes penetrated into the wraiths of New York winter landscapes, the playground of his and Nessan's relationship.

When I went to see Gerald he quickly took me off to another location, another room, down a few streets, this one peopled by women whose torsos rose from the floor in orange dresses, silent lanterns, red lipstick daubed on their mouths like fruit. They were enamoured of some drug which gave them visions of a heaven where I imagined the flat rooftops of New York to have suddenly sprouted palm trees.

White sheaves of paper, delicately twisted at the centre, so there were funnels at either side of the centre, twirled through grey skies in the Mid-West, hundreds of them,. The mind was a chaos. White paper was white backsides, the backsides of New York lechery; white paper was the white, aghast faces of hopeless men wandering without their children in the Mid-West; white paper was snow. One day there was snow everywhere. This was near Nessan's place of birth, a mound of a hill on which his family home had been, its white timbers, the harp hanging from the tree beside it.

In the journey there was Ireland, Nessan's vision of Ireland, Ireland under snow, and also another Irishman's journey across part of America, the hallucination of Victorian Ireland under snow in his mind too.

Gerald had ended up in San Francisco on that occasion; his long, sandy coat had seen and prevailed over much dust. After a few days among a street of sand dune coloured houses with gaping, sand dune type turrets on them, Gerald, furnished in a suave suit as if he were a business man, black suit, white shirt, broadening river of a blue, white polka dotted tie, was taking off in a plane from San Francisco airport to New York. There was irony, juxtaposition in everything he did. He'd partly learned this from Nessan. But the irony, the jokes were to forget Nessan.

The job of forgetting Nessan proved difficult. During the war he had served in a ship in the East; the ship was blasted from above; it was a little quagmire of fire on the ocean surface. But Gerald was still one of the few survivors; a bed of pock marks on the left side of his face for a while. But they had disappeared when he took to heroin – 'horse' – on the streets of New York, when he opened foil paper to look at substances white as pet white mice and smell them to ascertain their purity.

There'd been a time of late when he'd been shuffled between sanatoriums and his body bore the brunt of this shuffling. He abandoned himself to the landscapes of America. There'd been one sanatorium on an island off New England and another in Kentucky; the train journey to the latter had been demarcated by the blood-red clay outlines of Virginia, the vessels of brighter red running through the earth, by the grey, Grimm brothers forests of North Carolina. In a sanatorium in Kentucky he'd been reminded of Nessan's story of his visits to a young mystic dying of tuberculosis in a sanatorium in Brooklyn in the early 1920s when Nessan first came to New York and how the sanatorium became a place of revelations. On each visit Nessan made he got a further revelation about the future history of the twentieth century, especially about the events at the end of the century, the young man standing, facing him in a bare room, a Slav, a recent immigrant, an incurable. This episode had happened before Nessan had known many people in New York.

148

He'd picked up the trail of the young man because a man in a bar had told Nessan that he was the most astonishing talent of his time. The young man wrote poems and he died having burned all his poems in a fire in a tin chamber pot in the garden of the sanatorium. What Nessan remembered of the poems he put into his own work and the charred edges of the poems were passed onto Gerald beside an expansive window in a sanatorium in Kentucky. Gerald saw that he too had been an intermediate for Nessan, having died where Nessan was concerned and Nessan having picked up what was relevant for him from the relationship. A woodland copse outside a sanatorium in Kentucky became yellow ochre and brown, yellow ochre in vacuums, and these colours, the colours too of wet bark in autumn, transported Gerald back to New York where his coat had the colour of wet autumn bark and his face had the damaged, perplexed look of a tree in autumn or a piece of furniture made from damaged wood. The colours of trees changing in New England, the technicolored panoramic twinge in them, was in his face too, moments he'd savoured from his pursuit of a cure. But you couldn't cure love that had been lost when you were thrown out of your best friend's life.

When Gerald met Nessan he'd been wandering through apartments in New York for a few weeks; he was between apartments and his bumping into Nessan did not so much revive memories of their meeting over dinner as alert Gerald, visibly, to the idea that Nessan might have a floor space for him. There was a sheepish, cowering, pleading look on his face that Nessan did not resist. Nessan made room for him in his bed, Gerald had forgotten the love he'd felt for Nessan on first meeting him, it was a pragmatic exploitation for him, which was ironic because it was Nessan who was in love with and folded a knowing pragmatist – one of the pragmatist's eyes always open, the conspiring, disassociated white to be seen in the dark – at night. The conspiring, dormouse-look gave way to trust, fluidity, holding his body straight. Gerald was with Nessan when Nessan's book was published. Gerald stood beside Nessan. It was Gerald who had the extraordinary shirt, full of Mexican colour designs, lemon Aztec tongues among the other colours. The world was falling down when Nessan's book was published. But it seemed to conquer the world and Gerald and Nessan, lovers, were indifferent to the myriads throwing themselves off skyscrapers. Nessan was a success when bank after bank capsized across America, in rhythmic succession, a wind from a Methodist hymn passing over, blasting the roofs off and ripping tulle covered hats of Methodist female songsters off their heads, lavender being the favourite colour of hats of women caught in banks that autumn when the news of those banks' collapse was announced. But as old men jumped off skyscrapers, like Icaruses, baring their ewe-pale chests in a final recklessness of carnality, tearing their suits and shirts out in two directions as they flew, Gerald and Nessan were in one another's arms. 'You were the first female I made love to,' Nessan said.

Gerald reported the pornography to me, explained that he'd had a fat arse. It was late in Greenwich Village. January rain was falling. Mist. It was 1949. We were on the street. Gerald said goodbye to me. The graffiti on the wall behind, white on grey, jumbled some words about Hiroshima, 'horse' and future apocalypse with a depiction of an erect phallus which looked like a subway train that had zigzagged out of control.

The soldiers, soldiers on a battlefield, soldiers making friends; Nessan's poem. The battle was over and people were guilty about there having been a battle and a victory, so there was largesse and friendship among the winning side. Two soldiers getting to know one another. A relationship during the American Civil War. His poem. Nessan's dual background, Jewish and Irish. His background was illuminated for the world to see at last like a children's party performance long delayed.

Bonnie did make love that autumn. It was after a visit to a children's party. Carmine, rouge – pink flushed with light and seared by darker pink – hats flustered around an area of performance – an illuminated Chinese screen show. The man behind the illuminations was a boy with almost tonsured blond hair on the top of his head and with skin on his tall and merry form baby pale and delicate. When he revealed himself there was jubilation in his presentation of himself. Bonnie had been about to depart, having just dropped in to affirm, like everybody else, that they had not been fossilized and made ashen by the money crisis, but when she saw the boy she remembered her ambition to be in the theatre and had all that longing reawaken in her,

150

that reawakening happening alongside the belief that to touch that broad, white forehead of the boy might bring her remuneration in terms of success with fate. He had a forehead that was broad and pale – pale as a fragilely held together, near-albino child – but there was nothing fragile about him, and that tested you in your ability to resist it. The adults there, the droppers in, aunts of and patrons of different children, the casually called in world of adults distant from the children – there were few parents present – all reacted to the boy's manifestation of himself as if he himself were going to afford the main excitement of the evening. But Bonnie was solicitous to him and moved closest to him, close enough to extract words from him. About his profession, about how he came to be in it. So charmed was she by this exultant blond head that she risked her reputation by asking him home for orange juice that night. They could talk, quietly, about the theatre she said. She'd produce decanter after decanter of orange juice. He needed refreshment she told the crowd and her place with its sympathetic stripes of cretonne over the windows would offer him the right atmosphere. When some of the faces in the crowd looked mangy and disbelieving at her she mentally told herself that she'd offer him so much orange juice that he'd have to be aiming his white penis over her toilet every few minutes. So she moved off, arm in arm with the boy, rather than leaving him to get to her later for fear he'd lose his way. The conversation was strictly theatrical as they moved off. Bonnie linked arms with him as she might with a newly ordained priest. A few children followed them down the street and when the children were out of ear range of the party one boy became rude and insinuating and boastful of what he knew to two smoky-faced and eel-mouthed little girls. 'He's going to put his elephant's trunk inside her.' The little boy had a cowboy hat on, which he'd worn in lieu of the pink paper hat, and his sage, cobalt eyes were on Bonnie's prissily strutting backside. The young man did put his elephant's trunk inside Bonnie and not long after they'd got in. They made love in the big bath tub, coffee coloured at the sides, Bonnie's mother asleep, and Bonnie decided that this was Bohemian. She wanted to follow this young man to his source, a hotel by a lake where he performed with others, actors, magicians, jugglers. The boy was not a boy but older. Under the bathroom bulb she saw a grim line in his forehead. His penis was as white as expected. It emerged from his trousers like something slowly arising from under a theatre stage – some surprise of a scenery accroutrement. It had been years since she'd made love and she lay her head back on a pillow he'd put under the taps, a brown pillow with gold tassels, and said sluggishly, 'I've realized my own potential tonight', meaning she'd realized how much of a nomadic spirit she had, something very suspicious for she'd soon be up and on the move with her hair dyed an innocuous, little-girl peroxide. Life, adventure, the outer frontiers of the cosmos, were beginning for Bonnie Muir in her fifties.

This hotel to the north, a theatre in it, stayed in her mind, the idea of it, a holiday with entertainment. The young man had been on a summer break from it, touring with the apparatus of his profession. Winter was the time for it, he declared. It was by one of the smaller, satellite lakes of the Great Lakes, a pearly eyed dot on the map. She savoured the address. If she couldn't find a job there as a juggler maybe she could work as a chamber maid and observe the tricks of the professionals and learn from them.

The fact that Nessan's fame coincided with her making love after so long, arching her legs in the air and ultimately clenching the white buttocks of a young man until she squeezed them to the red intimacies of them, made her feel that she was on a par with him, that they were setting out anew from the same starting line, it increased a sense of kinship for him in her and made her rear to see him as if now she could see him truly as an equal spirit who was waiting to welcome her. This fraught ambience in her made her rush to pack up her business and sell it. But then when she had it sold her mother became very ill and that illness forced her over her mother's bed and her mother's fitfully moving breasts. Bonnie didn't make the first tidings of the newspaper headlines of Nessan's success. Nessan was left to exhaust them alone – well, alone, except for Gerald.

Gerald took Nessan into the first years of the new decade. There was a very dark rain over Greenwich Village after I'd left Gerald and that rain took me back to the rain that Nessan and Gerald, mutually, resisted, the black, thick rain on the street early in the

152

1930s. A rain that accumulated over things in clouds, so long had been its duration, and would not let up. But Nessan and Gerald had their own shared fantasies to protect themselves against the rain; the fantasies enacted between them in their rooms. Sex became scarce between them and instead there was Gerald's devoted, slightly anxious attentions to Nessan, the still adolescent frame of him sitting on the edge of a bed, poised to jump up for Nessan but an agitation in his body and his fingers, already like that of a drug user, preparing for the drug user of later years, a tomato coloured shirt on him with mandatory black check in it. There was a crucifix which was new to the room and Gerald most often sat beneath it, as if to emphasize the similarity between him and Christ.

The rain on the night I walked home from meeting Gerald was thickening by the minute, the rain on days of Irish cattle marts, the rain of the lost soul of rural, 1940s Ireland, an Ireland which had not experienced the war. It was the rain of an Ireland I was foreign to and I wished I'd been part of because that would have made me real for myself; its truculence and torments and the Hell-fire of its spindly spired churches' confessionals would have tested me. I would have been driven out with anger by its torments and that anger would have made me make something; in Kentish Town in London, or alternatively in a lost piazza of council houses in Coventry or Wolverhampton. But as it was I was aware of it lunging west of Dublin, that darkness, and now walking out of the borders of Greenwich Village the thickness of the rain here made me connect the darkness of Nessan's life with the folden, ever spilling within itself, darkness of rural Ireland. The shadows cast up by the meeting of pavement and wall under heavy rain here were little signposts that had carried Nessan, huddled, along towards his Irish background. He'd been thinking of going to Ireland when he was conspiring to leave Gerald. Gerald had become a burden. Gerald had been dragging him down, always waiting there for the next move from Nessan, always waiting to pounce on Nessan's turns of energy, always waiting for inspiration. He'd been an extraordinarily, even a chaotically, a haphazardly attractive young man, the good looks accumulating in the shields of dark hair on his cheeks. But the good looks had occasionally fallen off to reveal an empty package, more often of late when Nessan was meandering alone through those Jack the Ripper, London-type

153

streets in January 1932. Gerald's anxieties had begun being effervescent. He'd begun leaping up from the bed on which he was sitting when Nessan demanded something. He insisted all the time on having the aura of Nessan's slave. His fingers grouped together as he sat on the bed, wondering what he should do next. There'd been distraction in the eyes that looked to his fingers. And he had noticed how Nessan had been allowing himself more and more into the proximity of women at parties, especially women known for their good looks, as if Nessan could not distinguish a good-looking woman himself but had to go by reputations to know whom to approach. There was something heterosexual in the surprise of ginger hair around his genitalia, an impatience, an urgency about him. He'd caught the whiff of his posterity and wanted to lean towards it, create it.

Nobody was ultimately sure who left whom. Gerald went off in the direction of a café which he and Nessan often visited together, with an advertising tableau of a huge heap of steaming navy beans outside, and never came back. Nessan about the same time, at a midsummer jamboree, wealthy American ladies hopping around as carmine Pucks, in an overlapping event, under Chinese lanterns which tussled with one another to give light, wilfully disappeared into the crowds and the light, abandoning Gerald to the literary personalities and the maverick millionaires. Nessan wading through the crowds and the shadows of crowds until he found a spot far from Gerald where a lantern threw a gold light, interrupted by a surrounding column of little pink Chinese marchers on the lantern, onto an empty space which seemed specially made for Nessan, Gerald left somewhere, half-heartedly whisking his hands through the air, in rhythmic movements, not far from his waist, in an effort to express his lostness, his bewilderment, his dementation.

Gerald never turned up at the apartment after that. How the two accounts of the dissolution of Nessan's and Gerald's relationship cohered with one another no one was exactly sure afterwards, but the undeniable truth was a Nessan who was on the move around town in spectacular shirts, demonstrating himself against the background of America's grief as if he in his success and his prime moment was taunting America for her earlier neglect and even distortion of him.

The publisher of Nessan's first book, Gerald's father, in a

café, over coffee, one eye behind a fin de siècle monocle, his hand to the monocle as if it was a siren going to issue a warning, stated to other literary people seated at the table, they too over coffee and the scattered remains of a lunch, that this young man had run the gamut of his talent, that there was no more, that his heart and his innards were drained. How much of this prophecy came out of bitterness the listeners were not sure but they were treated to the sight of Nessan falling over on his face, with three examples of red brick 1930s skyscrapers to be seen through a huge window behind the fallen body, like three harpies or three fates peering into a café that was foreign and exotic for them, holding exotic vegetation, sparse furnishing and the faces of the literary people against an overall white as against an ice-rink blankness.

Three

'Hollywood.' Bonnie arrived on Hollywood Boulevard in a yellow ochre outfit that made her look like a maggot, covering her, long slim coat, a hat with a wave of a plume over it, yellow ochre like the rest of her outfit. She arranged that she arrived on Hollywood Boulevard. She'd been transported there by a slow bus determined to show her the sights of the depression. Even clouds heading West looked like refugees, low, fat, jammed clouds, the first clouds in these lines being the ascendant ones, the most voluminous. Gregarious buffaloes could not have been so packed. But that had been before she'd reached the Rockies and it was obvious the clouds could not climb the Rockies because on the other side she was in a different world, a clearer one, a more lucid one. Here there was no depression. The light in the air saw to that, heavy light spiralling to the heavy blue of the sky. There was the thud of meringue surf skimming the borders of this world. It elated this world. Then there were the occasional gossiping palm trees arching in pairs over her head. Their magnitude reminded her over and over again that she had escaped. Her son, the script-writer, had welcomed her as she arrived from her journey of escape. His dark glasses had worriedly reflected the scars on her forehead, a triad of very definite lines which related to the trouble she'd had in shedding her mother into a nurse's hands. The nurse had moved into the house with very sizeable bags in her hands and stern eyes that stared ahead as if her face was a locomotive that was going to go through the white walls. Many of the furnishings around those white walls had been dismantled and the place looked bereft, but for the odd fist of a cactus, as if the occupants were waiting for nomadic years to begin. Mrs. O'Dowd had the look of a temporary lingerer when Bonnie was going because she was told that she too would soon be going to Hollywood. That was the only way that Bonnie found she was able to disengage herself from her mother, with the promise of an early trip to Hollywood. Mrs O'Dowd, at first suspicious and doubtful, her shoulders crooked with suspicion, heartened at the news and realized that this was the chance she'd always been waiting for, a trip to Hollywood. That old frame, in jeopardy so many times, became resolute and firm and inhibitingly renewed. Mrs O'Dowd looked a girl on the verge of dancing. Death receded as the prospect of gates opening to film studios signalled to the mind. Mrs. O'Dowd was going to go to Hollywood rather than to Elysium, about to enter alternative gates than those of Elysium. If there were any parts for grand-mothers Bonnie should look out for them, was her last admon-ition to Bonnie. Already she'd stolen Bonnie's most lascivious knickers, a carmine pair that wound down your legs like Christmas decorations and she might have been wearing them when Bonnie was going for there was a pertinacious look in her outstretching eyes. Already there was more than a hint of future rivalry in their relationship. Bonnie, for her part, imagined stuntmen in tops which cascaded down among the meshes of dark hair on their chests – little redundant wriggles of hair overlooking the material of their tops – and jealously guarded the idea of these stuntmen. If they were to be found she would not let this bony old creature, though surprisingly revived, near them. Ultimate farewells were delicate and saccharine, hands waving. The film studios of Hollywood, stretching like headstones in a cemetery, waited now. But there were no auguries of film studios as Bonnie stepped out of a bus to be greeted by a son in a dark suit, white shirt, his dark glasses reflecting the hurriedly dyed blonde curls, the little-girl lips,

160

talismans of departure from former self for her, his face momentarily subsumed in impassive white as she embraced him, the face making a little detour into the charged light, as he took one step back on the light blanched pavement sanctified by stars' feet, as if to proclaim distance from her or new status – wealth, fame, membership of the empire of the rich. All these elements collected about him to make him appear wholly different, wholly more integrated as he stood there. Her hands lapsed from his chest. The muscles were tighter and more defined. There was almost disappointment in her first recognition of growth and advance in him until he made the gesture of picking up her case with familiarity and leading her away, his other arm linking her arm, to a waiting piece of transport, a black automobile which confounded them by its bigness and immediately sped off when they entered it, down the boulevards, out into the hilly precincts, driven by an outrageously giddy black man with one elbow out the window, sticking into the blue that lifted the land and the ocean into the sky. The tour through the hills was for the benefit of her inspection of Los Angeles and to give her a view of the homes of the stars, and eventually they wriggled up an avenue to a mansion near the ocean, drawing up outside it with a sigh of satisfaction from the black man whose blackness was more than accentuated by the glacial whiteness of the mansion and the polar bear rims of the swimming pool to the right hand side of it, those rims around water that was a make-believe, child's picture-blue – but everything here had an aura of make believe – and Bonnie got out and marvelled at the place her son's fortunes had brought him to but not without some trepidation in her vocal chords.

Nessan was working as a scriptwriter for a millionaire producer. He'd been doing this for a few months, having been picked up from a party in New York where he'd stood like a cool empress, his back erect, and drew attention to his torso, in a white shirt that looked a cracker you could pull so frail was the impression it gave, and to his blond, quirky and upstanding topping of hair, and was quickly transported to California whose climate seemed more suitable for his neatly laundered and light-as-a-feather shirts and for the blond, woodpecker signature of hair above, that hair, though diminishing, making a last stand of identity. In California his physique had prospered, white silk shirts billowed outwards and he held

161

himself with almost decorous erectness. There was a seemingly long ingrained familiarity in the way he hosted his mother in the house, introducing her to the crevices of it, and he liked standing a lot by the swimming pool, as if this was his special place to conduct business, hands in his trousers' pockets. The millionaire producer waddled in from other mansions, a little walrus of a man, in grey pin-striped suits, a little fat cigar always at his garrulous East European mouth and muffling his East European accent. His mansions had grown out of the fortune earned by his films. They'd mushroomed, a fecundity of them in this area of the coast. Nessan liked standing by the pool whose water threw ripples of light on him, secretive gleams which inculcated him with the spirit of the place, water, light, ease. From this vantage he ordered Bonnie's approaches to him by his laconic ancient Roman stance, which was fed by all the suggestion of water and light of the constantly mobile and constantly whispering atmosphere of an interior Roman pool with lichen slapped on the walls and the azure of the nearby ocean slapped on the pool itself. California had its own Roman ocean always near to slap its imprint on things and for the first weeks Bonnie was addled by its light, drunk with it. It heaved towards her, visibly cowering her. But she came to grips with it. And all the time there was the image of Nessan by the pool, giving to eternity the image he wanted it to have of him.

'Nessan.' Bonnie called to him one day. 'Nessan'. She moved close to him alongside the swimming pool. 'What are you thinking of?' He said something like – history, time. 'So you think you're Jesus?' The words exploded from a brand of shining lipstick purchased on Hollywood Boulevard. Nessan said nothing. Arms folded he'd been contemplating the battlefields in his epic poem and thinking how such grand conjectures would never come to him again – the wastage where fires had been in the aftermath of battles were the wastages in his mind. He'd have to go on pretending to people that he still had some panoramic arc of a theme in him. He'd have to keep one step ahead of them so they'd never know. In the meantime reams of white paper accumulated in the house, pile-ups so high that the sun-shocked tops of them were activated, mechanized where the height reached the level of the window through which blew friendly breezes from the swimming pool outside by which the scripts could see their author preen himself near naked,

162

standing on a diving board and exercising his body, systematically manipulating his limbs.

Bonnie was getting clearer pictures now, after the first heady Californian days. Nessan in raspberry swimming trunks, arching his bum. They'd been left alone. No one had come to the house but one, occasional servant. In this meringue ghost of a house, bits of the meringue almost melting in the heat, Bonnie was able to see how they'd become two performers, deserted by all the other performers, left alone on a vacuous stage, and these performers included history, past, or were these things props – in more senses than one. Props to keep the excuses going. Without these excuses there was almost a macabre ripple in the air. An atmosphere without past was an atmosphere of unease. Nessan's limbs were brown as an acorn in the autumn but she longed for, she pined after the white, breastless, more or less featureless body he had as a child. She'd been many months here, but the realization of the extent of that time only impinged on her when Nessan's body was radically brown and when that body transfixed itself on the diving board for seemingly endless pauses. Bonnie's eyes followed the movements of that body towards the tip of the diving board when those pauses were broken. It was as if by following that body she would come to the source of a mystery for her. Was this her son? Or was it a new person? In his very movements, in the rhythms of them, Nessan had freed himself from old patterns. And the question arose in her. Had she altered too? Was she a different person too? Had she bounced off her banks? In this stream of change with its eddies and flows she was meeting another person as a free person, a new person, a person without the burdens of labels such as son or offspring. Bonnie was in love with Nessan. But she was not so in love with him that she didn't notice that he was sneaking off from the house, leaving her to wander around by herself. And in the meantime her mother was writing. When was she coming to Hollywood?.

Her mother did come to Hollywood early that winter. She and Nessan and Bonnie did tours of Hollywood. The Keystone Cops were nothing on them. A woman from the Mid-West wearing a black furry tail on the back of her black hat and a long coat on her, itself like a tail, her hands in a black muffle, that was the renewed version of Bonnie's mother. She was able to move now, getting out of cabs, going towards restaurants, as sprightly as a Keystone Cop. Bonnie's mother had followed the example of Bonnie and put dye in her hair, black dye so her hair was parted with fierce precision at the top, raven colour. That bold old face looked out of the dye. Bonnie's mother was eager for Hollywood. They were greeted by the celebrities of Hollywood whenever they entered a restaurant. Jellyfish of producers zoomed upwards from tables, thinking that Mrs O'Dowd was a celebrity because an old European actress who resembled her was in Hollywood at the same time, a woman once a citizen of Russia, now exiled in the western perimeter of Europe. So Mrs O'Dowd achieved celebrity in her own right and was asked out to parties by herself. Bonnie and Nessan were left at home. At one party, she told them, she was given a wheel-chair, a relic of the Civil War, to reign from in the course of the party. It was always given to the oldest guest as a mark of respect. Those parties were dotted with the paraphernalia of Europe, already Europe was moving to Los Angeles, old men stranded in the middle of parties, standing, with moon-like, semitic eyes looking to the focus of the party, certainly Mrs O'Dowd at the party in which she'd sat in the wheelchair. An old man with a flair for lunacy and a hat, always urging upwards like a balloon, in his hands, took a fancy to her and drove the old lady to the ocean into which sinews of sewer pipes ran at the point where the automobile had pulled up. Mrs. O'Dowd disdained his advances. She came home after all the new-found life of fun and gave herself up. She was too old for it. She left soon after that. Back to the house, which was being sold, and the nurse. Bonnie and Nessan then had fun.

It was the late winter. Against the cartoon backdrop of the depression in the rest of America, Los Angeles was panicing. The palm trees seemed to be grabbing all they could get. Middle-aged men ran amok in cars along the boulevards, sun drained to a blinding white in contrast to the overseeing, lean, charred stems of palm trees. Bonnie and Nessan took to the boulevards themselves in a chauffeur driven car. They were racing for the madness of it. They had caught the disease of the moment, fear of what the future would bring and knowing what they had just now, however they had got it, using it. However they had got it indeed! Nessan often wondered how he'd come to be here. Bonnie often wondered how she'd come to be here. Nessan had slipped into this scenery before he'd known where he was. He was a languid part of it now. Hands drained into his trousers, white silk shirt, he standing motionless, profiled, on the far side of the swimming pool to you. But there was more in his life than meditation as Bonnie was to discover.

The required script was not coming. The task set out for him not being achieved. And he was creeping more and more to the bars by the port, one of which, that most frequented by him, had an interior of gaudy pink, 'Valentine pink' the lady of the premises proclaimed, and very often harboured a milky, sheepish, standing wolfhound, the companion of a little man from Liverpool, England, who had three distinctive layers of stomach in his sailor vest top, and who sat up on the bar stool, curled up and contorted like a fat Arab concubine in a photograph taken out of Victorian archives. Into these bars came disillusioned sailors who had visions of Hell on sea and who were intent on annihilating their bodies, having foregone all acknowledged and taught axioms of gender. The lady of the pink bar was often arrayed in a Spanish flamenco dress of many colours, a butterfly's wing of a dress and, though her immediate ancestry was of County Donegal, she'd churn the outspread frills of the dress as she was clearing glasses as if she was going to perform a flamenco dance. Her lips were planted on her face as if they'd come from a Hollywood star, scarlet. And she had innuendo for the sailors. The men's room in her bar was scribbled with graffiti, the whole wall, ripples of lettering going over it in horizontal patterns as if it was all by the same hand and telling the same story, and in the middle of the waves and currents of lettering a whale-like, lost piece of the male anatomy. You stood to piss and got lewd messages in biblical language. Your head got dizzy with the scribble. Your stomach seasick. And the sailors would walk in and philosophically assess your piddling figure. There were rooms upstairs where men went with one another. In other bars, further out, near the pier, pink poodles ran around like fireworks.

Nessan found a young man in the pink bar who fulfilled all the fantasies of his adolescence, a young man who disrobed and had a chest and arms billowing like a torso of Greek sculpture, gold rings and the shine of gold rings on his fingers. But the fulfillment was a fantasy in itself because this was the house of fantasy. There was no reality in the body, no love in it; a member which protruded, the same colour as the walls in the bar. Nessan touched the sea-tan of the chest muscles and found a fathomless emptiness. The young man left him in the room, and when Nessan woke up and looked at himself in the mirror he saw that he was old. What had happened between them was animalistic and a ruddy streak on the bed proved it. Nessan then went to a bar where a diminished old man on a bar stool was reciting a pornographic speech. Some Mexican boys who'd come to the door by mistake smiled, hair on them like friendly coals of accumulative curls. A priest wandered the ocean-side in search of lost souls. Nessan rushed past him. The tattoo on the young man's left buttock had a Viking-like, trident-bearing Tarot card figure. Nessan's blanched hair was going but his eyes in the night were very bright, very blue, very young. For a few weeks after that he kept his fantasies and his body to himself, curling up his limbs in his bed in the mornings. His mother brought a tray of breakfast things. The bed was over-large, a wedding one. There were muffled noises from Nessan as Bonnie tried to rouse him. There seemed nothing in life, nothing in life worth living for. Then gradually he remembered he had a script to complete and he roused himself, getting on with the job. And when sufficient work seemed done, in the afternoons he'd go off with Bonnie.

Those were the happiest weeks, weeks which combined work and excursions with Bonnie. Something in the form of what felt like a script was coming and in spring Nessan's pose was luxuriant under an ilex tree in bloom, on a slope, he standing beside Bonnie. Nessan drove his own automobile into the countryside and found spots, still pastoral, despite the general inclemency of the southern Californian landscape and there they picnicked, Bonnie running excitedly back and forth between the picnic blanket and the picnic hamper which was dumped, as a rule, just beside the automobile. Standing together they surveyed far-off outlines of ocean, Nessan's arm quietly sneaking around Bonnie's shoulder. Bonnie's curls bloomed upwards at the back now, a primrose bouquet, an irregularity among the rest of her hair. That bouquet developed into a fox's tail of a plume, standing in the air and then hanging down at the end, raggedly. When that event occurred Bonnie and Nessan were considered a unit in Hollywood. Hollywood was a series of film premières, producers with Chinese landscapes on their ties – white birds over mountains and calm oceans – waiting at the tail end of claret carpets, cigars stuck in their mouths like babies' stoppers. Hollywood was a conglomeration of cinemas where premières were held, a series of studios, starved looking places, a few cafés and night spots. It was the gluttonous seizing on the day. But into this Bonnie and Nessan strode, another couple, Nessan in a dinner jacket leading his lady. Nessan still had that blond hair, over his dinner jacket and its accoutrements, for the cameramen. He was a possible, unidentified star as he guided his lady, lightly holding her arm, in the glare of lights a vague unfocussed look on his face under a complimentary suffused vagueness of hair. Those eyes of his had a way of leading him forward though in an aquiline fashion. Nessan had merged into Hollywood's consciousness of itself, a mystery, and Bonnie too. Bonnie had sized up her possibilities for the part and entered the decorum of film premières, of public rendezvous, in a loin gripping black dress, an invisible tiara around her blonde curls, making them stand up now in a shock of self-assertiveness. That Nessan was a protégé of a single film producer he was reminded from time to time when the film producer arrived in the shadows of the door of a large room and distractedly flipped a cigar against his dual peaked upper lip time and time again. The script not quite ready, he looked on Nessan as part of his harem. Nessan the scriptwriter had a muscular body and the producer wanted to know if he'd take part in a pornographic film. Not quite coming up with the script he could do as an actor in a pornographic film. The principle of his sojourn was arbitrary. He'd been given a reprieve by a film producer who'd taken a fancy to him.

In the meantime he launched himself on film premières, on the entrances to cinemas, on the bustle of the crowd merging to enter the auditorium from the foyer to view the film. He was a perplexed androgynous face in the crowd, disconnected from it in his vagueness, but part of it none the less. People came to expect him and were almost reassured by his strange presence as though by a good conscience. They also expected his strange mistress. Not many people questioned where they came from but they were allowed to integrate themselves and when they disappeared people generally wondered if there'd been a suicide or calamity, because the mistress had seemed dangerously on edge sometimes, precipitously dolled up and crackled by age.

The producer's flipping cigar was ceaselessly in action in the background, it clicked like a clock on the verge of alarming. In this circumstance Nessan's mind jolted and remembered how he'd come to be here: the aeroplane journey, the apartment left in a wrecked state, bottles everywhere, so many bottles that whole sections of the apartment had turned to glass. The last visions of New York, demented, despairing, but frozen snails of queues of people, snails with frequent wriggles in their bodies. The faces in the queues, often southern, black faces under signs for navy beans, little steaming pyramids of navy beans in pictures above the heads of the starving with news of the amount of cents you paid for the beans. The beans in the pyramids the same colour as the genitalia of that fat producer. Or had they been the colour of naked prawns? Either way, there'd been some kind of sexual transaction between Nessan and the producer between the time Nessan had encountered him at the party and Nessan's time of hurrying from New York, reams of reviews scattered in his apartment like a despoiled roll of toilet paper to affirm his genius for the producer and reassure him he'd made the right decision. At least Nessan in some reverence for them had picked them up and sorted them out, feeling somehow in his languid state after drunkenness that there might not be any more. He could not recall, as he held them, the details of his sexual experience with the producer but it did seem to say if Nessan did not work out as a scriptwriter he'd make do as a facility for sex. A streak of a semen stain – or was it a jet of premature age? – over a review seemed evidence of this. The clock was clicking all right and about to alarm on a new identity for Nessan, that of an exploitable body which the producer seemed already to be imagining, the contours of it, the possibilities of the chest, from the doorway.

The script refused to be a final script. It became a poem. Nessan began writing across the clean, white, sun-sprayed Californian paper. He began writing about his life, his fears, in prose, in something that resembled prose but the prose was busheled into the shape of a poem. The page became crowded, populated by tiny scratches and baroque comas. Nessan wrote about his childhood, adolescence, his lovers, his work, his fears of his talent dilapidating, his drinking, his fear and yet his awe of death. He incarnated his life on paper on a night of glossy stars in the dome of the Pacific sky. The words bustled on the page. They ended like this. 'I have searched through many nights, many cities, but I think I've always been seeking to trace footsteps back, not just back to childhood and the child trudging through the corn, but back to ancestry, some diminution in ancestry, a moment of loss, loss of a person, loss of, separation from a country. I am a post-country person, a person that lost his country but can still grasp, under the Godly and suggestive Californian night sky, a sense of it and its pleasantness. It lies up there among the stars, a pasture of stars, a galaxy of its own.'

Bonnie came upon this writing, almost by accident, peered sidewise at it as her lean hands pulled back some paper to denude it, was swayed by it, felt her body swooning under its impact, wanted to hug him to her, hold his rough physique, that is his rough face but his tender chest, to her physique, decipher his despair with her body and thereby calm him. She did this.

On a night of drunkenness for both of them, bottles swirled about the air in their hands as they both camped like Indians in a big bedroom, seated on the floor, she managed to capsize into a bed with him in the very pretence of wanton, whorish drunkenness on her part, drunkenness of a very aged, shrill and flushed whore, the papier mâché flush in her cheeks the only convincing feature which bore her into his bed.

What happened between them was very little. She pressed the feigned drunkenness of her body against him to find out his secrets, the secret of where he went to, the secret of a part of his nature which she knew he was hiding from her, knew by the very evenness of the way he stood at times and by the distance in him, the glamorous, ever-renewed distance. He had a fund of richness which he was keeping from her. The wayward son would give in to her tonight.

But Nessan did not give in to her after all. After initially being assuaged by her, sleeping in her arms, he woke in the middle of the night, startled, wrested his form from her and made off like a dragon on fire into the Hollywood night.

A murky pink door opened for him. He was in a house of tortured delights. A sailor's Jewish looking nose inclined towards him. Nessan grabbed the smile. He and the sailor retired up stone steps, almost the steps of a medieval castle, to a room upstairs, leaving behind the pink phosphorescence and a woman's blonde head like a sunflower over the phosphorescence.

169

In a bed with the sailor he recalled or thought he recalled how in the middle of the night a woman, his mother, had tried to feel, beneath the armoury of his underwear, for his balls, his pink balls. Those pink balls were unleashed now. The sailor arched his buttocks towards Nessan and Nessan's posture capsized. He no longer had an appetite for this kind of activity. It was just repulsive for him. The sailor turned towards him and took his head in his arms as if Nessan were a loveable donkey.

Nessan was converted in the following nights to something he did not quite understand. He wandered down Hollywood Boulevard. Bars beckoned. But this time there was not the allure of the stooped and fragile figures inside. There was a new muscularity, a new knowingness in his body. The lights of the night were a new and onward calling language for him. Nessan remembered something of his childhood, was lucidly parallel to some event of childhood. Then it was gone. Something about his mother grabbing his naked and laundered body from a bath when he was a little boy and reaching for the pink and featherless bird of his sexuality. As if all the events and contortions in his life were explicable by this one event. Anyway he felt a new liberation, a new comfort, a new design in his body. He walked as though the travail of some wicked infiltrator had flown out of it. There was a new grasp on himself and on memory, and in memory now he saw smooth hills, hope. The Mid-West was for hope in him.

The figures in the bars were far off, remote now for him. Through a window he detected the silhouette of a male figure reaching with desultory motion for a cocktail. The cocktail was an onyx, urn-like shape against the iridescence of a row of bottles on a low shelf behind the counter, the light on the bottles like light at the end of a city sky at night. But the jagged mobility of the onyx shape could not attract Nessan in out of the night, the call of a fellow male for companionship. Nessan walked on into the night, towards the affirmation of some new evangelical disposition in his genitalia.

But before such affirmations there was the settlement of debts with the film producer. Having finally given up the idea that he was a scriptwriter, however demure the image was for him for a while in his white, body soaked shirt, Nessan decided to settle debts by performing in a pornographic film at the producer's wishes. The lascivious eye of the film producer was at the door prior to the shooting of the film, sizing up the possibility of Nessan's waist for pornography.

Nessan's biceps had widened in California as was evidenced when he took his clothes off for the film and he was proud to walk naked among girls with candy pink taffeta veils over their faces and shrouds of pink on their heads, their breasts covered in the same colour but their lower parts bare. The curveture of a woman's naked thighs, placidly resting on cushions roused manifold desires in him now. He strutted around naked with a penis sticking out and then pendant like the bold instrument of a horse or the cheeky one of a stone Cupid.

The clapboard was taken away and the action began. Nessan had to walk towards a girl whose pubic hair was showing in a dark vortex. As he was doing this he was supposed to slip on a banana skin into the girl's legs. All this was what happened. But near the girl's pubic hair Nessan remembered again some horror of childhood, his mother trying to snuggle him into her mound of Venus as they lay in bed together and he made off, grabbing a white towel which had a slim pink line through it. He made off to a bar by the sea and there after eyeing a sailor up and down absconded with him to an upstairs room. Pink poodles yelped below, one poodle with a ribbon around its ash and silver neck and a startled plume on its head. This poodle bolted and ran riot around the stone floor. Two paper lanterns with stories on them clashed into one another. Men's buttocks gesticulated with rippling movements to one another and legs slowly but certainly writhed towards one another. In an old and familiar pornography Nessan bent and kissed the backside of a boy. The hairs of eighteen slivered like a balcony of water reeds over those buttocks. Downstairs a woman in pink lit up like lightning as she emerged into the single bright light in the bar which was over the bar counter, lipstick on her like a blowaway piece of bunting. The boy's face turned towards Nessan and Nessan remembered in the white-lily anguish of the face the surprise of innocence, of youth, of waywardness that was still open to correction. 'Young man, you shouldn't be here,' he told the boy. But Nessan stayed here seven nights. In those seven nights he wandered like Count Dracula in dark rooms and through dark corridors through every kind of vice. He explored old brutalities of sexuality. There was one room in this house where a man who looked like a torturer from the Spanish

Inquisition, black leather over his face, whipped you. Lending his body for this correction, his trousers down, Nessan had images of high mass in the Catholic church, the solemn, pontificial figure of a priest in gold attire looking outwards at the flock from the altar, his shoulders slightly crooked. 'Come back to the church you who are vagrants,' his figure seemed to say accusingly, pinpointing the vagrants in the congregation. Nessan jumped up with a start, pulling up his trousers, surprising his torturer, thanking him cursorily for the treatment and made off to a room where naked sailor boys, their sailor hats still on them, frolicked with orange lollipops, daubing spare liquid of the lollipops on one another's bodies. They greeted him as if he were another member of a baseball team. 'Where's the woman?' Nessan said. 'What woman?' 'The sweetheart in your lives.' Bourbon had burrowed poisonous tunnels to his head. The boys looked uncomprehendingly. One seated young man kindly offered Nessan a lick of his lollipop. 'Lick this and you'll be all right.' Nessan screamed into a cavern of a series of cave-like rooms. Afterwards he wasn't sure if the rooms were in his head or real, if any of this was in his head or real, but his mother and the film producer came for him and found him sitting naked by a fountain in a stone room, gibbering to himself about being sodomized by a dog, a mural on the wall behind him depicting two groups of boys confronting one another in Ancient Greece, their hands raised in outrage at one another, only cloaks on them, often claret cloaks and their genitalia showing like alternative faces.

So Bonnie had come to the source of the distance in Nessan's nature, his sexuality. She had braked on it. Mountains seemed to descend upon her, mountains with Irish names. 'O God, this gift to her ancestry.' She had allowed herself to hear rumours of this sexual disposition before, feasts in Paris at the end of the last century with clumps of bananas, plates of delicately arranged oranges and then naked boys, men with only bowler hats on them, fountains of moustaches trailing into the incandescence of their cigar smoke, drooling over the boys. The men's trousers left behind in Indiana or Vermont. Men had gone from the States for these European traditions. But her son. Her son among the Turkish cigars and the boys with sweetly perfumed genitalia. Bonnie was aghast and perplexed. Nessan had betrayed the purity of his upbringing, the purity of the naked body he'd leant against sometimes as a child.

The events that followed would always be a muddle in her mind. It was as if she'd taken an overdose of a backwoods' bottle of spirits and couldn't remember. But she did recall the producer approaching Nessan's naked body and saying 'perfect' in a European Jewish accent. Maybe it was Nessan's speech that the producer was saying perfect to but Bonnie was so troubled, so sickened, she stood there for a while and then made off, packing her clothes with dazed abstraction, drifts of thoughts occasionally around her, lead in her heart. The whole of history as she knew it had been changed and its meaning destroyed for her. From that day on, for a number of years, she had no son. She began life again as a bedraggled unit, a long, lizard-like coat already on her as she packed for fear she might lose her resolve. That resolve would take her into the centre of her possibilities as an artist and thereby throw her into a place many miles from the ones she'd been acquainted with, territory on the Canadian border. Bonnie found herself there by the end of the year, a new personality, a new woman, the past obliterated on her face, almost in a dazed way, and a crown of Toulouse Lautrec henna hair on her head.

Nessan, a very sober and changed Nessan, packed his bags and returned to New York early in the New Year. He groped his way there virtually. New York threw new colours into his face or maybe it was the light that brought them out. His face and particularly the back of his neck had turned almost red and purple and there was anxious grey in his balding hair, silver almost. Silver hair rested around the salmon skin as it might around the skin of an old sealine dwelling Donegal man. The Atlantic ocean of his ancestors had washed colours into Nessan's complexion. There was an embarrassed tugging about the movements of his body in New York. He had to readjust his body to the grey, ethereal skyscrapers in the grey January light. What had been mellifluous and smoothed in him in California was here carbuncular and awkward. Nessan walked to the apartment of an acquaintance. His own apartment had at last gone, without hope of reprieve in his life.

The apartment of the acquaintance was spread with the detritus of talent: bottles, a few ramshackle typewriters with the arrow of a folded sheet of typing paper stuck into them like mascots, books, old, musty, dead books, ashtrays on which much neglected and dense ash was powdered. All these things accumulating into the wainscot cobwebs which had patterns like the manifold framework of the masts of Victorian ships. Drink, there was mostly evidence of drink: drink in the face, drink in the staring eyes of his acquaintance, crouching on the floorboards, drink in the gills. Last night's drink had washed into the face like an estuary deserted of tide and, wet, reflecting, the cold non-lyrical morning sky. The man's face, his deadened, wishing-to-be-dead eyes, were a mirror of Nessan's face. Death, dropsy-sought death, dropsy. Death sought death for signs of life or twitches of irregularity. Finally, in evasion of almost inevitable speech, silence having lasted so long, Nessan was offered a swig of a masculine bourbon bottle by a masculine arm. Dark hairs clung to the end of that arm and were exhibited by force of habit though the macho manifestation had lost its meaning. The healthier promises of that arm belonged to another era.

Nessan walked through the grey, fog faint, early year streets. He walked and walked. The network of fog-enfeebled high rise buildings and of fog-daunted street corners around him, Yiddish family names and occasionally whole snatches of Hebrew legend dented into shop signs, often lopsided, as if merry and drunk from poverty. A thread of chill and despair drew him on in a kind of dreadful fascination. It wound him through the streets and outer precincts, the secret, shadow plunging enclaves of those precincts, of the area of New York he'd been most familiar with. Those streets now had a different face, a withering, almost melting look of poverty, something doleful about it like the face of an old Greek woman who is trying to decide whether to call for help or whether to die vituperatively. The face of New York had changed. It was mesmerised by its own dilapidation. Nessan walked on and on, through afternoon, evening, into the Hades of night. Men with bottoms pink as those of pigs rested on lavatory bowls in open doored latrines, looking out, a menagerie for inspection. You could judge their eyes and choose the best of them for a prize. This was under the ground. A man reclined on a lavatory bowl, spent, a pea tin with a gapingly open top on the ground beside him, almost a talisman, the patterns of peas jocular, the jostling emerald peas on it the only reminder of food. The bottoms when you saw them retained a healthy pink. Was it an over luminous pink, a garish pink, one that was baby-like but a prelude to the pink of the fires of Hell, a New York version of Hell, flames like street signs dancing and kicking?

Nessan walked into the street lights of Broadway. A man in a Harvard cap had a tray dangled in front of him, spanking red apples on it and little bouquets of shoe laces like neatly tied tussles of maggots among the apples, red light falling on him as if he were a character about to begin his lines, emerging from the nether regions of a stage. His form was twisted though, like that of a spastic child, especially his midriff which was out of control, all contorted, a modern athletic sculpture. Nessan stared, further on, at a heap of a little girl on the ground as if she were part of a waxworks display, standing over her, looking from what seemed like an immense height above her. The little girl returned him to the Mid-West, the little girl creatures who were scattered like rubbish alongside the railroad beside runaway despairing fathers who'd decided to cart their favourite child with them. Although her eyes were on the ground the little girl's forehead twitched in rubbery lines in acknowledgement of him looking at her, taking the trouble to stop over her. She was grateful for the attention, for the witness. Again the raspberry lines of patterns on her dirty white dress looked to better times, times when comforting visuals were important. Her subdued and unhurried suffering, the nonchalant onlooker, the tableau of both of them, the one apparently dying, the other impotent in his attentions to her, soon drew an audience wider than the one the little girl had had, people stopping to stare, people going home from the theatre, middle-class couples, this another theatrical effect, snow replenishing it, snow tumbling into the focus of the street light, merry, theatrical New York snow, the scene emblematic of the times they were living in, one person looking at another person's suffering, perhaps going to carry it into and shape it in another, more hopeful era, the onlooker, too, degraded but not too degraded, hair on him like that on a patchily shaved white poodle, an uneven discoloured crust of it, something about this lilac and purple lumber jacket, hands in it, suggesting poetry. Yes, this young man was a poet. Men and women moved on, one woman in a fur coat warm and soporific as a tan beer, and silky and assured as the skin of a dog in a comic cartoon. When that garment was gone there was a further destitution about the

175

scene, as if the little bit of extravagance, the little bit of frivolity in the colour of that garment had alleviated the suffering of the scene and offered, by its contrast, some hope that this decor might be available, too, ultimately, to the destitute, that roles could be switched or argued with. Nessan felt the squalor, as if its intensification was in part caused by him and, embarrassed, he shuffled his feet, not knowing whether to stay or to go, to open his mouth or stay silent, to help and risk being called a molester, or to ignore and forever damn himself in his conscience.

All these dilemmas were solved; Nessan was rescued when a figure emerged from the arc of the street light and tottered towards the little girl, a male figure, probably the girl's father, a large crust of white bread outheld in his hand, like a ghastly hatchet. Nessan moved on, proffering no civilities, ridding his shifty presence into the streets which were being faded out in white. There was no end of suffering that night for even in that obliteration Nessan saw cripples, men lying in the snow moaning, a week's beard clinging to their thrown back mouths, like clouts which had stunned them. Only sleep wound up the sights of the day when the circuit of Nessan's trip had been done and sleep in an alien apartment at that which in sleep was absorbed in dreams as a grey, black place; it became a whole landscape, this apartment, a terrain on which a fugitive Nessan wandered under a moon, the earth of this terrain grey, parched and riddled with little crators on the inclines on either side of the road Nessan wandered on, crators like goldfish mouths, bulbous and gasping for breath. The whole of Nessan's world had been wrung dry of colour, it had been drained of all hope, incentive and lit by a moon alcoholics see on the outer edges of intoxication. Nessan wandered in dreams and in waking, a listless, sick light on him.

There was comfort in excess of alcohol, but Nessan never got too drunk – even in the conspiracy of drunkenness with his host – not to realize the progression of the facts of history, that the hunger queues, going for miles, endless, connected with the starvation queues in Dublin and in Cork during the Irish Famine, people waiting for the pittances from empire and from history. Social diagnosis kept him sober, kept him distant from his companion and drove him into the streets. In the streets he found the vigil of the crowds lulling, panoramic, evocative. They were reshaping him. He was no longer just seeing himself.

He went as far as the subway lavatories and surveyed the excrement left in bowls, comment on what the social system had come to. For some reason he had escaped. He was an outsider. He could mete out some assistance in his new guise as an angel. The angel Nessan had gained in being away.

His work was taken more seriously and it did not take him long to be awarded an overwhelming grant, given to him with the stipulation that he travel with it. America deemed him important enough to be put in Paris. But first he partied, ducking in and out among celebrities like a boxer dexterously splaying punches. And only once or twice did he think of his mother. He blamed her for everything now: for the desecration of his innocent sexuality, for the inflammation of his genitalia, for the perverted scouring of his juvenile nakedness. He cursed her from an otherwise placid party frame for having usurped his sexuality when he was at an early age and for having navigated his life, thus far, by implication of dark, tantrum-bubbling, Catholic, possessing, but oddly lucid and distant spirits. Those spirits were in abeyance now. Nessan had taken control of his own life, of the gestures of his sexuality. He faced a woman at a party and desired her.

She would not let her mind think of him. She would not let a sliver of him come to her attention, lifting her head that now was the colour of primroses in spring except that these primroses were a bit too blonde, a bit too awry. Bonnie had found her way to the north and was performing in the plays of Shakespeare in the theatre of an hotel, realizing her dream to be an actress in a room where everything, including the ceiling, seemed to be falling down and the floor seemed to have a dip in the middle of it. Couples, apparently unaffected by the depression, wandered in and out to see snippets of the performance, the women holding their backs very straight, ritualistically, as if they were present at the last moments of a cremation ceremony. They seemed unaffected by the economics of the depression but allied to events in the greater world. This made them inattentive to any supposed frivolity for too long. They had obviously mastered their economic situation, these couples not dragged down by economic events, but they harkened to the ripples of history and were worried by them. Gauche women in black could be seen anxiously standing by the lake's edge. These

177

people had hybrid European names and gave impressions of European mountain summits in their stance, always an intimation of books in their conversation, secretive battalions of books in their homes. This whiff of culture from his clientele was sufficient excuse for the bald Irish hotel proprietor, with a wart like a standing walrus on his nose, to indulge in his favourite preoccupation, the theatre, and welcome all kinds of players. The two worlds moved parallel to one another and even denied one another. Men, bent and dressed as red beaked birds, let out from a rehearsal, could be seen wandering obliviously by sublimated looking women in black, standing beside the lake's edge, looking out over unconsolable expanses of water. The bent backs were not so much a theatrical gesture as a copy of the proprietor's bent back. Most characters in the plays here went around with bent backs as if hoping to please the proprietor by this general distillation of his physical demeanour. It became contagious. Bonnie, as Gertrude in *Hamlet*, went around with a bent back too until the point when Polonius, the character with the most bent back and the greatest excuse to have a bent back, was found killed, and then she straightened up, in a bolt-like movement. There was a big bed drowned in a black quilt on the stage. Bonnie was dressed in purple for the part. One night when she and Claudius sat on the bed it gave from under them and a German woman in the audience panicked and screamed. The proprietor was from County Kerry in Ireland. He was a tinker and he told the German woman that being an Irish tinker was equivalent to being a Jew. Bonnie went on with her performance, hearing this story later. The bed lay on the floor for the rest of the evening. Bonnie slept in it that night, not going to her bed in the hotel, and dreamt, under the black quilt, of Ireland and treks out of Ireland, the Jewish history retold.

Nessan began having dreams of a child before he left for Europe. The banquet of Europe called. All that dressed up news about Germany. But those last nights in the New World he dreamt of a child, a very particular child, a boy in a blue and white striped vest. Homosexual until now, never believing he'd have a child, suddenly an imaginary one was created for him. Or was it a mental photograph of a child to come. Either way his ancestry had an imaginary child before he left. Out of Ireland, Famine, emigration, death and the debilitating alientation from personality and the inner fixed point of personality a child was realized or rather took over from the memory of these things. There was a newness about the child. He was a modern child. American. He had the gangly legs of the 1930s and a beaming face under raw blades of blond hair. Nessan was bringing something back home.

Bonnie dreamt of the same child as Nessan left for Europe. She dreamt of the child in the big bed under the black, deathly shimmering quilt. But it was Nessan as a child. The blond boy in the blue and white stripes. The blond hair over the face in a flowerpot and dangerously askew shape. There was red on the cheeks. Red which had faded later. She woke and started to scream. She knew she'd never see her son again.

First stop was Ireland; first sight the coast of Kerry, an island. Rain smudged out the coast and the jut of the island, benevolent late February rain, an emission from the general softness in the air. You could see little alternative throughfares in the rain, busy throughfares. The predominant colour was blue. On this island, Nessan was told, saints had come once to have their bony bodies and herring bone ankles flailed by rain for Christ. Towards evening, after a desultory standstill by the ship, a lighthouse started up. It blinked from a beach near another beach where an Irish hero had gone ashore with German guns during the Easter rising. It was a sign. We've put on our best clothes. You can approach us now.

Dublin was narrow, colloquial, tricksy streets; streets you walked along and were salvaged in your lost state by a pub which took you without your wanting to go into it and gave a man's face over a high counter, the man's face the gravedigger's in *Hamlet*, waiting for you, toothless mouth open with a grin. 'A Yank, are ye?' There were lemon gossiping daffodils in Dublin and a Huguenot graveyard by the street most frequented by Nessan, a verdant oasis on the severe Georgian street. Not that Ireland needed verdant oases. It was a spongy mess of dark and youthful green. It was not the land deadened by history that Nessan was expecting. There were mentally deficient jigs on old men's faces and conundrums on young men's sparely toothed faces. One pub sign led to another, an urgent arabesque of

179

messages, gold lettering on lavish green, dun planted on purple, secretive browns wending their way into dark grey. Dublin was a kaleidoscope of pub signs; they were ikons against which the 'Yank' with the blond, listless, shedding hair which revealed a salmon head in patches and with hands harmoniously knitted into his purple and mauve jacket stated himself. He felt alive in this city. He felt endangered in this city. The whites of the eyes of old poets gleamed with seduction and entreaty just inside pub entrances. Nessan did not go in. The poets fumbled with gnarled sticks as they sat on diminutive stools. Being ignored by Nessan they turned with some barb to their nearest companion. This was a city of the scintillating discontent. The poets and the novelists were luxuriantly coated polar bears with pockets in their lank bellies where they could obliterate you. But their smiles were still bear-like smiles. Nessan sauntered faster. The sins of every other city were invoked here as if this city had priority over all other cities. There were long, winding queues outside confessionals, frigid groups which stretched into the rain by the tortured pillars of churches over brief flights of steps. The names of lovers from other cities echoed in the mind and the gestures of each lover were recalled here as if these lovers could be reckoned with at last for their worth. A woman's red hair was remembered, the locust cloud of freckles over her face.

In the lavatory of a pub off Nessan's favourite street Nessan stumbled into the ways of the flesh again. A boy, a farmer's son, his penis embarrassingly white. 'I'm from County Kildare.' His boots carrying dung. The hair on his head was the red of the hide of a spectacular calf. They both looked down at his anatomy. He'd warned of a father who was on his trail. There are dangers of mortal sin in this, Nessan told himself, but they are allayed by the beauty of the boy's reaction, looking down at himself as if he is seeing himself for the first time. The boy came from a house which had pillows on the beds, big as clothes trunks. There were whispered confidences, whispered pieces of information. 'It's not raining outside any longer,' the boy suddenly declared, as if that was the reason for them staying here, his head still looking down. The penis disappeared into the thick trousers, already diminished, an ephemeral realization. Nessan's fingers dallied on the last manifestation of it. Then he went off, rallying his figure for the cold outside. There were black pugilistic clouds in the sky, one audacious dash of ermine. The Irish tricolour over an important looking building frantically urged further movement for Nessan. Horse dung on the street, wet on it, miles of emerald posters, dancing chorus girls on them, the odd, drunken-looking, onward-coming bicycle, further poky urinals, shrines, statues of the Virgin; this was Ireland.

Nessan left Dublin. He'd felt alive in this city. He'd felt endangered. A low undulation of blue mountain dipped over a gleaming, prostrate street, giving absolution to the entire city. Nessan left Dublin with the smell of a boy on his fingers, a boy who'd return to his big dungeon-like beds and probably never know the liberated auras of the flesh again. But before he left Dublin Nessan had stood in his hotel room, naked to the waist, before a portrait of an Irish patriot, hoping that the patriot would at last notice the snowdrop colour of Nessan's flesh where his waist dipped towards his loins. There was no answer from history. Nessan made off down a river, on a dingy boat, having addressed his grandfather from a window looking down on a dark street. His grandfather had left the cornfields once for America. Now Nessan had returned, still with an unrequited harvest of the flesh, searching here in Europe, where the journey had begun, for some clue which would make him whole. 'Star of the Sea'. A guesthouse gaped opposite. Over its black door a light. Páid O'Dowd mingled with Nessan that night, another waist, another steep incline from waist to loins, another tableau of longings, no less real for being part of an emasculated history and a part of other people's myths. A grandfather of Nessan had broken from order once, broken from inheritance, and so had sundered the connection in his descendants between the roots of their being and themselves.

Everywhere in London women sold spring flowers, at every corner, and between corners: crocuses and daffodils and narcissi. Nessan stayed in the East End, near the river. From his window he could see a woman pulling up her skirts and urinating in an adjoining yard, the yard of a pub. She was the pub landlady. She wore a man's cap and startled you when you went into the pub with the pipe coming out between her teeth. On one occasion Nessan watched her wheel up her skirts in that yard and lie back so a customer could make love to her. In the pub working-class men sat over lemonade. No indulgence here. No trespass. Words only went so far. On a wharf young men stood but they were standing only for fresh air.

Nessan was not the only one who watched the pub landlady urinate. From a window across, a little boy and a little girl watched, a cap on the boy's head, too big for him. Nessan at least made contact with these voyeurs.

Nothing doing here. Veniality. A few kipper-thin women entertained him, white dresses on them. Cocktails on a tray. 'And how is American literature these days?' A young man with tie loose and colours on it like those on a heraldic naval flag, scarlets, golds, made a speech from his seat of two cushions piled on one another about the importance of the working class in modern British literature. Nessan left England, having forgotten that he'd been half seduced by a woman on a couch, the couch from which the cushions had disappeared, the depths of it charred without the cushions and the woman's dress up in the drunken sleep he'd left her in, revealing black knickers with a gold, royal-looking message on them.

Paris next stop; city of carnival, colour-light lit urinals. Paris was dotted with pissoirs, mother-of-pearl lights on them. The coloured lights actually belonged to a marquee Nessan attended but afterwards, because of the drunken state he'd been in in Paris, his mind had decked the carnival lights on pissoirs. Not that it mattered. Nessan was drunk and gluttonous in this city. Young soldiers revealed themselves to him, white apparitions from behind their dark coats, their faces under the mother-of-pearl lights the faces of juvenile Egyptian mummies. Nessan was an adamant, an athletic party-goer in this city. There were lots of rich Americans to be duped by his frenetic antics. Bottle usually upheld in the air, Nessan parodied an earlier self. There was scope to move again here, a mortgaged reprieve for an old way of life. Any day the creditors would come. But still people danced and sang and tipped their fingers over the white flesh piano keys. The connections with the rich brought Nessan south, to the Mediterranean, a boat on the Mediterranean, a little tiara of lights on the sea. This was safety. Music nestled into the boat at night, jazz. Nessan walked a parapet on land and under a quiff of coloured lights looked out to his temporary domicile. He did not drink much here, stayed away from the parties, stayed away from the boat at night, and so was able to gaze at it. Paris had slashed open an anarchy in him that he never knew existed. Boys, young men, pissoirs like carnival citadels, a drunken dance from one of those citadels to another, the French way of pornography, ultimately an apartment, a woman depicted on the wall, a Goddess, flat leaves encircling her, a pattern of flat leaves, as if they were being juggled in her outstretched hands, morphine then, a little throughfare of it, meticulously injected into his left arm, and then all Hell: rats in New York, fat, carnal-looking rats invading underground lavatories long after the humans were gone, approaching the lavatory bowls as if the last humans had been swallowed down them in their emaciated acts of sitting on those bowls for respite; the vision down those bowls which rats' black saucer eyes could see: Hell and screams and maggots and churning, brown coated, gangly 1930s tramps, the tramps having surrendered control of those gangly limbs. All the tramps merged into one solitary tramp and Nessan could see that this tramp was himself. When he'd returned from California he'd stopped to stare at an automobile parked alongside a kerb, an automobile white as a Little Italy wedding dress, festooned with leaves from a tree late to shed itself, brown leaves all over it, finicky and clinging leaves, and Nessan had felt as he stared at the burgeoning automobile his own absolute estrangement from wealth, prosperity, from the prospect of wealth, from material ambition and even the possibility of material ambition and in that absolute estrangement he experienced an incarnation into the journey of an ancestor, as he made his way across America, distraught from loss of country and near loss of sanity which had resulted from the on-driving, unrelenting memories of that country, the cruel, attacking sleet of memory and on the street too there was a sexual exaltation in that incarnation, a oneness with the frail, naked buttocks of an Irishman in a strange house in the United States, in a strange room in history.

From a window on the Lido in Venice he saw a man, a woman, a child on a beach, the man in a full, breast covering, striped swimming costume, his shoulders expansive and his pose, as he stood, commanding. Perhaps at that moment the reality of a flaxen haired boy in a blue and white striped vest became immeasurably nearer. Nessan thought of the red-haired girl he'd met in New York and decided to return to find her. He evacuated a room in a palatial hotel and took a train, his back turned to the apocalyptic world of sea and sky and city which was Venice.

In New York he found she had gone, departed with her husband to a small Central American country. He sorted out all the vestibules of his life and left, by sea, for Central America.

There had been trouble in the hotel that year, a change of manager, no more Shakespeare. Bonnie demoted to a chamber maid. Lucky though to have been kept on. The young man who'd originally given her the address of this hotel had never turned up in her stay here. There'd been a general absence of jugglers, magicians, magic lantern show operators, a shift of emphasis having happened in the entertainments before Bonnie had arrived, Shakespeare having taken over, the more serious side of the proprietor. The young man had disappeared one winter morning and had never been heard of again, except in one dispatch which said he was reading Tarot cards professionally in Detroit, seen on a square modelled on an Italian square in this industrial, otherwise nondescript city. Bonnie was comfortable as a chamber maid; she could harbour plays in her head as she worked, until her mother was forced upon her by the sister who'd been looking after her. After her mother's house was sold her two sisters took the proceeds and Bonnie's mother was pushed from one to the other for care. But any solicitude they might have had towards their mother eventually dried up and a penniless, near corpse-like mother was handed over to Bonnie by the younger of Bonnie's two sisters. Anyway, Mrs. O'Dowd, suspecting that at last death was coming for real, wanted to be under Bonnie's care. There was also an excitement for her about rooms which had a burnt-out sense of the theatrical people who had once inhabited them and of theatrical events which had once occurred in them. Bonnie had been too busy thrusting herself into her career as an actress to notice when the money had been divided up, but now, when a penniless mother, who looked as though she had all kinds of disease grafted onto her skin, arrived, she did notice. It was Christmas 1934 and the landscape was tucked into snow as in some proverbial fairy story. Events moved fast and what

184

happened would always be etched into Bonnie's mind as something larger than her life, bigger than anything her life could cope with and yet by the draconian nature of these events making her heroic, spectacular even, giving her the part her life always seemed destined for, but one which when it came she suddenly realized all the clues and the bric-à-brac of premonitions had anticipated it would be for real. If some moments in life purge the soul this was one for her. But it gave her no time to philosophize. Her hair was a white wool again as she confronted the situation she found herself in, her eyes blue with Ireland and strength.

The city Nessan sauntered through near the turn of the year evoked many other cities, the turbulence of narrow back streets, cobbled passages and steps, the labyrinth that got more and more complicated as you walked through it and suddenly and dramatically smashed and offered a precipitous view of an eggshell, delicate hued ocean, hands out to grab you for ceramics, for sex, and in the evenings the night-clubs. In one night-club a dance by five, plump, pink bears, bears which shed their costumes and revealed themselves to be naked men, fig leaves marginally diminishing their nakedness, the gold, saucerlike shape of a jazz instrument under the supervision of a man in a white shirt, whose scarlet braces seemed to be bleeding from sweat, peremptorily beaten when the men shed their costumes. One bear still had his clothes on, the sixth, the fattest of all, a phosphorescent one, who entered from the wings and prowled among the men, dragging on a cigar, lewdly inspecting their stems of Indian-exotic chests. Pink bears were not the only pink thing in this city. There were pink rats, a contagion of pink rats let out of some drug in this port, an interim city on his voyage. Rats in his head, Nessan stumbled into a church in which he saw a statue, the top part the Madonna with raven hair, the lower part a whore, her brazen naked legs, slits of scarlet on her toenails. In a cemetery Nessan sighted the tombstone of someone from Dublin, the tombstone in the shape of a cross. Over this city and its profuse, continually agitating jazz bands, was a mountain with a plateau top, a demure mountain which spliced a cloud or two. In fact all the bears in the show had been phosphorescent but Nessan only noticed the consuming phosphorescence when the sixth bear, the bear disengaged from the chorus, emerged. This bear obsessed Nessan in his eddying journey through the city, the weight of his stomach, the confidence of his lewdness. In this city there were no harangues of conscience and very few reasons for restraint. Orgies seemed to be happening everywhere, orgies on people's faces, Latin, chimpanzee-rubbery smiles. Faces of figures crouched on the edges of narrow laneways which had graded falls, long steps which came to an abrupt halt, seemed to reach up to you, leeringly advertising some little known, regular orgy. Figures huddled together in a bath house, pink, piggy bottoms. What were they doing in the expansive bath? Nessan was praying in a tiny church, prayer the other side of this city, not a prayer that asked you to repent but prayer that was a twin of debauchery. Outside dolphins squirted into the air from the sea. There was a memory in this city, a strange memory, an ancestral memory of conjugal love. Two bodies coming together in purity, woman and man. Nessan's face looked boyish and his head was visited by a golden crop. When it was time to go he knew he was parting from a place where some bolt in a mechanism had fallen into place, some part of a machine. He had turned his back on an old self and found a holy heterosexuality. But the shrimp pink dresses of men in a chorus still waved, a goonish chorus, wands of white plumes coming out from the men's hands, from among the dresses. A small membrane of a stained glass window in a church seemed to peep in at this show; another hallucination.

Arrival: the first months a city in a country on the verge of revolt, mountains churning over the city, like the ocean that took the *Titanic*; a white square, drinks in the open there, one of the company at the table an American nun in white. She was joining the revolution and she stomped her legs on the ground, showing a bit of flesh above the boots, a gruff farmer. Veronica's husband was leaving. He'd been persuaded away to New York. Nessan was given the opportunity of this woman. The hair of Veronica's husband had a black, fruity gleam, riding purposefully, in contours, to the abrupt denouement of the quiff over the forehead. A white shirt covering the upper part of his body and closing him off at the neck, he looked searchingly at Nessan. You can have my wife because I like your poetry, the look said. It would honour the flesh of my chest and of my broad shoulders if you had her. He was anxious that Nessan be seduced by his wife. It might cause a flutter in his academic, literary papers and allow him to be grafted to a poet's dream, to stand in for the poet for an instant thousands of miles away in New York, among the detritus of the poet's imagery, the first manifestations of the twentieth century, bridges and skyscrapers and people wearing lumber jackets as if the whole weight of an offload from a cargo ship had suddenly been hoisted on their shoulders.

If there was one person who'd never doubted the fact of telepathy it was Bonnie O'Dowd. It was her belief in telepathy which enabled her to cope with the worst moments of her life, the awareness of the waves and waves of reverberation those moments sent out, reverberations which garlanded her in a heroic ikon. That posterity was attentive to her predicament was the only reason she went on, through her mother's death and the circumstances of her mother's death. A corpse, a corpse on a sleigh: Bonnie having been fired from her post in the hotel, America under snow, the journey among other vagrants, with a corpse, knocking on her eldest sister's door, being assailed with lizard, air-beating, Christian arms. 'Whore. Whore of Babylon.' Bonnie in the snow saw a land of readily available oranges for her position as whore of Babylon, oranges and tangerines and cumquats. 'You're carrying dirty diseases.' Bonnie suddenly had a vision of insects with shrimp-pink backs crawling over her private parts. 'And that son of yours. He's a sodomite. We read it in the papers.' The news of Nessan's homosexuality had become public just as he was turning heterosexual. Bonnie's sister had gone mad: mad from religion, mad from Bibles, tawny Bibles which Bonnie could glimpse inside just as the door shut on her face. Bonnie went on with the corpse of her mother and buried her in a paupers' graveyard beside someone's mail hatch, only anonymous stones, some still visible in the snow, by decree denoting the various graves, a man collecting mail, his back bent, as Mrs. O'Dowd was buried by a fat, former bar owner who had a long, whimsical moustache – other, ungoverned hair on his face – and many tales of his proprietorship of the bar. Bonnie Muir or Bonnie O'Dowd as she now introduced herself, was on the move, one of the many, apocalyptically moving tramps under the sky of America's northernmost inner states.

The city led in spiralling, circular pathways to a damaged El Greco storm sky. The vengeance of Heaven was imminent up there. Easter, and Nessan and Veronica and the American nun in white trod the circular paths, ascending. Down below, suddenly, they saw, as sun and blue sky returned, gold and yellow calves in the fields. A man writhed past them, carrying a cross, a Ku Klux Klan hood over his face, the eyes of a government agent looking out from the slits. Later they watched a bull-fight in the lower portion of town. There was sunshine there. The bull was festive. In an enclosure for the rich there were many white clothes and much doldrum-fat belly. A girl in white opened a bottle of champagne, the smile on her European, haut couture, the red expectation of lips between fascist cities.

During the next few years Bonnie Muir travelled from city to city, working as a charwoman, mopping floors, standing in lines of skeletal people at early morning, for jobs. Her figure narrowed even further and her hair exploded on top, a bereft clump of grey, the clump not knowing which way to dangle. She pressed the same winter coat against her body for years, black. Under the advertisements for kipper-red and kipper-thin sausages and for the dung-heaps of beans with rosettes of steam over them, she became another of America's nameless, 1930s tramps, whose former destinies had been among the middle classes, with loved ones, and in sedate and comfortable homes. She took all this as martyrdom: the crown of thorns, never far above her head, gave her a desultory, an accepting look. But, in the end, it was Nessan who woke her again and gave her life purpose and shape again, in fact made her give birth again in a way.

Nessan's father died in August and Nessan returned to the United States; a little aeroplane, sparely and tensely shaped as a silver grasshopper, swept him from New Orleans to the Mid-West. There Nessan's major portrait was done, a photograph taken of Nessan's head against the cornfields, his hair a stubble, having vanished in parts, the human features in the portrait almost dark and scoured by a further inner darkness, an intense, almost negative wondering, but the negativity was saved by the pubescence and richness of the lips. This was Nessan on the border of love.

I fumble with drawers, take things out, get rid of them. Maybe because death is near. It is autumn and the Dublin suburban sea rushes in with a rage, with even an untarnished-looking white foam about its mouth. But it is bits of paper that refer to Nessan that I come up with more than often and I leave them or I leave them tidier than before. Little shuffles of paper accumulate, a photograph of Nessan, a different one, he in a white shirt, an Irish mass card almost. The sea growls outside and Radio Eireann cackles, a transistor coming to life, the battery deciding to work after all, pop music coming out, an avenue of pop music, a Grafton Street of pop music. There is another boy in a record shop window. He stops to look. An Irish boy in a pink shirt. An Irish pop star. There is envy in Phineas' eyes. He too wants to be a star. But he'll do it in a different way.

They moved from the city. They were going on a journey. There had been an uprising. Indians had been crucified around one village and the American nun had disappeared. She wore a red scarf around her wimple now and was said to be organizing reluctant rebels from the back of a mare, waving a despotic stick, the mare particularly stubborn and dishevelled. Story refracted on story and the number of those crucified increased: it became myriads, myriads and myriads in peach and crimson blousons on crosses in the mountains.

The journey too from the city was reluctant. Partly on foot and partly on mule-back they went. Tourists, unabashed, photograph from an American ladies' decorous magazine, in a land of murder. Veronica chose her dresses carefully for the individual days. Nessan put his hand to his forehead, checking the horizon, in a civilized sleeveless jersey, alive with lime and soft emerald phalanxes. Veronica organized the mood of their journey, continually fetching bottles of mango juice from a satchel, replacing her sunglasses with a more comfortable and larger pair, the sense in her militaristic femininity – slacks and blouse she might have had on one day – of the journeys she'd made as a child, to and from Europe, so many journeys they'd

become a subconcious rhythm in her, an omnipresent dream in
her. She had authority over sea and landscape as long as she was
journeying. So murders were a point of interest for her and
fleeing bandits an initiation of a series of animated gestures with
a camera. She commandeered Nessan. She pushed him out of
any misgivings he might have had about the journey. It seemed
she was always behind his back as they went further, pushing
him on. Sometimes at night they slept under the stars. Veronica
said, looking up, that they were guests of the stars. Celibacy
prevailed but Nessan felt a different body on him or rather a
different aura around his body, that of a pale man with blond
hairs all around his pale, expectant flesh. One morning they
found a body without a head in the grass, the body a blackened
and abandoned tree trunk. Accidental corpses were common
here; they were a motif in this country. Evidence of hatreds so
murderous that even corpses appeared to have been further
abused. All around in the sky were vultures who seemed to have
red on their tails, making them like women out in evening
dresses for balls in the court of a military king, a dictator. In the
palace in this country women had a habit of turning up in
cannibalistic red. Lips were so red they were a uniform artificial
flower imported with the women into the palace. Up here there
were no artificial flowers. This was a home of perennial and
tumultuously combined runs of flowers. A lesser, more dehyd-
rated, landscape gave way to a landscape of pagodas of
mountains sitting over lakes, and the mountains in those lakes,
exactly, turned upside down, and Indians coming to the edges
of the lakes, dribbles of bystanding, curious Indians. A costume
would suddenly confront you on a forlorn Indian, birds,
snakes, crocodiles on the Indian's costume, a whole legend
being narrated. But the wearers of the legends were dumb.
They'd been stunned into silence, a telepathic, fearful silence
that went from one to the other. Only the costumes and the eyes
spoke of horrors feared. But up here there were flowers and the
smell of flowers incumbent on random, spring-like breezes, the
sky often languidly furrowed with cloud that articulated an
original, purple colour and seemed indeed to presage spring.
Here the seasons were as enmeshed in one another as the
flowers. That fact, norms having disappeared, gave a drunken
freedom to the movements of Nessan's and Veronica's limbs.
They were entering a zone of anarchy. Not that the terrain

below had been devoid of anarchy. But there there'd been some semblance of the seasons. When Nessan had returned from his father's funeral the coffee beans had turned a dried blood colour under a scouring storm sky in the corner of landscapes, and at night squashes in the fields gleamed like alternative moons under the moon. The fields in daytime, coffee fields, squash fields, were occasionally punctured by a scared little scarecrow of a girl, her hands almost afraid to hold on to one another behind her back, and the look in her eyes tenuous too, a separate fragment of her. On the steps of a cathedral in a town by the sea, Nessan, washed by eddies of blue from the autumn Pacific sky, accompanied in the immediate picture by a little girl who was standing behind him, holding a bunch of flowers bigger than her for an expected funeral, saw, in this town where fish-tin greasy men, who'd applied for jobs as spies for the Third Reich, were playing backgammon on open-air tables, visions of children in a Europe which was disintegrating, his own possible children, a little flock of children in bathing costumes bent over a hole in the sand, hen-like bottoms in parrot-patterned bathing costumes on the little girls.

There had been a decided sense of masculinity in Nessan's limbs on those steps – his loins in particular seeming to have magnified and become a new attribute, those of a youth he'd known long ago in the Mid-West. Now that he was on the verge of total masculinity, physicality was being passed on psychically from a web of remembered heroes, boys in white in the baseball team, or boys half stripped but wearing muscles of painterly gold, on the wrestling fields. Nessan was on a par with the masculine presences of long ago. He had achieved a delicate masculinity in the balls and felt he was about to be effortlessly consumed in an affair. But before the affair there were reflections: on war, on global catastrophe. All the dahlias, chrysanthemums, carnations, lilies, especially the lilies of many colours in the little girl's bunch, even lilies of blue, seemed to forecast a coming war by the intensity of their being, by the way they gathered up light and almost drained other things of colour. They were an apparition in themselves. The Virgin going into Heaven? Lustrous curls of cloud around her. Inside that cathedral no doubt there'd be a Virgin wearing extravagant livery and crookedly crowned. That lady's eyes would have no awareness of war. Nor would her giddy, scarlet painted lips.

But despite that well-nigh imbecilic state Nessan trusted her, the idea of her, to bring him and the world through world catastrophe. That was the slogan the wall mosaics of medicine bottles advertised that day, the Greek-ikon gold in them. Men's hands lazily drifted over backgammon tables. Children, images of children, flourished in Nessan's mind as a testimony to man's survival. The children were placed on an endangered beach in Europe, in endangered corners of Europe. Nessan and Veronica would bring their marriage to the perimeters of Europe and thereby heal the memories and the troubled psyche of those places. A beach in Venice, changing huts, sand, children bent with spades: a platform for their love in the necrophiliac intensity of Europe's ancientness. This was yet a dream. Nothing very much had happened between Veronica and Nessan when they got to the village where they were going to stay, Veronica unloading what seemed like a mule's back full of American fashion magazines, pictures spilling onto the ground of couples, much like them, women in oaken and dun shades stepping out onto the terrain under Africa's largest mountains, one particular mountain a favourite in the fashion magazines, an imposing, cloud frilled slab of a blue mountain under which distant zebras' and giraffes' disappearing backsides were just caught by the camera, a silver or gold electricity.

Veronica ordered the house. She'd been here before, Vassar girl. She put things away, she shifted things, she draped sofas with redundant crimson rugs, making them ready for an occasion, all under an Indian woman's worn shoe of a face and silent, almost ill-wishing eye. The largest room was painted a total white so objects had status: a painting, a gong, a typewriter – a pointer towards the creativity that was supposed to happen here. Despite the seemingly perilous distance of the place from everywhere, New York was everywhere here: some of the freshest aspects of New York's art world, a magazine open on tell-tale a literary criticism, a painting by a renowned female recluse, the political rantings in book form of a part-Marxist and part-American John the Baptist-type-mystic. The place, this house, had been lived in by eclectics, erudites, nimble-fingered typists. The house had been vacated by someone else to make room for a literary affair.

Afterwards, when Nessan was dead, there would be a photograph of him here, in a striped vest, he not unlike a child, a flag of fair, sun kissed hair on his head, a guilty look on his face, a dark blob of an unidentifiable flower reaching to him like a snake to a snake charmer, heterosexuality having torn asunder the pose he'd kept all his life up to then, making him see water again, not the reassuring water of the East River under Brooklyn Bridge but the limitless water of the ocean. He'd been dragged away from safety, from art, by the frenetic rigmarole of love.

31 October 1984. Hallowe'en in Dublin. I followed a boy along Grafton Street today. Around by College Green and Westmoreland Street. Over the Bridge. Into North Dublin. He disappeared into a block of flats and left me staring at graffiti. O God, this land, but always the merciful sublimation of the sea nearby. Am I going mad now, mad from loneliness? Maybe I should see a doctor or a priest. They're all after me, I sometimes think, and then I look around and see no one in the room. Well, almost no one. There's Phineas. His provisional I.R.A. ghost. His junkie beatification. Phineas is the participle of history, of the real in this lonely room. There are otherwise no connections with anything. I have no parents, wife, lover, offspring. But then I start clattering away on the typewriter and the ghosts, the immediacy of this city disappear. There's a temporary salvation. Then the phone rings. It's a penniless boy in a crowded pub in central Dublin.

'How are ye? Can I come out? Can I bring a friend?'

'No, I'll meet you.'

I want the lights again and the crowd and the angularity of a youth in the context where he might be my son, a sandy anorak on him, a ewe-pale face on him under mendicant drapes of blond hair and a fuss of a military-style anorak on his erect and somehow distinguished shoulders as he talks about art or politics. I want the purity of a compassionate encounter under gaudy and adulthood-oblivionizing lights.

On the second of November, the day of the dead, family groups sat munching picnics of obligatory biscuits beside graves, candles on the graves or in the hands of alternating family members, red carnations, the symbol of mourning, on the lapels of city suits, stuck on breasts, biscuits crunching methodically in people's mouths, red carnations wandering about and faces holding communion with the dead in trances with the dead. Nessan beside Veronica, on the ground, had a reverential red carnation in the lapel of a black suit, for once the two silenced without a pose, but in memory carrying the most romantic pose of all: lovers, held together by the silence of death, by the particularity of clothes, by red carnations they bore which had metamorphosed from symbols of decadent cities to divine, to funereal tokens. They clung together in awe of the opera of death in the stars, in the candles, in the skeletal, hypnotised, glittering outlines which wandered about. A star fell from the heavens, making contact with the hymn of a spluttering candle. On this night they saw what they took to be God's left hand over the coming history. Afterwards they didn't talk to one another. Nessan looked like a frightened boy wandering about in the hope of accidentally bumping into a mother's nightgown.

In spite of their departure the biscuits crunched on, the candles kept lighting, the carnations kept wandering, in a more and more disorderly fashion, until it was dawn. Then you saw people in a mixture of Indian and European clothes, Indian faces often under the mushrooms of black Spanish shawls, but only men of European origin in suits, jagged, embarrassed suits that had come in piles from some boulevard shop in a dusty ice-cream of a city.

7 November 1984. Rain, a trudge through the black rain of evening and night, then the ketchup of a red-fronted pub. Human beings file in, mainly male human beings. There's bustle and assured conversation inside. I'm packed between bodies. At least there's that warmth and solicitude. A journalist rears over me, a bear of a man in a sky-silver suit, the profound pits of his arms exuding trails of expensive deodorant. I listen to other people's conversations. Later I go home, part of the way on foot, along by the sea which has thrown up a wild black sky up there and has frantic sentries of light further out. Near the Martello tower in Sandycove an old soaked fungus of a pederast still holds out. Tonight I give up this business for ever.

A lamplight goes on in my house. It's got a fleshy kind of white around it. It illumines books and records. The detritus of the bourgeois homestead. A diary open on an appointment with

194

a learned priest. I'm seeing a priest, an ear for the suburban rich, and confessing my life's sins. Confession. But confession demands truth, not sins. I'll try to organize the truth for him. That's something I've been unable to do for a long time. Truth would involve the whole of me, the heterosexual as well as the homosexual. That damaged heterosexuality that I have been too weak and too battle-unworthy to recover, too set and too approved on the margins of society and of the mind, rather than willing to enter, be part, kick over the structure of people's expectations of you, bring the blood-rusty existential sword into this realm of boys in iron-leather jackets, of home-going, seaside-sauntering flotillas of bankclerks, of glass bank buildings that aspire to reflect the moods of the volcanic Dublin skies.

The flaxen biscuits of the Day of the Dead were left over: they were munched guiltily in the days after. They became a deadly treat on the tongue. Lilies watching, the white, healthy heads of death picked and arranged by the Indian woman. She resented and cast malevolence on their bed of love. The world and history were shut out by the lovers, by Nessan and Veronica. Their love-making became an inexhaustible universe in itself, became an alternative passage of history, the gestures of penises, of breasts, of the fragile pink brinks of people. They excluded history from the bedroom, a possible insensitive visitor. In the wet recesses of Veronica Nessan found again childhood, adolescence, young adulthood. Untamed desires, dreams of naked young factory workers. All was permitted here. Every fantasy. Young factory workers again naked Greek archers with only a foolish clothing of little wings on them, the exacerbations of a French painting in a drawing-room book. He tore at the genitalia of young men. They allowed him and welcomed him there. He awoke, safe, not just redeemed of, but enriched by these contraband conjugal adventures. In the past there had been an erotic history which should have been drawn into evolution but which, for some reason, had not been, had stood still. Nessan had lived his life until now as a puny chested parlour boy in the straitjacket of a snowy sleeveless jersey. That had been his mother's beastly ordinance. She'd wanted him like that, stopped still, for the menu of her own demented needs. Now at last Nessan had grown up. Overnight he became a 33-year-old encumbered sculpture of a man.

★

21 November 1984. Two women fought on the street today. On Whitefriar Street. Near Whitefriar Street church. 'I'll put your head through your television, Missus,' one said to the other. Threats have become modernized but the worst ones still said adjacent to the church: absolution can be quickly attained. Neither of the women went to the church. One brusquely hurried off with a sack bag full of Dublin working-class foodstuffs: tins of peas, cornflakes, jars of jam with Bingo prizes flaunted on the labels.

Further fantasies: like naked cupids strolling across Iowan fields, prim little bottoms on them, but, Hell, his mother following them, shooing them as if they were a flock of geese. What was she doing in these fantasies? Get her out. Nessan jumped up with a white sheet over his front or at least his back jumped up, a corpse suddenly coming to life with its shroud. The cosmos of sexuality between him and Veronica was a subterranean one: it was buried. It spoke no language but its own and was extraneous to everything but itself. Nessan lay on Veronica again and boats bearing a chorus of burnished brown heeled Ulysses glided over the Aegean ceramic-blue, motorized towards the destiny of an island which was a piece of plumage on the sea, a solitary palm tree coming out of it like an ostrich feather. This was an island which had escaped from a New York subway advertisement for some mendacious candy. The lack of poetic respectability of it all. And an Indian woman who came in and insisted on emptying a chamber pot full of urine, staring at the surface ripples of the urine as if she saw rapids of prophecies in them.

3 December 1984. A relapse. Some wayfaring child brought home. Nothing happens. He's come for talk, come to be fed through the beak as if he's a starving blackbird. His mouth opens for morsels and then, after food, closes appreciatively. There's philosophical outpouring in a Dublin accent. It's all too familiar. Late night I show him the door. Outside the sky over the city looks like black balloons, the way the city lights spread above the horizon has etched out shapes. Black balloons that gleam in a liquid, excited way.

A young man came before Christmas. An American

196

archaeological student. He'd braved washes of blood on the landscape to get here. A healthy armed 22-year-old. His whole presence invoked an uncomplicated part of the American landscape and American psyche, but if you listened to him long enough, to his tales of ancient, infant devouring stone Gods, or to his tales of coming here, you knew there were shadows there. Shadows as sleek as the dark rivulets of hair on his arms. There was black hair on his head, lots of it, liquorice, lustrous black hair over the extreme lantern of a red, cowboy's shirt. The boy tossed around the house and eventually, on an afternoon, ended up in bed with Nessan. The boy had a new gospel of amorality, having learnt it from Indians along the way. There was no way Veronica could have known, she'd been out, away, but she did know. The boy forgot to shut the lavatory door one day and made a pathetic sight, the undersized knees of him. Then he went. So much for those heralds of the sensual.

20 December 1984. Just before Christmas Gerry flies into Dublin. On an unexpected visit. She's going to spend Christmas in Austria. I meet her at the ground floor, raised level bar of a high-rise hotel. The sudden phone call from New York is still sending jitters through me as I walk into the hotel. I'm wearing a fawn anorak and I know I look ridiculous. A woman, somewhat fat and slobby, grey haired, stares at me. I was married once. The crease on my back disappears. It was to the wrong woman.

Yes, she wants to walk through Dublin again, see the streets, taste the place again. There's a hygenic distance between her and the place. Between her and the scene of her marriage. She's a rich woman now, editorial consultant on a cookery magazine. This Christmas there's been a huge spread of an article about Christmas puddings by her with French Impressionist shaded Christmas puddings represented. But her passion, she declaims, is still literature. So after the plum puddings a brief shopping excursion in Dublin and then Austria. Is so-and-so's shop still there? Yes. Right where it used to be in South Anne Street. I'm talking to a piece of wood, to a transatlantic halluci-nation of a person. There's been no suffering, no feeling, no starvation, no want of any kind in this person for years. The body has gone dead. It's become an image, a self-satisfied tussle of extravagant clothes, an outward traffic of perfumes. One particular perfume hits my nose and reminds me. No, I'm wrong. I'm trying desperately to kill her; this woman was my lover and loved by me once. Yes, she'll find antique gold rings in South Anne Street. There will be a particular shop window her figure will remark on. In Dawson Street church a choir of Protestant boys in scarlet and white will be waiting to uplift her, to crash the cymbals of memory. She'll be back then in a city of torrential soft skies where she was in love once.

What came between me and Gerry? Death. The death in the air in this country. Death and hybrid greys in the genitalia. What came between me and my sexuality? Money, greed, lovelessness, but primarily the air in this country. Old discarded tyres by the Liffey, huge cylindrical shapes by the Liffey – a new architectural feature just as the round towers were of old – a coal heap under a defeated terracotta crane; sky that was impotent, unmoving. Here a cesspool of the spirit, graffiti, a pornographic mind, gestures that transacted other versions of impotence, of frail daring, snowdrop-fingered protest.

A Christmas of flowers, a literary legend: poinsettia, hibiscus, oleander, jasmine, then the banana tree, the mango tree, papayas, cumquats, guavas, stars in the night a mimosa; then a fireworks Judas who was a merry friar with an entrenched, crooked grin; from other valleys reverberations of fireworks or were they reverberations of guns? A new shirt for Nessan: a gift, white with a blue people of pigmies on it or were they children? Its cleanness and newness almost abrasive on his body. A bowl of sweet-peas on the table, cherished, stared at for days and days over Christmas. There was no need for words with sweet-peas there. Nessan on a hill in his shirt: a photograph. An Indian grinned some distance behind him. The sweet-peas on the table were rampant pinks and blues, a fleshy dress of pinks and blues, Cinderella lifting her dress and leaving the ball. It was another year. Veronica was pregnant. Nessan, blond haired, a boy in a black jacket, alone in the room, stared at the sweet-peas. A hand reached out of time and tried to wipe the grime from his collarless white shirt. His mother's. He had defeated her. A child was to be born to him. But the ocean of anxieties in him increased. He could not cope with the imminence of adulthood. He was an acolyte standing there, awaiting the ceremony.

*

The ocean was rising in his mind as they were leaving, the swell on the surface of the ocean. There was the tumult of the past weeks there and the tumult of history. Trees coming in to bloom in far-off Berlin; a grandfather of his who'd left the moon of a gold autumn land. There was newness and abstraction in Nessan. The twin states of a man who'd just heard a sentence passed on him, who knew he was going to be cut down in his youth and yet was suddenly all the more aware of his youth or aware for the first time of his youth. 'Our short, short lives.' Some expiration of his grandmother's in his head. Life indeed was short; our time on earth was short. There was an acknowledgement in him of the brevity of life and the difficulty for the artist to fight against that brevity and make something of meaning that would challenge and even scar that brevity.

That it should come to this. Andalusia, Castile; saucers of light in the valleys of the latter in the evenings, hordes of flowers committing mass suicide over the rocks by the sea in the former. Killiney, County Dublin, in the 1920s, butterflies' wings impressed against the light of the sea with patterns standing out like patterns on gossamer dresses at the viceregal ball. The 1930s in Dublin, hearse-like automobiles nosing into Grafton Street, fascists armed with grey overcoats and with black, spidery, insinuating umbrellas and a solitary Spanish Republic supporter on the top of Grafton Street, a red handkerchief tucked into his bowler hat as he waved his walking stick to a duck taking off from Saint Stephen's Green – his travelling papers to Spain were poems sticking out of his breast pocket. The 1940s, all those cafés, the cafés of the world, arenas, tables bedecked with somnambulistic people: Dublin, Lisbon, New York; a newspaper in Arabic closely examined by one of the white suited exiles from war for coherent news. The 1950s, 60s, a lame, deadening landscape, the 1970s some kind of release, gaudy nuggets of neon signs over bars under which boys with ballerina, bejeaned right legs stood. The 1980s a counting of those boys, boys with all manner of waists, pale buttocks tatooed with baby red figments, butcher shop, hanging, skinned calves of pale boys, all the boys doomed and merging one by one into the face of a drowned boy in the Liffey, he our symbol, his hair blond and a nursery-blue denim suit on him and his face on a January morning merging in turn into stages of

199

putrification, of decay, until there is only rot and grey left of him, grey like the Dublin January river with its perimeters of venial buildings in which venial men tuck themselves into the pubs and spit out witticisms from under quasi-intellectual, toothbrush moustaches with rat-like, infinitely manicured teeth occasionally glowing. That it should come to this, youth, loveliness, hope, sturdiness, erectness. A wish for the world. A wish to be part and to help. A wish to be loved. A wish to have offspring. The offspring is a boy found floating on the Liffey, killed by the frantic fingers of Dublin pederasts. Before the church is a urinal and I stop to pee there; it is by the Liffey. With its toadstool brown walls and its slanted and effulgent litanies of graffiti on the walls it is a shrine and a church, not only to the dead boy but also to a dead era of the spirit, to a political failure, a failure to create a land where people can be open with one another, a failure of compassion in a land of Spanish Inquisition, black-cloaked prelates who emerge and re-emerge, ectoplasms, from soaring marquees of black limousines.

'There is an appeal to the eye in beautiful things, in gold and silver and all such; the sense of touch has its own powerful pleasures: and the other senses find qualities in things suited to them. Worldly success has its own glory, and the power to command and to overcome. The life we live here below has its own attractiveness, grounded in the measure of beauty it has and its harmony with the beauty of lesser things. The bond of human friendship is admirable, holding many souls as one. Yet in the enjoyment of all such things we commit sin if through immoderate inclination to them – for though they are good, they are of the lowest order of good – things higher and better are forgotten, even you, O Lord our God, and your truth and your law.' Some little working-class girl is there in the Pro-Cathedral in her Confirmation outfit, as if she's forgotten to take it off, praying, an ostrich tail of white. At least she's relinquished the veil. She's staring at the altar, asking for martyrdom, focussing all the debilitation of her life on the altar and its subliminal possibilities. A wretched old man and woman, or maybe more, shuffle into the confessionals, breaking up postures in which they sat like illuminated invalids, under windows. No, I can't do it: I can't. Goodbye, God. Cheerio.

★

Going to the boat, there was a terrible, a palpitating sense of foreboding in Nessan. In this harbour city he'd clutched a few reviews. Some recent poems of his had come out in pamphlet form in New York and people had thrown stones. He'd fallen from his equilibrium of grace again. There was nothing there people said, he'd been a nebulous and mometary display of talent. People had pushed him off their boats. They felt slightly offended with themselves that they'd ever detected talent in him, as if they'd slept with a saccharine perfumed prostitute. The limbs of young men were in Nessan's mind on the boat; sailors confronted him with their apricot arms, an elegy. That had been Nessan's world. He could be no more. A child was to be born to him. To make room for the child he dived into an ocean of city chestnut trees in blossom. He was back there among the cities he'd never visited: the city he'd tried to escape to, the ultimate city. He'd run and run and he'd never got away. Now he was back. In his mother's arms. She was waiting for him. Her arms. He'd failed to make it to a place of escape, of oblivion. There were no city trees then, just the Mid-West and a harp hanging from a tree which played the songs of Ireland. A young man left the blond autumn hills of his home, to create chaos, division, separation for his posterity. Now that separation, that non-cohesion had been healed. There were many stars over the ocean and a dream of an ancestor who'd stood naked by a window in the Mid-West, knowing the lack of cohesion within him, the androgony, the man-woman, the dual God, but suddenly coming to terms with it and accepting it as the way life should be.

A friend of Nessan's, a novelist, wrote to him from Berlin shortly after Nessan's drowning, not knowing he was dead, informing him, it seemed from the muddled writing on the postcard, of horse-chestnuts in blossom on Unter den Linden and of young men in uniform invading, like rats, the precocious and, it must be said, inviting colours of the sidewalk cafés. A young man, blond like Nessan, but who as he wrote the postcard had a blonde German woman beside him. By accident the grist of all-American, radiating masculinity in his blondness. That too composed a paragraph on the postcard, the woman beside him, the pose he was in, but also the world he was watching, the streets, the soldiers, the soldiers continually straggling en masse in the centre of boulevards, like children in the wake of a huge military procession, not wanting yet to give up the ardour and the intoxication and the transmutation of the parade.

3 April 1985. I get ready to go into town. I put on a jacket and stare at myself, ruminatively, in the mirror. The end effect of all my toilet preparations is a man who looks a bit like a woman dressed as a man, a beret on my head, holding up a defiant button of black, two splotches of purple on my cheeks, like make-up. My hair is still black and is oiled behind my ears as though it's going to end up in a suppressed bun. There is the freshness about my appearance of one who is about to appear on music hall and sing songs while he, or she, nonchalantly swings an umbrella. Yes, I've got the umbrella too. To get rid of some of this aura about my appearance I put on a long fawn coat which drags down on me and makes me look as if one part of me, the coated part, is going on an espionage mission, while the other part, my head under a beret, will belt out songs in front of backdrops of dizzy Paris streets. The lower part has the armour of the pervert, the child-seducer, while the upper part has the livid respectability of the theatrical transvestite. That's what an early swim in the Forty Foot has done to me, a swim with a few racing naked bodies under the blotchy, scudding April rain sky. A swim with a few temperamental solicitors who've decided this is good for them. I say farewell to my reflection and make off.

I stand for a while waiting for the 8 bus with a few suburban drug-addicts who advertise their addiction by stomping around like elephants in a cage, hands in the pockets of their black leather jackets. There are signs between us. They think I might be a film director and are open to having a part in the film. The bus comes and saves us from some petty rain.

I didn't go to the learned priest. Instead, I thought, I should go and have my confession heard with the humble. Otherwise it would be no good. But that didn't work out. At least I joined my hands in prayer as I knelt in the Pro-Cathedral. That did me good, my hands grafted together, too nimble, blanched, a gesture which commanded attention in the church, those isolated, aged, sincere hands. I did not have to go further. I was forgiven and sent back as an inspector to the streets, to the clubs. That's where I am going now. The places of sex, of gaudiness have to be known too and located within the prose of reverence. There's Dun Laoghaire passing, its juncture with Monkstown at Carrick Brennan Road Church. On the other side of the road to the church, among foliage, at Clifton Lane I once had an amorous encounter, in the dark, with a pupil of a local posh protestant school. I'd always recall his face, even from the night, and not many years later he turned up, grinning, pale stoat faced, as a compère on an Irish television programme in a suit that fell around him like ash from a cigarette, grey tinctured with black. Off Rock Road are wastes by the sea. There an oil truck driver let me put my hand inside his trousers. He was from Corofin, County Clare and wore pale blue denim. He'd leapt out of his truck when he saw me. We'd met once in a pub in Dublin lit by rose shaded lamps. He'd had black curly hair, tough Spanish hair like many people from the West of Ireland. This was the only homosexual experience he'd ever had he said, or ever wanted to have, indulged in after years of trial visits to Dublic pubs, his penis in my hand in the night in Blackrock with orange lights about and the smell of him, of the Atlantic and of epileptic, half fallen castles in Clare. There off Merrion Square is a little basement theatre out of which I walked one night in the mid-sixties with the main actor, a boy of seventeen, blond, who was later killed falling from a redwood tree in California where he'd gone and started working as a lumber-jack. From the basement theatre we'd gone to Mrs. Gaj's restaurant and over red carnations next to a table where sat a piper, who'd once been a friar and was destined to die from drink, I told him about the Spain of my boyhood until the whole restaurant listened and the piper took what was in fact a tin whistle and played 'The Lament of Limerick', music which portrayed the mood of Irish aristocrats before they left Ireland for Europe in 1691. College Green, the Bank of Ireland, the young of Dublin hesitant there, faces stalling in case you want to have a good look at them. I walk from the bus, down an alley, into a club where Nessan's face greets me, Nessan in a blown-up photograph over a dance floor, Nessan, his new shirt slightly open to him. This maybe was all a game. The story of Nessan began in a Dublin night-club, music thumping out, a backing of aggressive war drums and a dis-connected, elastic leg or arm or head daring in places on the perimeter of the dance floor, the crowd getting its beat ready before it assembles for the night on the centre of the floor.

Because they could not bury him, people gathered in haphazard crowds that summer in New York, to remember him, bringing flowers to tables with them, red carnations, bowing their heads over open-air Bohemian tables, girls in dresses patterned with lettuce leaves, a new breed of fan for Nessan, girls who might have considered throwing themselves under a train when Rudolph Valentino died if he'd written a few verses as well as having been in films. People who'd not bothered about Nessan in life were in mourning for him in death, if they were young ladies, having first smeared their lips with moulting rose-petal lipstick. Nessan was a cult for a summer, refracted from one open-air table to another, the legend of his death, until all of New York became a pale blue ocean for those people, in the intensity of fathomless and hallucinogenic light trapped between skyscrapers, light in which drowned poets in festive shirts floated. Nessan had come back, by detour, to the city whose pinnacles of skyscrapers and whose steel arms of bridges had allowed him to escape – and be euphoric about escape – for a while. But winter nestled in and Nessan was forgotten as people went inside from the open-air tables, drawn by the temptation of Mrs. Kehlibareva's Bohemian-warming borsch, with the conspiracies of chess games going on inside, dulled Slav faces, looking up from their games as if, remembering some Czarist atrocity, they were momentarily imbecilic. It was 1936 going on 1937 and when it snowed that winter bodies were dragged by horses through the snow, faintly, as in a defective moving picture, haunting the nightmares of New York Bohemians, a disease picked up from Bohemian cafés and from events that were throttling the world outside; the wind coming in through a slither of a crack in a window in Nessan's former apartment where two ballet dancers from a small and experimental company now lived, one male, one female, and howling like a breathless and huge wave on the ocean the night the northern ocean squeamishlessly took the *Titanic*.

The Dalkey sea throws tantrums outside; it is May, the rain already a persistent summer rain which often ends up in Ireland making the season a nation-wide miasma of wet cabbages.

204

There's a boy beside me, a youth, in a blue and white striped T-shirt, a rucksack discarded at his feet, his journey slimed into his blond hair. His eyes look at me earnestly and in a very taciturn, demanding American way as if I'm going to offer him some instant moral truth, his arms folded and his chest muscles emphasized. I feel like a child who should have prepared a lesson for a teacher and hasn't. But the boy is patient. There is silence between us. We knew we were going to meet for a long time. So words and tracts can wait. Silence juggles between us like a pinball game. Who is going to speak first? It is Nessan's grandson.

Epilogue

When Bonnie O'Dowd started living in New York in the early 1940s the events which had the most impact in awakening her numbed and almost autistic mind were the pageants presented by Jewish people to point to their fears about what was happening to their fellow Jews in Europe and to try to attract the public conscience, yahrzeit candles borne aloft on platforms in Central Park, the whole of Jewish history presented by lines of chorister-looking boys in white, by figures draped in the costumes of Jonathan or the Queen of Sheba. On nights when ponies neighed bearing ladies up from Carolina on buggies through the park, Bonnie wandered into the park for a further account of Jewish history, staring at the stage and knowing that this was God addressing her from the burning bush of the theatrical scenes. He was calling on her to awake from the long hurt of her life, the sleeping acceptance that had come on her mind, and to undertake a task. The task was at first mysterious but the New York buildings looking like a collage of paper led her to it. She started collecting Nessan's papers, scrubbing latrines, emptying rubbish cans full of sickly apple cores and of minced chewing-gum papers to support herself.

There was an incalcuable task before her, making order of an unorderly life and of what came to seem at times like a darting poltergeist in a mardi gras shirt, a crimson shirt with white moons spilt over it, the costume of an outing in California. But Bonnie was undeterred. She challenged the skyscrapers which held Nessan's enigma, the evanescent morning vacuums of light, the rock pool illuminations thrown up between patterns of skyscraper outlines. She sauntered down corridors in public libraries with an Amazon air of defiance. She carried piles of books like a professorial expert. She secluded herself in New York Public Library and read and read. Her reading matter took her far away from the subject of Nessan and the environs of his life, and she became, for the first time, learned: she embarked on the *Iliad* and the *Aeneid*, in English versions, and the mind of this charwoman became epic; she saw beyond New York and even the war. She placed her time and Nessan's time in the context of history and she was able to award Nessan a place on a blindingly lit, skin sanded beach with Sappho and overlap the voice of his prayer with that of Saint Augustine. She had vast, interior plans for Nessan which she carried with her, always, around New York so she became unworldly and even visionary-looking. Bonnie lived inside herself for those years and was safe until Veronica sought her out and drew her into her world, tempting her with little tea parties in New York and then in the summer of 1943 a ticket to New Mexico where Veronica was staying. It was the first time Bonnie met her grandson, and he was staring resentfully at her when she encountered him, corrugated black on his head, a bowl of sweetpeas near his head with a varicose light through them. A gaggle of female graduate students surrounded Bonnie, a woman in black, sinister moons of black glasses around their eyes and one of them eventually, in New York, abducted the papers Bonnie had collected about Nessan and never gave them back. It was then Bonnie started to die. There had been a flash in the sky that day and a new sort of epic started. The papers had been a loan. They'd never come back to Bonnie. On Bonnie's first day at the home Charlie Chaplin visited her in her dreams and commiserated with her.

Then a young man from Ireland came, a faded, distant kind of emissary, a Greek legend; both of them were impotent, they had nothing, they communicated in a well of their own position-lessness in the world. Neither had props. Bonnie's papers, her

210

work for a few years, had gone. Perhaps the girl with the gargantuan, red, fleecy-paper-flower lips had not known where to find her. The young man from Ireland often brought red carnations to her bedside. He never got the truth about Nessan or anything like it. Instead a collection of lies, half truths, savoury fantasies, the mischievous ticklings of an avidly working imagination. She was encouraged by the success of some of her stories to further stories, forgetting that the real story too had been demented, that the real portrait of Nessan could be achieved too by circumspection and fiction. One way or another Bonnie O'Dowd or Bonnie Muir, call her what you like, became a fictional character on her deathbed, sitting up with the excitement caused by this, expanding her arms to show the lengths and breadths she trod in her life, forgetting this time that it was all true. The young man left and she wasn't sure what to think except that he'd looked sad in his buttermilk colour polo-neck and that he seemed oddly doomed for his gentleness. Many a time she wanted to touch the liquid blackness of his quiff but she daren't for a new propriety and a new shyness in her. The young Irishman wrote to her after he departed and then the letters from him stopped, but by that time her life was filled with reconciliation with Veronica and her grandson and by the time she died in December 1950 the first of the multifarious books on Nessan had started to come out, a point in her mind where the letters from the young man had stopped, the meringue dawn sky just out on the sea from Cobh from which so many ships had set out for America. Bonnie died a literary legend in her own right and was given a literary funeral, black shapeless bottomed literary figures there in the hush of a December fog, agitated red carnations in the tableau, a skyscraper just about peeking through the fog, morphine in some people's eyes, the bird's foot of morphine on some of the hidden arm veins, the whole population of Mrs. Kehlibareva's restaurant there, a population which was wont to sit now in uniform, forward-facing positions, like an orchestra, as if waiting for some heavenly apocalyptic band to start up. The final ikon for Bonnie was thrift store, affected black, red carnations and fog, the possible charade-atmosphere redeemed by a genuine mourner, Bonnie's grandson, fourteen years old now, lava-like, fermented acne already on his face and delicate, mourning anemones in the whites of his eyes. They'd become friends; he'd brought candy to her in the home in Brooklyn. He'd felt guilty for having been an abrasive child. He'd been a man at thirteen. He held her hand as she died, a delicate giant toadstool-top of a hand. She talked of harps and of candy factories and of red wine, Mid-Western dawns, dawns over the fields scattered with the odd lonely pioneer dwelling, a dwelling of muddy brown timber beside the spire of a windmill and a collection of devoted, flame necked hens. She died talking of home.

The bashings for Nessan came and went, the critical bashings: Christ stoned outside the town walls. In the meantime, his son withdrew from literature, out of hatred and repugnance for the world of it, and opened a string of garages in the near desert terrain of Arizona. They were monuments of ingenuity in the deprived landscape and Fintan grew up among them, offsetting them against his literary inheritance, playing the two off against one another, but the game not succeeding as it should because often on the door of one of his father's garage offices you'd find a picture of Walt Whitman or Leo Tolstoy or beside a row of red cars like ripe tomatoes a second-hand book open on a poem by Fintan's grandfather.

Fintan was born in 1967 and he went away to college in the Mid-West in the fall of 1984. But before the end of his first year at college, all the nearer to Europe now, fascination with his troublesome and unintegrated ancestor got the better of him and he flew to Ireland. In the plane coming over County Kerry he had the bold hair of Nessan as a boy, troubadour stripes of it lit up by the sun that came in and for a moment sent a bit of incandescence over a promontory in Kerry, a lazy smile on his indented lips and a reckless and independent cascade of curls over his forehead, which half hid the smile by throwing a shadow across it and so mitigated his unpardonable American unashamedness. The chest, which sat forward from the body, was part of the unashamedness, the gondolier T-shirt of awry blue and white stripes.

He'd grown up with constant contact with California, even weekend trips there, the Californian coastline a fringe in his mind, the razzmatazz of jammed beaches where people went to annihilate the mind, surfers symphonically coming in at evening. There was always the chatter of Californian beaches wherever he went, even in the Mid-West, and there he kept his

Californian tan. In December he'd been a swaying furnace, still in white campus shorts. But, despite all the temptations, he was true to Nessan. The Californian tongue, a collection of a few spare part words, was a deflection point from the huge burden of ancestry he carried. Changing huts on Californian beaches, casually peach coloured, had been a metamorphosis from an ancestral motif. There'd been hallucinations on Californian beaches of Ireland, journeys and nights of possession.

This boy had wandered on Californian beaches, nuclear arsenals in the distance, a sun-splotched and soldierly shouldered Lazarus, a Lazarus who was conscious of being a Lazarus. He knew he carried the message of his grandfather's poems, release, resurrection, the immaculately laid out new garment. But he had to go to the place he'd been released from.

He arrived in Ireland Easter 1985. Instead of staying in Dublin where he arrived he headed straight to Belfast. There he had nightmares, men with explosions of blood on them, blood the way crimson appears on Hawaiian shirts, intermittent white also on the shirts. He headed on from this grey city with its grey inoffensive river and encircled Ireland, a rapacious hitchhiker, rucksack on his back, chest stubbornly thrown forward as he straddled the roads between lifts. His nose took him to Kerry, to the outer promontories. He gazed at the sea and then turned back to Dublin. Across the slovenly Midlands. Dublin was full of pubs, of backstreets. Musicians were driven by the rain into pubs. He was keenly observed on entering. He knew there was a person in this city who had visited his great-grandmother; he knew the person's name; he knew by way of family folklore; he knew that young man had had hair black as black olives and that he'd had exaggerated, cartoon, quizzical features; he knew for some reason that that man must be lonely now.

Veronica had dropped Bonnie for a few years after having made initial contact; she'd blamed men for it, men as lovers. But in fact Veronica's withdrawal had levered a general withdrawal, a general pursed-lipped cessation of interest in Bonnie. There were other goals in the literary climate, other nuclei. Anyway someone had made good capital use of Bonnie. Letters from Nessan to Bonnie were turning up in campuses all over the United States; affidavits, supposedly, to some graduate's persistent research. But Veronica came back to Bonnie, repentantly, when she came to live permanently in

New York. She brought her son. She'd become a Roman Catholic. She dressed in black. She came with a rainbow of dried flowers on the first day, a muted rainbow which dropped particles of itself in the corridors, mostly particles of the blond stems, a mottled dust. There were long exchanges between Veronica and Bonnie, sessions; Veronica's son often present for these. He was the recorder, the link, gum in his mouth and the ballasts of his acne just beginning.

> Nessan, the holy deacon, loves
> Angelic pure devotion:
> Never came outside his teeth
> What was untrue and guileful.

Fintan had found reference to the ancient Irish name of Nessan in the *Martyrology of Donegal* in the National Library in Dublin, other records, other recorders, this time recorders who sat in round towers among solvent green pastures and among untarnished tentacles of rivers. An American boy smiling at the image he'd just conjured, paused on the steps of the National Library, under the green of the trees brimming with wet over the dogged grey building on the Georgian street.

The nights were full of lights, of clubs, of gaudiness that reached now down to the Liffey and threw their colours into the water which had once held only the skeletal outlying lights of Dublin. The days were full of green, of wet, of water; Fintan found a promenade by the sea where he could parade and announce his presence to the city. He knew that there was nothing in this city of men's changing-huts on stone promontories that stretched into the sea, of derelict garden houses by seaside railway tracks screaming with graffiti, of distant, manifold beating lighthouses, of tentative park bench conversations, to rival him. Every bit of Dublin had a myth, a legend, and especially the vestal Hill of Howth on the opposite side of the bay to the promenade on which Fintan walked. This comforted him and reassured him about his purpose in this city.

If you were entering a pub in Dublin about a month after Easter 1985 you might have been surprised by a blond American boy making a telephone call in a kiosk just inside, his eyes on you as he telephoned, music which had been threatening for a long time starting up in the narrow and diving

214

pub full of mahogany vestibules and of imposing barrels, a banjoist who looked as though he had stepped out of a Hunger Strike poster so severe were his eyes and his beard, the boy's eyes trying to communicate something to you, the stranger, who was casually bringing in the new green and the damp grey of Dublin, something about the nature of the boy's question making you suddenly pause for a moment in wonderment at its exact message, startling you out of your surroundings, the brown walls, the baleful smell of soggy maleness, the smell of sawdust with which someone had anointed half a floor, the city in general – low rain-lavender mountains spilt onto streets – and then the real surprise happening, a ray of sun peculiar to that narrow street in Dublin that day lighting up the boy's blue and white striped T-shirt, transforming him into a resonance of an Easter which you'd long hoped for in this shabby and slithering city but which had never come, never that is, until just now.